BLOOD
BROTHERHOOD

Also by John van der Zee
THE PLUM EXPLOSION

BLOOD BROTHERHOOD

JOHN VAN DER ZEE

HARCOURT, BRACE & WORLD, INC. • NEW YORK

to my father

BLOOD
BROTHERHOOD

1

Baxter Bragg is dead.

Someone waited for him in the dark last night, silent and remorseless as a marauding animal, until Bragg came alone, walking, in thought.

And tore him apart with a shotgun.

No random killing, this gunning-down-from-across-the-street; no stick-up or jealous reprisal; no sudden combustion of a quarrel. The intention was not the end of a life, but its obliteration by an act so brutally abrupt that it would be all of that life that was remembered. Is it possible to watch a man, to follow his comings and goings, to study his looks and the way he walks, learn his habits and some of his secrets, and kill him? To know and not care? If such a thing is possible, what isn't?

I had the news instead of breakfast. Another killing in the paper, huge headline, columns of facts, a photograph of a body in the street like a run-over cat; but this, a man whose voice is in my head. For whom I still have questions. How much of my life is gone with him?

Doug, my son, slouches into the kitchen, wearing pajama bottoms and rubbing his eyes. Six foot four, two hundred pounds, at seventeen. There's a whole generation coming along like him. I'll be too small to reach a public telephone. Sometimes he acts as if it's already happened.

"Whyn't you wake me up? I'm late." He looks around for coffee.

Not without malice, I tell him: "Somebody killed Baxter Bragg last night."

Doug stops, mouth open. I hand him the paper and he sits at the kitchen counter next to me, stunned, frowning. Bragg had got through to him, past the studied toughness and the stacks of *Car Life* and *Motor Trend*. Bragg and Sally Bragg had come for dinner. Doug was in our driveway, bent over the engine of his car, indifferent. Bragg walked over and began talking to him. He offered Doug some advice, handed him tools; they worked on the car together: Doug stood aside and watched Bragg, dirty and absorbed. An old guy who knew. Bragg told him when and how to start it, and Doug obeyed. The engine turned over and coughed to life. Blue exhaust filled the street. The two of them came inside together, beaming with satisfaction.

"Points," Bragg had explained proudly.

Now he is dead. I can see the realization of it in Doug's face. Anyone can die. Anytime.

I make him a cup of instant coffee and burn some toast. He reads while he eats, without looking up from the newspaper. He doesn't say anything.

Getting dressed, I can't seem to get my hands to work, they are trembling so. The more conscious I am of it, the harder it is to stop. My face in the bathroom mirror looks like some pale ancestor of myself. I drop the razor, pick it up, and cut myself with the first stroke.

I give Doug a ride to school; he brings the paper with him in the car. His hair isn't combed, there's dirt under his fingernails, and he's smoking a cigarette at eight-thirty

4

in the morning. No use bitching at him, not today. I'm choking with grief. My legs and arms feel as though they're made of glass. At the school, he thanks me and takes the paper with him, still reading it, folded over, as he heads up the sidewalk, falling in with the other kids.

Who did it? I don't know. Bragg had so many enemies, it seemed to make him immune. What man would want to do so many others' killing? He could needle a man to tears, but needled men don't kill. Or do they? Funny. He was the only person I could talk to about things like that.

I drive into the parking lot outside our building and park in the space reserved for my car. The building is one story, green stucco with a yellow shake roof, landscaped with trees and flowers like a suburban house that has been stretched to an exaggerated length. Our local, Construction Workers 252, owns the building, but we occupy only a few offices and a small auditorium, leasing out the rest to other locals, and to business and professional men, usually connected in some way with labor. Some of the brothers are already waiting outside, standing around a car, looking for jobs and favors. They stop talking; I nod to them and go inside.

In the hallway, Doctor Loeb, a young, black-haired physician with a squinty, pointing face, is standing in his office doorway, watching disapprovingly as I pass.

"Good morning, Mister Burke," he says accusingly, as if I should explain or apologize for what has happened.

"Morning," I say, and rush on. He gets most of his practice from our local.

Everybody in the office has heard about it. Beverlee, a frail redheaded girl who works for us as a secretary and is studying nights to be a schoolteacher, is crying into a paper towel. Dorothy, my secretary, is trading theories over coffee with Potter, our dispatcher: a hired gunman from Chicago did it, the National, the Minutemen, Black

Muslims, the CIA. I hustle around the counter, and through the gate with a hello, but Potter follows me into my office, hovering around the other side of my desk while I get settled. He's a smart, pushy young guy who barrels around too fast in an Italian sports car, and has an ugly scar running all the way across his upper lip to show for it. That's one habit of his I don't like. The other two are hanging around when he isn't wanted, and second-guessing me. He wants to be union business agent, a job I hold now since we can't afford a local president on full salary. I take a long time looking through the incoming mail, but he's still there, waiting, when I sit down.

"Well, what do you think?" he says, as if he already knows.

"The police will get them. They can trace the bullets."

"Not shotgun pellets." He smiles cocksurely. "There's no rifling in shotgun barrels, so all pellets are alike. It's impossible to match the pellets to the gun."

"Oh." Potter can see, in anything, an opportunity to make points for himself.

"It wasn't robbery, that's one thing," he says, hinting. "They found money on him and his car keys were in his hand."

I know then that I'm in for it, his whole theory on why Bragg died and who did it, motives, evidence, with everything boiling down to his single truth that nothing is what it appears to be. The telephone saves me. It's Rose, and I ask Potter to leave and close the door.

Rose sounds calm and unshaken, but when I ask her where she's calling from, she admits she's home, hasn't gone to work, hasn't even got dressed, can't get started. Sally Bragg has telephoned her. The union is helping with funeral arrangements, Sally's neighbors are bringing in meals, friends are coming by to offer condolences. Sally's all right, but she's afraid of being alone at night, and she's

6

asked Rose to come and stay with her. So Rose is going, moving in. They were never even friends, not close. But now she's going.

"What time are you leaving?"

"This afternoon," she says. "I'm packing now."

I tell her that I'll come by at noon.

I hang up the phone and open my door. The outer office has its worn, weekday look: Beverlee and Dorothy typing at the open desks behind the counter, Potter standing at the dispatch window, stamping the union book of a man who's just paid his dues, very deliberate about it, making the man sweat, two forlorn-looking workmen, laid off the day before, waiting on the other side of the counter for an interview, the framed local charter and the Brotherhood Constitution on the wall above them, pictures of the past local presidents and Tom Cannon, Brotherhood Chief Executive Officer, looking down from around the room, a faded American flag leaning in its stand against a citizenship plaque from the local mayor. I nod to the men and tell them to come in.

They follow me into my office and sit down, sheepishly, like schoolboys about to be scolded. Both have been in trouble before. Billy Hildebrand, a chinless, big-eared journeyman carpenter my age, forty-five, a capable man with a childish side that keeps him drifting from job to job; and Clarence Equals, a helper, an indifferent workman with blackened nails and a perpetual sneer who leaves jobs as often as Billy does, but not because he wants to. This time, both have been fired. Billy's wife had a baby, Equals explains, and they went out drinking, drank all night, and reported to work drunk the next morning. Equals got into an argument with the job foreman, the foreman became excited, and Billy took a poke at him and knocked him down. Both men were told to pick up their time.

7

"How do you think your wife's going to feel about this?" I ask Billy.

"I didn't plan to tell her just now." He smiles guiltily.

I look at the two of them. The rank and file. Bragg's hope.

"I'm splitting you two up," I say angrily. "You're finished working together. No more. Billy, I'll see if I can get you back on the same job. Equals, I'm going to find you something else, nowhere near where he is, and this time you better make it stick."

Equals scratches the back of his neck with what I know to be his middle finger.

"I guess you know Baxter Bragg was murdered last night," I say to them.

Hildebrand flinches. "Ohhh," he says, in what seems a moment of honest sorrow. "That's a shame."

Equals just shakes his head. "You couldn't get me to be a union officer if you gave me the job."

"Go home," I tell them, blindly waving them away until they are gone, and I'm left staring at the empty doorway. It's true. He's gone. It's just a job now. The days add up to nothing.

The phone rings again, and it's a man from one of the San Francisco papers calling to ask me about Bragg.

"Is it true he was a Communist?"

The old question: he was, he wasn't—as if that could explain everything about the man.

"I don't know. He got his men a contract for six fifty-one an hour. That would make him a pretty good capitalist, wouldn't it?"

"What about your national?" he hurries on.

"What about them?"

"Do you think they had anything to do with it?"

"Well, they were opposed to him, but so were a lot of people. I know they offered him a job just a couple of months ago, but he turned it down."

8

He's disappointed, and grows curt, wanting to wrap it up.

"Police questioned you?"

"No, I haven't heard from them."

He asks me if our local has made a contribution to the reward offer, and I tell him that I don't know about any reward. That finishes it. I'm not worth his time and he doesn't bother to thank me.

I call Bragg's local after that, and ask about the reward. Twenty thousand dollars has already been put up to find the killer. Almost every union in San Francisco is kicking in, and individual pledges are coming in from rank-and-file men all over. I leave a message for Lenny Silk, the San Francisco local's business agent, to count us in for five more.

Noon. I drive to Rose's house, through the quiet streets of our residential town, winding up into the steep hills beyond, where the houses start thinning out and the trees start growing thicker. Rose bought her small house about fifteen years ago with the lump settlement from her divorce, organizing her life carefully, determined that the bad marriage was the last big mistake she was going to make, settling on this rustic house even though there were hardly any others around it, keeping up the place, painting and fixing, while other, bigger homes went up nearby, endorsing her choice, the house's value and Rose's confidence increasing together until the place became an obstacle to her marrying again, she's so unwilling to part with it.

The garden feels green and good. The lawn, fresh-cut and fragrant, flowers in half a dozen colors around the border, a hummingbird nosing in the climbers over her door. She opens the door wearing a bathrobe and slip, holding a brush and a mirror, her black hair hanging down straight and parted in the middle, Indian-style, not the way she wears it, but the way I wish she would. I follow her back to the bathroom and watch her putting it up, brushing and pinning, examining herself in the wall mirror, holding up the hand mirror to view the back of her head, setting the mirror on the washbasin with a click. Women always have the maintenance to fall back on; there's never nothing to do.

"Do unions do that, Joe? Do they kill people?"

"It happens." I stand in the doorway, trying to seem hard. "One union in Chicago had ten killings in twelve years, all political."

"Then there shouldn't be any unions. They should be outlawed."

She brushes, examines. Click.

"People drown. Should we quit teaching swimming?"

Rose has the firm poise and institutionalized good looks of a cashier in an expensive San Francisco restaurant, which is where she works. Prominent cheekbones, grooved smile, alert eyes. The job makes her too professional with herself. She can calculate a man's credit rating while flirting with him, and she must have a steamer trunk full of eye shadow somewhere in that house.

She turns from the mirror to me. "Could a man kill a stranger for money?"

"I guess there are men that could."

"And they call *women* whores."

Women. One minute they make no sense at all. And the next, they're profound. She gives herself a severe final appraisal in the mirror and shakes her head. "I hate being old," she says.

It isn't really true, but it's true enough. She turns out the bathroom light and we walk into her bedroom, all cool and dark, full of women's things, ruffled furniture and figurines, smelling of wax and soap and perfume. Beside her closet door, I stop and kiss her, and put my hand inside her robe.

10

"Oh, Joe, *today?*"

"Yes, *today.*"

She's all gooseflesh. I'm nearly sweating. We make each other the same warm temperature. How intense life is, close to death!

About a quarter to two, I leave to go out in the field and make a few calls, as I do every afternoon. My first stop is a cluster of unfinished houses in the forty-thousand-dollar class, even farther from town than Rose's place. The general contractor has complained about the men we've been sending him, and when I get there, he's standing inside a huge Swiss-style chalet, a burly, hard-eyed man named Marshall Moore, staring up at the beamed ceiling and looking not at all pleased at what he sees.

"Sorry I'm late," I say, walking in. "Things are pretty upset around our place today."

"You mean Bragg," he says, looking up again at his ceiling. "Labor's better off without him. I know he was your friend, but that's the way I feel. The son of a bitch made me sick."

I grab him by his shirt front and wrestle him around so he faces me, and I can feel his big fleshy chest rippling beneath my hands.

"The man's been shot!" I yell into his face. "He wouldn't have shot anybody. Doesn't that mean anything to you?"

I glare at him, my face inches from his, adrenaline racing, my legs trembling. The hammering and sawing in the house next door stop. Moore looks down at my hands on his shirt. A man I've never had a beef with before. Strengthless, I let go of him and back off, shocked at my own anger. Moore smooths out the front of his shirt and looks embarrassed.

I sit down on a nail keg. "The hell with it. Let's talk."

We get along all right after that. He has a legitimate complaint; we'd sent him some permit men who weren't

up to building quality houses, and he wants them all replaced with experienced book men. It's a relief to both of
us that we're able to negotiate. My anger has established a
perimeter. If he has any idea that Bragg's death is going to
change our local's posture, now he knows otherwise. We
agree that half the permit men will be replaced.

From Moore's place, I drive down to the County District
Sewage Plant. We've had a crew of men there for a month
or so, building some forms and pouring concrete, and the
union steward has been filing complaints. He says the
foreman has tied him down to one job so that he can't get
around to the men and take care of his union duties. I talk
to the foreman with the steward there, so that neither one
can hand me a cock-and-bull story, and it seems the steward has a beef. The foreman reluctantly agrees to put a
couple of extra men on the crew and let the steward float.

At four o'clock, I'm back at the office, and Dorothy has a
message for me. Doug has called; he has to talk to me
right away. What now? A wreck? Picked up for speeding?
Suspended from school? It has to be bad news. I go into
my office and call him at home.

"Doug?"

"Dad—" His voice sounds small, and there's a throb in
it as though he has been crying. "A man said he's going to
kill you."

The breath leaves me. My body is suddenly heavy and
numb, and the numbness spreads, hands, feet, face; the
thought of death alone seems enough to drive the life out
of me.

"What man?" I manage to say.

"Just now, on the phone. He had the hardest voice I ever
heard."

"Tell me what he said." I'm impatient with fear.

Doug recites it, quavering. "He asked me if I was your
son and I said I was, and he asked me if I knew what had

happened to Baxter Bragg, and I said I did. His voice changed then. It got harder, and he said, 'Well, tell your dad he's next.' "

As simple as that. Bragg, then me. And no reason why.

"It's just some crank, Doug." I try to sound offhand about it.

"No! He meant it! His voice—I never heard a voice like that, like an animal learned to talk."

I try to imagine someone who would do that, who would send a message like that to me through my son.

"All right. I'll call the police. Stay home until I get there."

I explain to three different people at the Madrone Police Station who I am and what has happened: a telephone clerk, a sergeant, a captain. The clerk and the sergeant are skeptical, then uneasy; the captain is skeptical, then curious. He asks me if I have any idea who it might be, and I tell him I haven't. It *could* be a crank, he assures me, sometimes they have an amazing feel for what can wound people; or it could be someone in the union with a morbid sense of humor. He says he'll send someone out to the house.

I sit alone in my office, the door closed. It might be just an opportunistic gesture, an attempt to use Bragg's killing to intimidate me, a threat and nothing more. Even at that, I am involved in what Rose spoke about with astonished distaste. Yes, unions do kill people. It is a part of the way they operate.

I don't think Bragg ever wished to die, but he may have willed his death by boldly courting it. He burned up his days himself. He was prepared. I am not. I am a bland, cautious man, of prudent dimensions: five foot eight, twenty pounds overweight. I make payments. I have a physical exam scheduled next week. I get lost in a crowd of four. I have never felt any desire to be a hero while awake and sober. I resent Bragg despite myself. He tugs at my ankles from death.

I am sitting now by our dining-room window, writing this in longhand in one of Doug's blank school notebooks. I have decided to write down as much as I can remember of what happened to Baxter Bragg and, in doing so, interpret what is happening to myself. I had thought the police would question me about these things, but Officer Hoxie, the man they sent out, says that is an inspector's job, not his. Hoxie is a tall, parched-looking cracker who is addicted to Pepsi-Cola; he has moved in with us as my guardian and protector. He says that the San Francisco Homicide Bureau will surely contact me, because the murder was committed in San Francisco. But what if I'm killed first? Even life and death, apparently, can't violate procedure. Maybe what I write will have some value as evidence. Or as the record of a victim's thoughts. Perhaps I can write fear from my mind.

Yet there is another reason, uncomfortable in its egotism and vanity. Bragg's death may obscure his life. Mine is already obscure. Probably my death won't even be remembered. What does that leave of me to my son? We are all embezzlers, trying to withhold something from the grave. Perhaps someday someone will ask Doug what it was that his father did that would make anyone want to kill him. And he can turn to what I have written here. I cling to the belief that what is written honestly and in sweat is as much of a man as it is possible to snatch away from death.

2

Baxter Bragg used to say that there were only two kinds of people in the world, those who want to change things, and those who want them to remain the same.

He believed that all the selfish, frightened, privileged, lazy, and incompetent people of the world had a common interest: squeezing work out of the capable; that the rules for doing this had been set in law, custom, convention, and morality; and that the people who actually did the world's work were too busy to do anything about it.

He believed all of this so strongly that he made me believe it, too.

"Look around you," he'd say with patient intensity, as though speaking to a child. "Look at business, government, the military, the church, education, the press, organized labor. Look, and then tell me honestly that it isn't so."

"All right," I told him once, "I'll look at you. You're the president of a labor local. You make a good living selling work that other men do. That makes you one of the squeezers, right?"

We were at an Area Steering Committee meeting at Toad Fuller's house in Maple River, sitting outside around the swimming pool that Fuller never used, listening to the crickets compete with the noise from the highway.

"Absolutely," Bragg answered. "There are things about my job that make me puke, and every one of them's connected with that. I'm on the other side of the wall, with the big bellies. The difference is, I'm tapping around for a hollow sound. And when I find it, I'm going to push with everything I've got, and I'm going to break through."

In his sly, cozy way he turned my own argument against me.

"Look at yourself," he said. "You're the president of your local, and you don't want to be. You quit and they re-elected you. You're with the people on the other side of the wall, the squeezed, but you're only with them emotionally. You haven't realized yet that it's only people like you who can change things. People who have the option to join the squeezers, and don't. I think that this contradiction between your true feelings and your job is what made you quit, and what's bothering you now."

It was a thought that had come to me only at night, as I lay in darkness, awake and afraid and alone. We hardly knew each other when he said it.

"Such serious faces," said Josie Fuller, smiling behind a plate of cheese slices and crackers. "It's only a job."

"Yeah, what are you two talking so deep about, anyway?" said Toad, following her with an armful of cold cans of beer.

"Keeping the union from dying," said Bragg, taking some cheese and declining a beer.

"The Thinkers," Lenny Silk chimed in from across the pool, his young, dark, even features slack with disinterest.

Toad handed me a beer and I cracked it open. "The union isn't dying," he said. "They don't turn out for meetings and they don't vote, but they pay their dues. If they were unhappy, they'd yell." Toad is the National's Area Representative and the Chairman of the Steering Committee. He walked over to the other side of the pool, lay back in a lawn chair, and opened a beer for himself.

The four of us, Toad, Bragg, Silk, and myself, met every couple of months at Toad's house as the Area Steering Committee. The bylaws said we were to meet as equals; actually, each of us found whatever hole best fit him. Toad, as Area Representative, was our contact with the National, and anything important had to be cleared through him; Bragg, President of the San Francisco local, represented the largest single body of men. I double as President and Business Agent for our small organization in Madrone County, and Silk was the senior Business Agent in the San Francisco local. That, generally, dictated the order of the say we had in things.

Our union, the National Brotherhood of Construction Workers, was in those days a loose collection of dissimilar and often disputing locals. Some locals duplicated others, allowing employers to play them off against one another. Other locals were run outright by contractors, middlemen who kept labor costs down to lower construction bids. Our effective power to strike was limited, wages were comparatively low, and membership was declining. In twenty years, little about the union had changed, and what had changed was for the worse.

"I just wonder if there isn't more we could do," I said. "Retraining men out of work for new jobs, starting an apprenticeship program for Negroes, maybe, or even financing our own construction projects to make more jobs."

"Free riders?" Toad said contemptuously. "We can't afford 'em. A man's got to be willing to work to improve himself."

Bragg turned to me, his cigarette glowing out of the onrushing dark.

"Lonely, isn't it," he said.

17

"What?"

"Knowing you're on the wrong side of the wall."

We went on for hours, arguing and plotting and laughing, our voices carrying over the water and into the nearby hills and trees until only an occasional truck roared by on the freeway and the last dog in the neighborhood had quit barking. Then Toad started shifting around heavily, his lawn chair sagging and groaning beneath him.

"Well, boys, big day tomorrow."

And we got up, all together, and went inside to say good night to Josie, half-asleep in front of the TV, knowing that tomorrow would be no bigger than today.

"Keep the noise down," Toad warned us as we left. He liked his neighbors to think he was some kind of businessman.

There was a preordained futility about these meetings, as though talk were action and action accomplished nothing. The things that were wrong with our union had been wrong with it so long that they had become institutionalized; to change them you'd have to change the structure of the union itself, or replace the men who ran it; for all we knew, that might leave us with something worse. So we rolled along from day to day and month to month, heading downhill in well-worn grooves, so accustomed to things as they were that the fact that things were actually changing caught us by surprise. Even Bragg, who started it all.

It began a couple of days after Bragg and I had had that talk at Fuller's. I was in my office in the Madrone Union Hall, and I remember that I had just taken a real shellacking trying to get an industrial contractor to observe minimum safety precautions on a factory job. I almost had to beg, and he left me with an ultimatum. I was staring out the window, thinking once again about quitting, when I saw Fuller's Toronado nose into the parking lot, grow bigger, jump the parking buffer, and land in a flower bed.

Toad sat behind the wheel dejectedly, an elbow the size of a knee jutting out the window. His voice boomed at me across the lot as if through a bullhorn.

"He's done it! Goddam beatnik!"

Without knowing who he was talking about, I motioned to him to come inside. He squirmed out of his car and crossed the lot, a big man with a little mincing walk, top-heavy with chest and fat. The floor of our building creaked as he came down the hallway, and he was grumbling to himself so loud I could hear it inside my office.

"Won't answer his phone . . . won't return a call."

He ignored the girls' hellos and Potter's big, bootlicking shout and came straight into my office, his face folded all over itself in a bloodhound's frown. I offered him a chair. With his odd build it always seemed a great relief for Toad to sit. He leaned back into the chair and it trembled. He spoke slowly, in a deep voice, breathing heavily from the walk across the lot.

"Goddam Bragg, lousy shit-disturber. Pulled a crew off a job. Accused a contractor of chiseling on material. Didn't talk to me about it, just did it. Contractor told me. What gives, he wants to know. What is this guy, an agitator? And it's nothing. A housing project. Bunch of blues on welfare."

The Area Steering Committee had an unofficial policy for disputes with contractors. Any serious difference was referred to Toad, who got together with the contractor privately to iron things out. He was flexible enough to satisfy the contractors, and persuasive enough to get concessions out of them. It was a good policy, and it worked as well as anything else we'd been able to think of. It avoided a show of strength, which we didn't have.

Bragg had ignored the policy. What was worse, he had ignored Toad.

"It takes years to get contractors to trust a union officer.

Years. Just to get them to take your word. Who'll trust me now?"

For a man who physically doesn't look the type, Toad is one of the touchiest people I've ever known. He can take anything personally. Even as he was speaking to me, he kept taking fleeting little looks at me as though to read my reaction to what he was saying, wondering if I already knew what he was talking about, was in on it, had conspired against him. He made it hard to be yourself around him.

"I could have cleared this up in ten minutes. Now it's out in public. Everybody looks bad. Cannon's even on my ass about it. He wants to throw Bragg out. I'll have to bring him up on charges."

He stood with effort, walked around my desk, picked my telephone up off the sill, and set it on the desk in front of me.

"Call Bragg's number and say you want to talk to him, then put me on."

I didn't like shilling for Toad, but he was in such a distrustful mood I didn't want to say no to him. Besides, what did I owe Bragg? I picked up the receiver and dialed, while Toad stood watching me with his huge arms folded.

"Baxter Bragg, please."

"I'm sorry, Mister Bragg isn't in."

"Do you know when he'll be in?"

"No. Would you care to leave a message?"

"Yes. Tell him to call Joe Burke."

Whatever road Bragg had chosen, he was galloping down it alone, convinced that he'd be followed.

That afternoon, some Negro boys got into the materials Bragg's men had left behind: lumber, roofing, glass, tools, paint. They smashed windows, started fires, smeared paint over the walls. The police were called, and a sullen crowd had gathered when they arrived. The policemen,

20

frightened, talked tough, and the crowd responded by calling them motherfuckers. Arrests were made. Rocks were thrown. The police had to call for reinforcements. It wasn't a riot, but it could have been. People were milling around the areaways watching other people throw cans, bottles, and garbage out the upper-floor windows until after dark. The project was a bomb, and its fuse had been lit.

On the late-night television news, the screen went jagged with the fury of the place. The camera swung about wildly; black figures ran back and forth, objects were thrown, children shouted. A few people were interviewed, while kids waved and pushed each other around in the background, yelling and pretending to throw things. One huge woman, dressed in the white uniform of a nurse or cook, spoke directly at the camera, shaking with rage.

"You say we run these places down. Landlord run 'em down. Landlord is you!"

Suddenly, Bragg was there, and though I had talked with him and knew him slightly, seeing him like that surprised and startled me. He was strangely at home there, in all the wreckage and shouting and deep communal anger, as though some terrible pressure within him had been equalized. His black hair was as long as a girl's, and he had a shaggy black mustache, like a Mexican bandit. He wore a sort of improvised uniform, wool postman's pants, a work shirt with a red workman's bandanna knotted about his neck, and fuzzy boots like regular boots worn inside out. In all this, there was an unnerving air of random calculation, as though everything had been assumed deliberately, for effect, and even if you didn't fully understand the effect, he did.

"Why did you take your men off this job, Mister Bragg?" a reporter in a trench coat asked him. Bragg looked directly at the man, but his voice and the words he

21

spoke were aimed beyond him, at everybody there, and everybody watching.

"I'm tired of going to banquets and hearing beautiful speeches about the sacredness of public funds, and then finding myself confronted with the naked reality that leaves those beautiful words empty of ethics and empty of morality."

He had the gift. He could speak to a hundred people the way he spoke to one. And he was speaking of an issue far beyond a contractor's cheating on a single job.

"The more people you steal from, the less of a crime it is. If a man holds up a gas station and gets caught, he goes to prison. But if he steals from a whole community and misuses public funds, you've got to go out on the street and yell your head off, just to get a hearing."

Around him, where there had been only threats and screams of rage before, there were now approving voices.

"Oooo-weee!"

"Rip them mothas!"

"Then you're in favor of what's gone on out here?" the reporter said disapprovingly.

"There's been a theft, and people are yelling 'Stop, thief!' I blame the thief."

The reporter's tone became scolding now. "Kermit Stephenson says there isn't going to be any hearing. Do you have any comment?"

Kermit Stephenson was the head of the local Housing Bureau. His father had built a successful street-paving business on the same kind of chiseling that Bragg was complaining about now.

"Yes. Tomorrow morning, when Mister Stephenson goes to work, he'll find a picket line outside his office. It will stay there until he agrees to allow this matter to be heard openly. There will be another line out here to see that work isn't resumed until these tenants' rights are respected."

"Where will you be?" said the reporter.

"With the others, on the line."

It was as though Bragg had been preparing all his life for such a moment. He was improvising, acting instinctively, and his instincts had been bent to his will.

The newscast returned to its gray summations. No good. Bragg had shattered it as if with a hammer's smash. Feeling limp and excited at the same time, I walked out to the kitchen, threw a punch at the refrigerator door, took out a beer, and cracked it open.

Our union!

In the morning I went to find him. Thinking about what had happened, I began to brood about it during the night, slept hardly at all, and eventually decided that someone ought to warn Bragg that he was about to lose his job. But it wasn't only that. I felt proud and scared and guilty, all at the same time, and I knew I had to see him and talk to him and find out how he felt about what he'd done, because he seemed stranger to me now than he had the first time I met him.

Guessing, I went to the Housing Bureau Office of the San Francisco City Administration Building, an ugly, slab-sided mod-suburban box. There were no pickets outside the building; the only sign of anything unusual was a truck from a local television station.

I rode an elevator up, and as the doors slid open, I saw him. He was in a little knot of people, a crowd about the size that gathers around a fight: news people in close and men from Bragg's local, without neckties, farther back. The people around him were smiling, but Bragg, ferocious with hair, looked serious and strangely distracted as he answered questions, perhaps already seeing himself somewhere else.

I had decided to forget about trying to talk to him, but he spotted me with a quick look that I felt had read me down to the color of my socks and what I'd had for breakfast. He waved at me to come over until I did. Up close he looked tired, and he needed a shave. He put an arm around my shoulder. He needed a shower, too.

"This is JOE BURKE, president of our MADRONE COUNTY local."

One of the newsmen backed off a little, and pointed a movie camera at us that started whirring. Another man stuck a microphone in my face.

"How do you feel about this, Mister Berg?"

"What?"

"We've won, Joe." Bragg bloomed suddenly with pride. "We've got a full hearing on everything."

"No shit?" I said, and the whirring stopped.

We left them in the huge, marbled foyer and walked across the street to a small, nearly empty coffee shop. Bragg talked all the way, waving his arms and mimicking Kermit Stephenson. He was full of ideas; there would be a rank-and-file delegation to the hearings, and a permanent investigation team would be formed to look into all public-contract work while it was in progress. I tried to tell him about Toad's trouble with the National, but I couldn't get through to him.

"We've sat around moaning long enough. It's our union. We've got to plan our own future."

I noticed that people on the street were sneaking looks at him. He was as animated as a child, and it wasn't until we'd sat down at the counter and a fat-armed waitress served us coffee that the fatigue seeped back into his face and I remembered that he was as old as I was. I offered him a ride back to his office, and he accepted.

He drank his coffee with his eyes closed, needing it. Finishing, he turned and looked at me, and then beyond me to where he'd been before, when I'd seen him as I came off the elevator.

"Joe, I think I heard the hollow sound."

24

3

Hoxie has told me to move away from the dining-room table. Apparently the light I have been working by displayed me perfectly through the front window. He says it would have been an easy shot for an eleven-year-old boy. So now the trees and bushes in our front yard have become a threat, and the walls of our house move in on me. I work now in the kitchen, alone, like a woman, with the moody hum and silence of the refrigerator.

The police feel I am safe at my job and in daylight, so Hoxie stands watch only at night. He reports at six o'clock, in time for dinner, four or five Pepsis, and an evening poring over Doug's old *Motor Trend*s. He's a likable enough man, easy to talk to, like most Southerners; and if he has the racial hangups, he doesn't flaunt them. But he seems satisfied to work within the limits of his job. Curiosity isn't in him. He is prompt and diligent and follows his orders, but he asks me nothing about how all this came to be. It doesn't seem to concern him. I can imagine the account he would give of my killing: "At approximately ten-fifteen p.m., a vehicle pulled up outside the victim's house and two shots were fired through the front window. The victim fell to the floor and expired immediately." He would tell it in police jargon, and he would begin and end with the incident. I won't have my life reduced to a report on a police blotter!

4

At our next Steering Committee meeting, Toad was so angry he was walking around his house with his fly open.

"How do you expect me to help you when you don't even tell me what's going on? I *know* these people, and I'm telling you beefs like this can be avoided if we talk them over before they come to a head."

His shoes were off, his shirt was out, his hair was sticking up. Outside, it was raining.

"I've turned down cases I could have won, to keep everybody friendly. And then you come along with this. You start taking every beef out on the street, the whole process breaks down. Chrissake, we have to live with these people!"

Bragg stood restlessly, pretending to look through the sliding glass door at the rain hitting the pool. He hated being told what to do.

"I'll tell you what the contractors are saying. Dump him. You want to do business with us, get rid of that Fidel Castro son of a bitch. You sound off on TV, I'm the guy who has to live with it next day. I had to clean up your mess. I'm the one who has to apologize and make promises."

"You shouldn't have," Bragg said, still looking out the window.

"What? Are you kidding? You know what they can do to you? They can take away your job and blacklist you so you'll never find another one. Sure, I apologized. You've got some mean, tough people pissed off at you. So I told them you'd come around and join the team. And you will!"

Now Bragg turned and faced him. "Whose union is this, anyway?" he said.

"Theirs," said Toad. Turning his back he walked over and sank into his green leather chair, putting his stocking feet up on the matching footstool. "My job's with a union, not the Welfare Department. It pays for a house and a few comforts. Without it, all I'm worth is union scale. I don't lead revolutions."

Bragg looked at him, then walked over and lay flat out on the sofa; it was so long there was room enough for him to spread all the way out, and still leave plenty of space for me to sit.

"Watch your feet," Toad warned. He's one of those men property seems to make fussy. Bragg gave him a long look and hoisted his boots up over the sofa's arm.

"I thought you were supposed to represent the rank and file," Bragg said, still staring at him.

Toad jerked his thumb into his chest. "Mister, I AM the rank and file. I want what they want—to make out. They've all got something on the side, a piece of a contracting business, jobs they do below scale, scabbing, screwing us out of union dues. They're ambitious, like you and me. Admit that, and you know all there is to know about what the rank and file really want."

I felt helpless, ineffectual, in custody. I could hear Silk laughing with Josie Fuller in the kitchen. Smooth, black-

28

haired, a dandy, Lenny tries his hustle on them all. Like him, I was taken for granted. They would decide and we would concur. Both men assumed my consent. All the way out here in the rain to be a stooge.

"We all have to accept responsibility for turning down grievances that aren't important. Good relations must be maintained."

I felt feverish, angry, frustrated at being there and being silent, grouped with Silk, an empty iridescent suit, listening to that inconclusive bickering. It was getting late and I wanted to go home.

Most of all, I was tired of the way things were: I no longer believed it was the way they must be.

"So what if the contractors don't like it? They couldn't treat us worse."

Toad looked at me as if he'd just realized I was there. Bragg sat up on the sofa, alert.

I felt naked, and hot with exasperation.

"I'm tired of eating shit," I said. "I don't care about the consequences."

My reputation within the union, if any, is based on coolheadedness, reason, and detachment, qualities that are more personal timidity than personal conviction. I was the least likely person there to say what I did in the manner I did, and it must have been that fact that made Toad pause and reconsider. He had either misjudged me or misjudged the situation, either thought disturbing to a man who prides himself on the way he handles people. I expected him to pounce on me, but there was no sound but the rain.

"They're talking union in my local for the first time in years," I said. "You get enough men doing that, you've changed the union. That's what we're all trying to do anyway, isn't it?"

"Joe's got a point," said Silk, standing in the doorway. Hair combed, smirking, reassured, he crossed the room

29

and sat down in a wing chair. Toad glared at him all the way. "Well, he *has*," Silk pleaded.

Toad was looking at all of us now, studying to see if we had combined against him. He had made a mistake and he knew it. He should have tried to get to Bragg alone, instead of dragging the rest of us in on this. He had no idea of Bragg's aims, and he'd underestimated his influence.

"You're begging for trouble," he said. "You haven't got any idea what you're up against. You don't know how rough these people can be. Just wait till the general contract has to be renegotiated. You go in with everybody worked up on both sides and you'll end up with a strike for sure."

He paused, but no one rushed to agree with him.

"There's still time to drop the charges and call off this fool hearing."

He paused again, until it looked like he was making a plea.

"Democratic representation," he said disgustedly. He turned to Bragg. "Satisfied?"

"It's like a fight between two men," Bragg said. "You beat him once, you've got the edge on him the next time."

Toad shook his huge head, dismayed. "Have *you* got things to learn."

When we left, the rain had stopped and a cold wind was sweeping the last few clouds from a black, sparkling sky. There were puddles everywhere, throwing light back up at the moon, and yellow leaves all over the walks, pavement, and lawns.

Josie Fuller, tiny, blue-haired, concerned, cornered me at the front door, her glasses on a ribbon around her neck.

"You're not even wearing a hat. You take one of my umbrellas along with you." Maternal interest. I miss it enough around home to appreciate it when I go out.

Toad was hanging back, looking hurt and resentful. I went up to him and told him I was sorry.

He was disappointed. "I always thought you had some brains."

Carrying Josie's umbrella, folded, I walked dejectedly across the wet, spongy lawn, stamped mud off my shoes when I reached the street, and walked up the glassy pavement to my car. I had just unlocked the door when a thin, strong hand squeezed my arm. It was Bragg, come up the street behind me.

"Thanks," he said. "We'll have 'em where we want 'em." He smiled at me with clenched, animal teeth. I had nothing to say to him. I simply nodded, smiled back stupidly, and got into my car. I started the engine and he walked on. I ran the wipers enough to clear the windshield; looking out I saw Toad standing in the light of his doorway, watching.

It wasn't until I had driven down the darkened block to the cross street and hit a flooded intersection, the car submerging and surfacing, that I realized that Bragg had said "him" and not "them."

I'd assumed he'd meant the contractors, but he hadn't. He'd meant Toad.

Angry, I promised myself I wasn't going to let him lead me into doing anything else I didn't want to do. Why should I take his side? Let him fight his own battles. Yet even as I was telling myself these things, I had the feeling that Bragg was saying what I ought to be saying, that his battles actually were my battles, and that if the time and the issue were right, I could no more deny him than I could deny my own conscience.

During the next month, I got to know Bragg better. His job, like mine, dictated attendance at meetings of one kind or another three or four nights a week: Building Trades Council, construction industry forums, regional labor conferences. At each of these meetings, Bragg, assuming my sympathy, would seek me out, anxious to talk. We'd have coffee in a restaurant together, or stand outside and smoke during a break. I knew he was trying to win me over, but I didn't mind. The meetings were dull, and Bragg was one of the most interesting men I'd ever met. By adding the things he told me about himself to the now constant gossip about him around the local, I was piecing together a picture of what his life up to that time must have been like.

As far back as anyone could remember, Bragg had been a rebel. Finished with school at sixteen—the first and last time he and his teachers ever agreed—he went to sea, and was soon in the thick of the waterfront disputes of the thirties. At eighteen, standing on a barrel on an oil-refinery dock, he made an arm-waving speech to the crew of a tanker and pulled them out on strike. He was named a delegate to the Mariners' Union strike committee. He wrote articles for the union's newspaper, circulated petitions and made speeches. He took sides in every election and campaigned hotly for his candidates; eventually he ran for office himself. Always, he inspired among some people worshipful loyalty, and, among others, murderous hatred. He left no one he met unmoved.

In time the union divided into factions, one of which was supposed to be Communist and one anti-Communist, and Bragg chose the wrong side. Twice he was tried and convicted by the union's Executive Board. Twice he was beaten up, the second time so severely he was hospitalized with broken ribs.

Flat on his back, unable to act, Bragg had contemplated his future. He was dead-ended politically with the Mariners, and he didn't want to go back to sea. He possessed only one real skill, a surgeon's sense of the inside of a labor union and how it operates. So, when he got out of the hospital, he joined the Construction Workers and started over.

Shrewd, experienced, he moved up rapidly in the new union by avoiding the mistakes he'd made in the old. More clearly than anyone else ever had, he gave voice to the fears and desires of the rank and file. But his militance now had a discipline to it that he had lacked before. Instead of just making speeches when he ran for office, he went around and talked to men individually at meetings and out on the jobs. He handed out mimeographed copies of his complaints and a description of his aims. He adopted his unusual dress as a badge of his service to an ideal: no fancy suits, no expensive shoes, no jewelry, no deals. The dissidents in the local began to gather around him. Most important of all, on election nights, Bragg always had his own monitors standing by, watching the ballots being counted. He had become sergeant at arms, recording secretary, and a business agent. Now he was local president, and there were men reduced to red-faced speechlessness at the thought of it.

Among most union officials and the leading contractors, the feeling was that Toad would have Bragg housebroken within a short time; yet now, just months after his election, Bragg was as noisily militant as he had been before. Knowing both of them, I wasn't surprised. Bragg was dedicated and he was tough, two qualities that Toad felt obliged to defend. He was also useful. To the National, Bragg was a problem that they were depending on Toad to solve, and while the problem remained, the dependence remained—as long as Toad didn't let it become too great a problem. So though he complained about the way Bragg looked and acted, and repeatedly threatened to take action against him, Toad mostly just waited and watched.

33

• • •

One afternoon toward the end of that first month, I was making a call down near the bay at an old Navy warehouse that was being renovated. The warehouse, idle since the war, had been bought by a commercial real-estate developer, who was splitting it into small industrial space. There were about thirty men in there, putting up partitions, painting, and installing fixtures, and the steward had complained that some of the men were nonunion, so I stopped by to investigate. I parked my car and walked around the building to the main entrance, which faced a wharf on the other side. There was Bragg, leaning against a piling, a paper rolled under his arm, chewing a toothpick and looking as though he expected me.

"Got something I want you to see," he said, unrolling the paper. It was a petition with about eight pages of signatures.

"It's against automation."

I started to laugh, but stopped at a smile when I saw how serious he was.

"Did you know that in less than five years, eighty per cent of all construction work will be done by automatic machinery? Not just the heavy stuff, but the skilled work —the finish. We've got to do something before it's too late. I know I don't have any business out here on one of your jobs, but my men have all signed and I need more names. Once we get the signatures, we can have copies made. One for the contractors, one for the National, one for the Department of Labor. . . ."

He rolled up the petition vigorously and stuffed it back under his arm. "Of course, I won't go inside unless you okay it."

I didn't know what to do. I didn't want to appear a fool in front of my own men, but I couldn't turn him away, either. I decided I'd say nothing to the men and keep my

34

distance from him. Then I could explain him away as an eccentric.

"No, no, it's perfectly all right, you go right ahead," I said.

We walked into the warehouse together, and the men inside recognized him immediately, looking up and staring, nodding to or nudging one another as we made our way around sawhorses and stacks of wallboard, the whole building echoing with hammering and sawing and electric-sanding. One kid with long hair, carrying a window frame, yelled something I couldn't hear because of the noise, and Bragg grinned at him. Most of the men seemed merely curious, except for the foreman, who looked angry.

They broke for coffee, and the warehouse became so quiet I could hear the footfalls as the men drifted away from their work, went outside to a catering truck, and then came back in and gathered in a loose circle around us, looking at Bragg and drinking from white plastic cups. Silently, Bragg climbed up on a forklift in the center of the circle, unrolled his petition, and read it to them, showing them the pages of signatures, names of men just like themselves who did the same kind of work—or used to— up against the same competition from machines—automatic sanders, sprayers, precut walls. There was a good deal of moving about among the men, and quiet conversation; they seemed more interested in the way Bragg looked than in what he was saying.

Suddenly, Bragg raised his voice as though there were hundreds of men in there instead of thirty, and the sound went clear up through the dusty air to the rafters.

"We're not against machinery. We're in favor of it!"

The circle around him grew silent and still. The foreman, standing off by a roll of tar paper, turned to listen.

"We believe in lessening the rigors of labor at the point

35

of production," said Bragg, "but only when the men it replaces are given certain guarantees."

There was nodding in the crowd at this, and an enthusiastic "Yeah!" from the kid with the long hair.

"A full week's wages," Bragg continued. "Holiday and vacation pay. A pension plan for our old age. We say okay, give us these things, and you can do the work with robots or trained monkeys if you like."

They were smiling now, and a couple of men laughed in a small, pleased way. Bragg waited them out, then picked out the foreman and looked directly at him.

"But until you provide us with all these securities, we'll tell *you* how the work is going to be done."

The foreman turned and walked away, and Bragg addressed himself again to the men near him.

"That's what this petition says. If you're for it, sign here."

They crowded in around him, reaching into their pockets for pens or pencils, borrowing them from one another, pushing through to get to the petition, signing, asking Bragg questions, then working back out to the edge of the crowd. He got all the names. He even got mine. The men shoved me forward to the center of the circle, and there was no getting out of it. I signed; they cheered. Bragg smiled as he took my name. He was using, as a writing surface, one of the compressor-sprayers he was trying to have outlawed.

That Radical, the contractors called him, for they feared Bragg less than the forces he might awaken within the union: independence, autonomy, reform. Almost every afternoon when I'd go out to the jobs, some foreman or contractor would take me aside and pump me about him. What was he really like? Why did he dress funny? What did he want? They could feel him pressuring them, but they didn't know why or for what.

36

About a week after Bragg had come around with his automation petition, I made a call on Howard Geer, the industrial contractor who had driven me near to quitting by his refusal to consider even minimum compliance with the safety regulations standard in union contracts. Geer, a thin, aging man with a corrupt bloat of stomach and proudly healthy teeth, operates out of a one-story cinder-block office next to an auto junk yard. When I drove up, he was outside wearing a windbreaker and a Panama hat, loading square white boxes into the bed of a blue pickup truck.

"I knew you were crooks," he said, seeing me, "but I never thought you'd stoop to this."

Geer conducts all his business in a chafing manner that alternates between sarcasm and embittered righteousness. Some people describe it as gruff charm.

"Well, you've got what you wanted," he said, opening one of his boxes. He held up a silver construction workers' hard hat. "Hard hats. Goggles. Respirators. Safety belts. I hope you're satisfied. You and that blackmailer with the two last names." He closed the box and shoved it into the back of the truck.

"Baxter Bragg?" I said.

"That's the one." He picked up three more boxes. "Lousy racketeer." He dropped one of the boxes and I picked it up and handed it to him.

"What did he do?"

Geer lifted the boxes into his truck, took a breath, and tilted his hat back with a thumb.

"I got a job over in the city, renovating a grade school. Public contract, no sweat, everybody's happy. Yesterday, smack at the noon hour, this hoodlum shows up with a gang. Walk right through a schoolyard full of children into the building and start tearing everything apart. Ropes, pulleys, plastering equipment, scaffolding. One of the teachers runs and gets the foreman, who comes to see what's up. 'You got a fire hazard here,' this pirate tells him. That gas valve is leaky. The men have no hard hats. And he starts reading off the regulations from the contract. Kids and teachers standing around watching. 'You know what this kind of thing can do to a man?' he says. And he shows them. How? He uses the men he brought with him. Each one of them's a CRIPPLE. One's missing an arm. Another only has one eye. A third limps. And the fourth one—the fourth one has NO FACE. It's just scars, like a Halloween mask. His Safety Committee, he calls them—they even chewed out one of their own men for working in street shoes. From now on, he says, safety regulations will be enforced as written, and he'll send this team around to inspect any job where a violation has been reported, so men can work without suffering these horrible injuries. All this with children watching. They finish up with a demonstration of mouth-to-mouth resuscitation, and ten minutes later the principal is burning up the wire. You better do something about this, he says; I don't want trouble with the school board. It's blackmail, I tell him. I don't care, he says, I don't want trouble. So here I am, spending my own money for a bunch of crap for babies who don't know enough to take care of themselves and won't want to use it anyway."

He slammed the gate on the truck bed and fixed the chains.

"I've seen 'em all," he said. "Harold Gibbons when I was a kid teamster in St. Louis, and Bridges when he called the general strike here. This one's the worst. He's nothing but a god-damned hairy maniac."

He opened the door of his truck, climbed in, and angrily started the engine. Just before he put it in gear, he leaned his head out the window.

"And it's for nothing," he said sourly. "The men couldn't care less."

He backed up, turned around, and drove out the dirt

road to the highway, trailing dust, the white boxes bouncing in the bed of his truck.

Confused and elated, anxious to talk to somebody about what had happened, I got into my car and headed back toward the local office. I had never known a man who took so much pleasure in making people uncomfortable. Or who was so skillful at it. Bragg seemed to be able to pick out a psychological advantage in any situation, and know exactly how to exploit it. He must have sat up nights planning some of the stunts he pulled, or have been anticipating them for years. All the arguments I'd had with Geer had produced nothing. Now Bragg had made him give in completely with one clever stunt. I was proud of him, and, at the same time, envious.

When I drove into our lot, four apprentice painters, kids of about twenty, were outside taking turns spray-painting a cut-out section of wallboard. I stopped to talk to them, asked the journeyman supervising them how they were doing, and questioned the kids about the work. They seemed bright, enthusiastic, different somehow from the kids we usually drew into the union, yet familiar. Then it dawned on me. Each of them had hair that was longer than normal, and was attempting to grow a mustache.

I went on inside and, after thinking about it, decided I'd call Bragg to tell him what had happened and thank him. I had a hard time getting through to him. There always seemed to be people in his office or trying to get in to see him. I wondered how he managed to get any work done, and as he talked to me, he seemed preoccupied. I told Bragg that he ought to know that he'd won an old battle for me, and that I was grateful to him for it.

He said something I couldn't hear to whoever was there with him.

"Hey, what have you got on for tomorrow night?" he asked me.

I couldn't think of any plans.

"Why don't you come over here to our business meeting and see how we operate?"

I didn't want to go. I attend enough meetings as it is, but I knew that wasn't the real reason. I was afraid Bragg would again be successful where I wasn't, that he would have a big turnout instead of the sparse ones we had, and that what went on would be interesting instead of a bore.

"Okay," I said.

"Good! We're in the Trades Union Building, and it starts at eight."

Promptly at eight o'clock the following night, I walked in the front entrance of the San Francisco Trades Union Building, one of those brick-and-stone fortresses out of the Crusade Era of American labor, drafty inside, with spotty lighting and grimy, landlord-green walls. Bragg's local occupies half a floor of the building, including a hiring hall, and I followed the murmuring sound of men's voices up a flight of stairs and down a narrow hallway until I came to a man who seemed wider than the doorway he guarded and had piles of black hair all over him. I handed him my union card, and he scowled at it as though he'd never seen one.

"Next door," he growled, handing back the card. I walked on down the hallway, the murmuring breaking into individual voices now, shoved open a heavy metal door, and entered a small dark room with hanging ropes and electrical switches on the walls. There was a velvet curtain across from the door; I stepped through it and found myself in the hot glare of an auditorium stage. Bragg and three other men were standing at a trestle table in the center of the stage, talking; he waved me over and introduced me around. Lenny Silk I knew, but Max Volt, the Secretary-Treasurer, was new to me, a little rat-faced man going bald at the back of his head. The other man, a bashful kid who was growing hair and a mustache in frank imitation of Bragg, had recently been elected recording secretary, and was scheduled to chair the meeting. He was being teased by his buddies in the audience. It was a big crowd for a routine meeting, a couple of hundred men, maybe, some of them standing, all of them talking, a few yelling back and forth, frighteningly alive.

We sat on folding chairs behind the table, and the audience gradually settled itself. Max Volt banged a gavel on the table gently and called the meeting to order. He introduced the chairman, who blushed and stared at the table while his friends booed, and then me.

"He looks like a contractor," someone said in a loud voice.

The kid read the minutes of the last meeting. This was followed by a report on recent grievances by the chairman of the Grievance Committee. After the report, the kid asked for comments and the hands went up. There were two microphones, one in the center aisle and one to the side, and whoever had the floor would stand before one of the mikes and talk. A short man built like a weight-lifter got up and complained that his foreman was picking on him; two fat, bald men, one at each mike, almost came to blows arguing over Vietnam; a Mexican kid with a big mop of hair got up haltingly, hands in his pockets, and, in broken English, complained that union dues were too high. There was a long discussion about the dues, and at one time men were lined up five or six deep at each microphone, and Bragg or Silk would have to break in occasionally and direct the discussion back to the subject. Finally, a resolution urging a reduction was proposed. They voted, and it passed. Bragg said he'd notify the National of the proposal and the vote, and the men groaned.

Most union meetings are puppet shows. Either nobody comes or nobody cares. This was different. Anybody who

41

wanted the floor could have it, and you could raise any issue you wished.

About eleven o'clock, a little man with red blotches on his face, wearing horn-rimmed glasses and a brown fedora, got to one of the microphones and began reading a long typewritten statement charging Bragg with conduct unbecoming a union officer, accusing him of being a Communist under direct orders from Moscow, and demanding his resignation. The other men laughed at him and tried to shout him down, but he read on doggedly in a shaky, angered voice, while Bragg leaned back in his chair, boots up on the table, listening. The man raged on until it stopped being funny. His anger had a fuming, lethal quality to it, an indignation too impersonal to be laughed off. Listening to him, you knew that he could get up and say what he was saying only because he was sure that there were others who felt as he did, bossed and cheated, in the union, yet against it, against Bragg the way Bragg was against the National. The man asked the angry, silent crowd to pass a resolution demanding Bragg's dismissal. It was an ugly moment, and the kid chairing the meeting looked around anxiously, not knowing what to do.

"Second," Bragg snapped impatiently, raising his hand.

"All in favor," the chairman said numbly. The blotchy-faced man voted, but he voted alone.

The meeting broke up abruptly after the vote, and Bragg left, walking past me without speaking, looking upset. I stood by myself for a few moments, watching the men file out, noticing the frequency of beards and mustaches among them, until I saw the man in the fedora leaving silently, alone. I decided I'd better find Bragg, and went looking for him.

He was in an office across the hallway, a small, cluttered room where he sat by himself, running his hands nervously through his long hair. I closed the frosted-glass door behind me, removed a binder from a chair, and sat across his paper-covered desk from him.

"Bastards," he said bitterly. "Lose one vote and it's all over."

He opened a desk drawer and brought out a quart bottle half full of bourbon, along with two dusty-looking water glasses. He poured about two fingers in each glass and handed me one. He drank about half of his in a quick gulp, while I sipped mine; without ice, it tasted medicinal.

"No wonder Cannon rigs elections," he said coldly.

We sat for a while without talking. He was in one of those disagreeable moods where he'd be against anything, and I didn't want to argue with him. He was leaning back in his swivel chair, not looking at me but off toward the wall, and I thought for a moment that he'd fallen asleep.

"Businessmen have it knocked," he said, thinking. "No fucking democratic principles."

There was a soft tapping on the glass of the door, and Bragg turned, slowly recognized the shadow standing there, and smiled wickedly, his whole mood changing.

"Want to see something funny?" he almost whispered. "Go open that."

As I got up and walked to the door, I heard Bragg roll his chair away from his desk. I turned the doorknob. A small, pale, older man, dressed in black, wearing a black overcoat, carrying a walking stick in one hand and a black Homburg hat in the other, was standing in the doorway, catching his breath.

"That's some stairway you've got there," he said as if he knew me, in a surprisingly deep voice.

He had thick, white, carefully trimmed hair with long sideburns, fierce, glittering eyes, and a tight, moralistic mouth.

"Foster Wilkins," he said tentatively. "General Counsel

for the Contractors Association. And you're Mister Bragg."

"No," I said, pointing behind me, "he's Mister Bragg."

I turned and looked back. And saw nobody. There was no one sitting at Bragg's desk, no one standing by his dirty window, and no other door to the room. Wilkins looked at me suspiciously.

"Over here." Bragg's voice came up from the floor.

Wilkins walked into the room, up to the edge of the desk and peered over.

"Mister Bragg?"

"Yes."

"I'm Foster Wilkins."

"I know. Have a seat."

Wilkins backed bewilderedly into a chair. I sat down, too. Bragg remained lying on the floor. Wilkins waited, apparently expecting Bragg to get up and take his chair or at least offer some explanation of why he was flat on his back.

"Go ahead," said Bragg, not moving.

Wilkins glanced at me distrustfully, then addressed the empty desk.

"I think it might be best if we spoke privately."

"Anything you have to say to me, Joe can hear. Foster Wilkins, Joe Burke, Madrone County local."

We nodded to each other awkwardly. Wilkins stared at Bragg's empty chair, at the desk, at me, searching for an explanation. Torn between his fear of giving offense and his fear of being laughed at, he decided to rise above both, and cleared his throat.

"Very well. Mister Bragg, the General Executive Board of the Contractors Association are very much aware of your remarkable capacity for organization and leadership. Being executives, they respect ability, even when it's opposed to them. They understand your sentiments, and they've asked me to make sure that you understand theirs,

44

so that relations between your organization and ours may continue harmonious. Briefly, they'd prefer working with you to working against you. And they've asked me to ask you if you'd be interested in continuing your work for your men on the employers' side."

"In what way?" said Bragg.

"As a consultant," Wilkins said delicately. He had crossed one leg over the other and was tapping his shoe on air. "You'd receive a monthly fee paid into a bank deposit box, to which you would have the key. You could use the money to establish your own business, buy a home, educate your children, anything you like."

"What would I have to do for it?"

"Simply help the Association deal with your men."

"That's all?"

"Generally speaking, we'd like you to co-operate with us more, and oppose us less."

"Just sort of take it easy."

"Yes."

"Lie down on the job."

Feeling the ridicule, Wilkins grew annoyed. "However you choose to put it," he said condescendingly. "We want you to lead your men less militantly, in the best interests of all concerned, and we're prepared to pay you a regular sum to insure your co-operation. Are you interested, or are you not?"

"If I was, would I be treating you like this?"

Wilkins made a face. He uncrossed his legs and fondled his walking stick as though he'd like to brain Bragg with it. "I see," he said, staring at the desk in front of him. He boosted himself up with his stick. "Thank you for your time," he said, not meaning it. I stood as he walked past me, his face pure hurt. But when he reached the doorway, the heat had flowed out of him, leaving the old, moralistic coolness.

"I hope, for your sake, sir, that your enormous confidence in yourself is justified." He held the door for a moment, then closed it behind him quietly.

Bragg's hairy head bobbed up behind the desk, teeth gleaming.

"Do you know what that *does* to a guy?" he said delightedly.

Two nights later, our own local had its business meeting, and by comparison to Bragg's, everything seemed managed and dull. Only a dozen men showed up, every one of them a steward, and half of them wouldn't have come if we hadn't raffled off a clock radio as a door prize. They sprawled over a couple of rows of folding chairs in our auditorium, yawning and scratching, openly bored, while Potter read the minutes of our previous meeting, the Grievance Chairman made his committee report, and I read a few announcements and presented the budget. Then I drew the winning ticket out of the local's ballot box, and, as luck would have it, the ticket belonged to the Grievance Chairman. The men moaned as if they'd all been cheated, I handed the Chairman his radio, the meeting dissolved, and the men headed for home.

Potter and I were left to fold and stack the auditorium chairs. I felt so low about the way the evening had gone that, while we worked, I tortured both of us by telling him how much more crowded, interesting, and involved things had been at Bragg's.

"You've heard what he's done now," Potter said grudgingly, as he collapsed a chair upon itself.

"What?" I said, taking it from him to pile it on the stack, expecting to hear another account of some minor mischief.

"He's merged his local with the San Carlo local."

I stopped, the chair still in my hands. For years, the

Construction Workers local in San Francisco had been forced to compete with the Construction Workers in neighboring San Carlo County. Jurisdiction of the two locals was identical, to the weakness of each and the advantage of all employers in both counties, who played one local against the other constantly. The problems that this dual jurisdiction posed were so tangled that no serious attempt had ever been made to resolve them. And now, apparently, Bragg had done it.

"When?" I asked, piling one chair and refusing to take the next, so that Potter had to pause in his work, too.

"I heard it in the car coming over," he said. "The rank and file of both locals voted to amalgamate, all the officials resigned, they held a joint election, and Bragg was elected president. I guess they'd been working on it in secret for weeks."

Weeks. Of the hardest sort of bargaining, with union officials who were being asked to abolish their own jobs. What patience it must have taken, with all the exhausting legal details, the scheduling, the phasing of existing situations into new ones. He hadn't told me a word of it, and it began to dawn on me how all of us who had been amused or outraged by Bragg's public acts had underestimated him. It was almost as if he had conceived his more colorful shenanigans as cover, and proved that none of us had correctly gauged his depth, his ambition, or his ability to exercise his will in private negotiations.

Potter handed me another chair. "His agitating days are over now. You watch."

"Why?" I challenged him, thinking of Wilkins' offer of two nights before.

"Because he's now president of the largest Construction local in the United States."

5

Tonight is his memorial service, and Hoxie is my chaperone.

Bragg had rejected formal religion, so his wife and his associates in the local have decked out the Trades Union Building hiring hall with dogmatic unorthodoxy: evergreen boughs, giant blown-up photographs, folk music. "A simple, nondenominational canonization," Rose calls it.

There must be a thousand people in the shabby, half-lit auditorium: all the professional Friends of the Working Man, city officials and other political dignitaries toward the front, looking beefy and at ease; union officers sitting stiffly behind them, and a large number of rank-and-file union men with their wives, people who don't talk but give each other quick glances and look down, embarrassed and frustrated, not knowing how to act, men with heads bowed, dumpy women wearing bandannas, curious and reverent in the face of death and ceremony. All the seats are taken; a line of standees stretches from one end of the stage along the side to the back wall, across it and up the other side to the apron.

Lenny Silk, standing at the door, greets everybody warmly and thanks each of us for coming. It's the kind of thing he's good at: tell him your name once, and he'll never forget it.

We find room to stand about halfway forward along the auditorium wall, Hoxie with his back against the wall, wearing a gray plastic raincoat, his eyes continually scanning the audience, hands clasped in front of him in the fig-leaf position. He might as well be wearing a uniform and a badge.

A quiet crowd, except for an occasional nervous cough, and the clear, sad voice of Joan Baez, floating out over the public-address system.

"We shall over cuh-uh-um, we shall over cuh-uh-um."

I hear a sniffle, turn, and catch a man in tears: Paul Eisan, the scar-faced man who headed Bragg's Safety Committee. A roofer, he had once been struck by a bucket of hot tar which left his face an eerie, expressionless mask of scar tissue.

A podium has been set up at the center of the stage, against a backdrop of pine boughs and Bragg's staring photograph. Below, in front of the apron, is a row of floral tributes displayed on wooden tripods. "Rest in Peace Brother, Brotherhood of Glaziers, Local Four." There are flowers from the Longshoremen, the Teamsters, even the Mariners; but nothing from the National or the Contractors.

The audience rustles, heads turn, and Sally Bragg comes up the center aisle, walking quickly, small, slender, about twenty-five or twenty-six, and very pretty. She was Bragg's second wife, and they'd been married only two or three years. A college student, she had come to the union to help out in the office during the summer, had been persuaded to move in with Bragg, and in the fall, over the screaming objections of her parents, had married him. I suppose they had predicted something like this for her. A fiercely determined girl, with a fluid, sensual body, she has a pawnbroker's shrewdness for getting what she wants. Hardened even further by the cold shock of what has happened to her husband, she moves now with taut purpose, head erect, tearless, her blond hair pulled back severely from her face, as much concerned with the significance of gesture as her husband ever was. Rose follows obediently at one elbow and Silk at the other as she walks forward and takes a seat at the front, the politicians making room for her. There is sympathetic muttering in the audience as she passes, injured, bitter, vengeful.

Having stood to look, everyone remains standing. The folk singer's soprano is followed by a slow, rich Negro baritone:

> "Sleep my love and peace attend thee,
> All through the night.
> Guardian angels God will lend thee,
> All through the night."

They better all have union cards, I can't help thinking. Or he'll send them back.

> "There's a hope that leaves me never,
> All through the night."

"Be seated, please."

Silk stands at the rostrum, and the sight of him there, handsome and amiable, is oddly reassuring. Whatever he says, it won't be anything graceless or clumsy. With a lot of bumping and scraping, people reclaim their seats.

"We have come here tonight to honor a brave man, who chose to live colorfully and dangerously in a world that is, for most of us, safe and drab."

He's already a memory, and no one seems quite sure what he'll be remembered for. To Silk, Bragg was a knight who had heroically fought life's greatest dragon, boredom.

"A great personality, an exciting companion, a warm personal friend."

Fireman Tom Sheehy, a labor skate and perennial delegate to the State Assembly, sees him as "a union man of the old school, whose name will be remembered along with Gene Debs and Joe Hill."

"A dedicated crusader for the rights of all citizens," an earnest Negro lawyer describes him.

There are eulogies from a mayor he'd helped elect, and a congressman he'd tried to defeat, telegrams from the governor, an assistant secretary of Labor, and the president of the AFL-CIO. He might have been dead five years. People are trying to put the pain and horror of what happened to him behind them, smoothing flat the ground he had turned over. Where is the man's feistiness, his raw hunger for combat, his anger? As I listen to the second-hand feelings, the easy condensations and baseless optimism, it occurs to me that perhaps, in the end, it is his enemies who knew him best.

Only one voice has any shame or outrage in it. A turkey-necked old-timer named Zip Coleman is introduced as a rank-and-file spokesman for Bragg's local. He sways drunkenly at the rostrum, wearing a shiny blue suit that's too big for him, hopelessly flustered at speaking in public.

"I'm no speaker. Had to get half a heat on to come up here. But I'll tell you something. We got to get them that done it, or we won't ever be men again."

He starts to continue, stumbles in embarrassment, leaves in the middle of a word, and sits down. An empty rostrum gets the thickest applause of the night.

They turn the lights up full when it's over, and the people file out, solemn, murmuring, squinting at one another. I see no contractors and no one from the National, but there are a few expensively dressed officials from local construction firms shuffling out in the crowd. Bragg had always got along better with the management of management than with the management of labor. They'd had no illusions about each other. I don't see Toad, but then I hadn't expected to.

I wait for Rose to break away from a group of women consoling Sally Bragg with a lot of sympathetic nodding and hand-squeezing. Quietly, looking harassed, Rose draws off to the near corner of the stage, and I walk over to her and we talk for a while. Her skin is tight across her face, as though somebody has hold of the back of her neck. Rigid, nervous, she speaks fast and softly. When I ask her what's wrong, she won't say, and when she hears Sally's voice, she jumps.

"Rose? Where's Rose? Oh, there you are, dear."

In some women stress forces to the surface a crisp, spring-steel authority, instead of tears. Hard, assertive, masculine, it makes the simplest request seem like a direct order, and must be the envy of all job foremen. Some schoolteachers have it, I suppose, and frequently the mothers of small, active children. Sally Bragg has it now, so pronounced that I feel she can go out in her black veil and issue commands to a firing squad.

"Joe. Bless you for coming." She sweeps back her veil and turns her cheek to me. I kiss at it, miss, she's gone, brusquely heading out, sweeping Rose along with her, three or four other people hurrying after.

"I'll phone you," Rose calls back to me, waving as she hustles away up the aisle.

Deserted, I turn to Hoxie. He's looking off in the opposite direction, and his hand is reaching inside his raincoat. I look around. A man is trying to get over to me, half restrained by another smaller man. It's Eisan, the roofer, and there is no reading any intention in his destroyed face.

52

"Let go," he says sharply to the man at his sleeve. "I got to to talk to him." Reluctantly, the little man lets him pull away.

He turns his shiny, plasticine face to me. "Burke! What do we do?"

Thinking all he wants is commiseration, I shrug. "I don't know."

"Tell us!" he shouts, distraught, intense, and so loud that the few stragglers remaining in the auditorium stop talking and turn to look. He really wants me to give him some kind of order, and he wants it desperately. The little man tugs at his sleeve again, urging him away.

"He's got to tell us," Eisan shouts at him. "He knows!"

Shamelessly, I use Hoxie as an excuse. "I have to go. This is a police officer." Pulling Hoxie with me, I turn and flee.

"Don't sell us out!" he yells after me. "You're the next!"

I almost run down the narrow hallway and the dirty cement stairs. Hoxie has to trot to keep up with me. His raincoat flies open, and I see his gun is drawn inside it.

"I thought he was going to try it," he says.

"Not him," I say, short of breath and gasping, "he's not the one."

My legs are shaking when we reach the street, and I have a pain in my side. People are out walking, cars and buses pass, horns are honked, an old man on the corner hawks papers. The indifferent busyness of the city absorbs me. Self-consciously, I assume a calm, exaggerated stroll, and Hoxie puts his gun away carefully, without opening wide his coat. Wanting company, a crowd, security, I offer to buy him a drink in a gin mill down the street.

It's a small place, just a bar with a row of stools and two small tables toward the rear, crowded and noisy, half neighborhood drinkers and half men off the night shift: printers in square newspaper hats, a baker, a tattooed dishwasher. Hoxie gets into a conversation about firearms with a man in an orange jacket and a red hat, who looks as though, wherever his car is parked, there's a deer slung over the front fender.

With no one to talk to, I have three beers instead of one, and the bartender sets up a complimentary shot. What the hell, things are going to be all right. This isn't the jungle. People look out for one another.

Eventually, Hoxie's gun buddy lays his head on the bar and falls asleep. With effort, Hoxie recalls me.

"Hey, what did that scar-faced guy want?" he asks me innocently.

"To bring the dead back to life."

"I damn near dropped him."

That seems to be the end of his interest. Feeling angry and neglected, I start needling him.

"Hoxie, how come you're only a patrolman when you've been on the force so long?"

Surprised, but not hurt, he thinks a moment and says: "Timing." He explains that as a rookie he'd walked a night beat on the main street of our small town. He was young, conscientious, eager to please; things on his beat were slow, so he'd decided to crack down on the only vice available, Irv's, a bar, much like the one we're in now, that was serving drinks after hours. At five minutes past two one morning, Hoxie had walked inside, caught the bartender still pouring, and announced that he was going to close the place down. He took a drink off the bar and brought it back to the station house as evidence.

"Bourbon and water. And a little napkin with it."

Proudly he'd reported to his desk sergeant. Nice work, Merle, the sergeant said, let's see your evidence.

Hoxie didn't know at the time that the sergeant was Irv's partner. He put the drink right up on the desk. The sergeant held the glass up to the light, then emptied it in a single gulp.

"I don't see any evidence," he said.

"Next thing I knew," Hoxie tells me sadly, "I was night watchman out at the powerhouse." He stares glumly into his glass. "It was timing, that's all. If somebody else would of been on that desk, it would of been a good pinch. It's been shit details for me ever since."

Remembering me, he adds: "Nothing personal, you understand."

Hoxie wheels us home; I'm too stiff to drive. It's late enough so there's almost no traffic, and he zooms through the empty city streets as though driving a squad car. I can't help sympathizing with him. This must be lousy duty: there is no way for him to distinguish himself. Either nothing happens, or I get shot, in which case he has to take the blame, and risk getting shot himself.

"You know," he says wearily, "if there's just one man who's out to get you, and he's willing to die to do it, there isn't much I can do to stop him. I thought you'd want to know that."

"No, I didn't want to know that." The calm and the drinks are wearing off together.

"Well, it's a fact."

We're crossing the Golden Gate Bridge, and suddenly alone. No houses, no buildings. It would be so simple for a car to come alongside us now . . .

"Why guard me at all if you can't protect me?"

"I'm not protecting you, I'm protecting the force. If you get hit, people start saying why wasn't this man given police protection? You've got police protection, so they're covered."

"So this is just bullshit, then."

He nods. "I don't like being a target any more than you do."

It's true. He's right there at the bull's-eye with me, and kicking himself for letting it happen.

"What would you do?" I ask him.

"If I was you? I'd take off."

"Where? I've got a house, a kid, no money."

"You could go away for a while and come back."

He makes it sound so easy; I know it's hopeless.

"They might shoot me anyway. I don't even know what they want."

The mad backwardness of it is infuriating. I can't even do things their way. Maybe someone is simply out to kill me, a nut or gunman who thinks I know something.

"God damn it, I haven't DONE anything!"

We jerk to a stop in our driveway, next to Doug's stalled car, and I start to get out. Hoxie grabs me by the arm and pulls me back into my seat.

"You recognize that car?" He's half-turned, looking out the back window. Across the street, beneath a shaggy pepper tree, a station wagon is parked with two men in it, sitting one behind the other, wearing hats. The engine is running and the lights are out. Suddenly, still dark, the car turns out.

"Down!" Hoxie yells. I sit on the floor, bent double, my knees in my face. Hoxie flops flat on the seat above me. An engine roars, coming closer; there is a chalky screech of tires, a rush of air, spun gravel. I close my eyes and clutch my body to me; a can is run over—pop!—exhaust noise fades up the street. Quiet. I look up. Hoxie is outside already.

"Damn! Missed the number! You get it?"

"No. I don't know the car, either."

"Well, it's no crank. They mean it."

"Are we going after them?"

Hoxie turns and looks into the car at me, shaken and annoyed.

"Just how bad do you want to get shot, anyway?"

My fear is no longer shapeless; it has features. A car,

two men, hats. Someone is really out there, waiting for me. They killed Bragg, they want to kill me. Even now, after the car and the men and the hats have gone, the desire remains there, in the dark.

THE CONSTRUCTION WORKERS FREE PRESS

The purpose of this paper is to represent the rank-and-file interest in our union. We intend to publish the membership's views in its pages, to promote debate, achieve unity and return democracy to our Brotherhood. We intend to be your voice. The future of this union is in your hands.

Baxter Bragg had started a newspaper, and it read as if it had come through my office window, wrapped around a rock.

Let's hear it for Tom Cannon!!!

I know we hear a lot of ugly things about our National leadership . . . bribery . . . rigged bidding . . . illegal contracts . . . embezzlement . . . perjury . . . contempt. Rumors, that's all!!! Ask the contractors, they'll tell you. Our National officers are clean . . . easy to get along with . . . understanding . . . reasonable . . . respectable. All that other stuff happened under the previous president . . . You know . . . the father of the one we have now!!!

The National had dropped all mention of the San Francisco local from its newspapers: meeting notices, letters, even obituaries had disappeared, reducing the paper's acknowledgment of the union's largest local to an assessment against its members of the weekly price. Bragg, scrounging, working deals with printers, writing most of the articles himself, persuading a draftsman to draw bad cartoons, had brought out his own paper, an eight-page tabloid.

A chunky, dapper black boy with a hat that had almost no brim at all and a black coat with a fur collar had come in early one morning with an armload of papers, and set them on a chair just inside our outer office door. "Papers here," was all he'd said. I thought it was the National's bull sheet, usually around for a week until we threw half of them away. Then the men started coming in and picking up copies. Some lingered around the dispatch window, pretending to be on business. Others just came in without a word, took a paper, and left. When toothless Joe Lucas came in and grabbed one, I decided I'd better investigate. He can't read.

NATIONAL TREASURER GORHAM IS CONVICTED EXTORTIONIST

There they were, the things we had barely dared talk about, in print and with names: an account of the beef at the housing project, or "scandal," as the paper described it; a long article accusing the National of catering to employers; the full story of Bragg's merger of the two locals and the National's opposition to it. The paper was intemperate, full of personal attack, raw disclosure, and accusations of conspiracy. People were called names: "bigot," "fink," "economic Neville Chamberlain." As I read it, I burned with embarrassed curiosity, but I devoured every word.

NATIONAL GIVES NO ACCOUNTING OF HEALTH AND WELFARE FUNDS

"How can he say these things?" I heard Beverlee ask innocently in the outer office.

"It's true. How else?" That was Dorothy, her voice harsh with sarcasm and cigarette smoke.

"Well, at least those men have the decency not to do those things in public."

Our union had become two unions. One old, settled, conservative, docile, comfortably corrupt, concerned with respectability: the National, Toad, the contractors. The other, Bragg, the rank and file of his enlarged local, and sympathetic bands of insurgents springing up in the big city locals of the East: militant, idealistic, disreputable, and unpredictable. I spent a lot of my time trying to figure out if I was on one side or the other. Or both. Or neither.

Anything that pleased one faction angered the other. I had the feeling that every act I performed in the course of my job was being interpreted, that all the papers I signed, letters I wrote, phone calls I made, and conversations I had were being marked down, not in one place, but in two, that they would be evaluated independently and judgments would be made, that I was a radical or that I was a sellout; and that my future depended hardly at all on what I did and almost entirely on what other people thought of what I did. I tried to do my work fairly, avoid lying, and approach each grievance with an open mind, but the job was becoming increasingly political, and as a politician I am a total loss.

I found myself accused of taking sides, praised or criticized for acts that a few months before would have been simply part of my work. No amount of explanation or denial could discourage people from their conclusions, and the usual conclusion was that I had made a secret deal with Bragg.

One night I had gone to Madrone Hospital to visit Chester Lee Wheeler, an old contractor who had suffered a severe heart attack. He lay in bed, propped up with pillows and straining to breathe, yet he wouldn't stop complaining about Bragg, who seemed to have gotten into his blood stream and wrung his heart.

"Why you always takin' that creep's side?" His mouth hung open like the mouth of a gasping fish.

"You rest now," I told him. "Here, I brought the *Sporting News.*"

I offered him the newspaper, but he brushed it away with his hand.

"What's he got on you? You can tell me. How long we known each other, fifteen years?"

"Nineteen," I said. Chester had been my first job foreman.

"And now you're on his side."

"I'm not on anybody's side," I said. "I just think, on every beef so far, that he's been right."

Chester rolled his eyes up and looked at the ceiling.

"If he's what's right, I'd rather be wrong."

To him, as to the other contractors, Bragg was impossible. They couldn't swallow him, and they couldn't spit him out.

Sometimes I was tempted to act against my own judgment out of sheer perversity, to deliberately call one wrong just to prove that I was acting independently and take some of the heat off me; but when it came down to living with the consequences of a deceptive contract, loss of wages, or phony seniority, I couldn't go through with it. Strangely enough, if I'd really seen things with Bragg's longer view, and had been able to overlook the present with his air of ultimate rightfulness, I probably could have done it. Sustained by some distant justification, he didn't seem to suffer life's haunting uncertainties one day at a time. Where other men sought to avoid conflict, he deliberately provoked it.

And now this paper.

I still had a copy on my desk when I heard his twangy, nervous voice in the outer office.

"Joe Burke! Where is that old man?"

He burst into my room, looking like an apostle employed by the post office, the girls outside gaping after him. Two big, tough-looking kids, one white and one black, waited behind him, unsmiling.

"You've read it. Tell me what you think." He fretted, his hands in his pockets, anxious as a boy.

"What do I have to do to keep my name out of it?"

"Come on now, I want to know," he insisted.

"Well, I hate to think what you'd say about these people in private."

He looked disappointed. "You better get off the fence," he said, suddenly sore, "while you still can."

He invited me to have lunch with him. He saw me hesitating, and I had to accept. Friendship, to Bragg, was simply loyalty, and to bow to the pressure of what other people thought would have been, to him, the worst sort of betrayal. Besides, he was good company, amusing and outspoken, with a vitality so intense it seemed to recharge my own. Perhaps he was short on mercy, but he had a good deal of charm.

"This is Grimes and this is Buxton," he said, introducing the two kids, who nodded grimly. Grimes, the white, was a dirty-looking youngster with a pinched, mean face and long blond hair. His mouth was black, gutted by heavy smoking. He wore a blue suit and a black shirt, and his hands were covered with homemade tattoos. Buxton was just big, six five or six six, rangy, with big hands and feet. He wore shades and had a thick, curled-back, disapproving upper lip. "Bad asses, both," Bragg said enthusiastically. "You drive."

Bragg was proud and excited about his paper. He had

sent letters to the National's weekly; they weren't printed. He'd attempted to take ads; they wouldn't sell him space. So he'd started his own paper, and bootlegged copies around to other locals all over the country. He was already getting long-distance phone calls from dissident rank-and-file men.

"We're mobilizing the rank and file for action, any way they want it, legally, conciliation, mediation, talkathon, conferences, or in the streets. Anytime, anywhere. We'll be there!"

We passed the tall hills and low towns of Madrone County, Bragg talking, the two goons in back looking lazily out the car windows.

Madrone is a commuter county, emptying during the day and filling up at night like an enormous, rustic dormitory. The only good restaurant open for lunch is a fish place called Federico's that overlooks either the mud flats or the bay, depending on the tide. That day was a mud flat day.

The restaurant was crowded with chattering suburban matrons, three or four to a table, wearing little pointed paper hats that I suppose meant they were part of some sort of club. We were led through them, across the main dining room, to a table in a corner, everybody eyeballing Bragg: the women, the hostess, our waiter. Someone was always staring at him, offended. Grimes and Buxton faced their chairs out at the room belligerently, tried to look up dresses, and ate their way through a basket of breadsticks in about three minutes. Bragg treated them as if they were children, or mutes, saying anything in front of them.

"Have you heard about Toad?" he said, looking at the menu. "The National made him a vice-president, to counter me."

They had dangled the title in front of Toad for years, luring him into doing one dangerous or loathsome job after another, refusing to give the vice-presidency to him because they didn't have to. Now Bragg had forced them.

"Well, he's got what he wanted," I said.

Bragg lifted his eyes and met mine. "That's his reward for twenty years of sleeping with a pistol in his night-table drawer."

He seemed to be studying my reaction.

"See much of him?" he said.

"Toad? I run into him at banquets, Building Trades Council. I get the feeling there's a lot of pressure on him. How about you? Do you hear from him?"

"Hardly ever."

The waiter came, bringing drinks: a Scotch for me, Dubonnet for Buxton, Cokes for Grimes and Bragg. We ordered lunch, and Grimes asked for a chili dog.

"Eat out much?" Bragg said cruelly, and changed Grimes's order to a basket of prawns.

"He knows everything I do," Bragg said when the waiter left. "Someone's informing on me, and I have a good idea who it is."

"Who?"

"It's either Silk or you."

All three of them were studying me now: Bragg, steady, inquiring; Buxton, blind to me behind his shades; Grimes, tiny-eyed and mean.

At that moment I remembered sitting once in a project manager's office, just a cubicle in the headquarters of a huge construction firm, trying to renegotiate a contract, and overhearing, through an open office door, Lenny Silk's bored, complaining voice.

"I know exactly what you mean," Silk was saying to some other, unseen, project manager. "The men are lazy. You can't get any work out of them."

Later, as I was leaving, I saw Silk at the elevator, and we rode down and walked through the lobby together. He was complaining about project managers then. They were incompetent and you had to do everything for them; and, worst of all, they were ungrateful.

I'd never confided anything to him after that.

Bragg was still watching me. "He's heard things only you two knew," he said. "Somebody's finking."

My stomach tightened. The rest of my body felt limp. Either of the goons looked big enough to break me in two. There was no point in denying it; as with everything else, Bragg would decide for himself.

"Tell me," I said. "How is that different from men in other locals informing on the National to you?"

He smiled, teeth clenched. "Simple. I'm right and they're wrong."

He laughed, but after the laughter, he believed.

A few days later I saw Toad at an interunion ceremony at the Madrone Town Hall. He was standing in a row with four other union officials, all flinching against the wind on the front steps, while the mayor made a short speech commending the men for their role in community affairs, and presented each of them a civic-booster plaque. Afterward I went up and shook Toad's hand and congratulated him on being made a vice-president.

"I'm so proud of him," said Josie, leaning out from behind him. "He's worked so hard."

Toad handed her the plaque indifferently. "Put this someplace, will you?"

He steered me over to a corner of the steps and took out a handful of clippings from Bragg's newspaper.

"Why does he have to do this? Why doesn't he wise up and knock it off? Quit causing all this dissension, all this uproar."

He spoke as if Bragg, in attacking the National, had attacked him.

65

"He doesn't even try to get to know people. Backs them into a corner. Calls them names. You've got to leave a man an exit. Say what has to be said, then shut up."

I told him that Bragg had this idea of the union as a social instrument, a voice for people who had no voice, and that his dedication to the idea caused him to be indifferent to those around him, without intending to hurt anybody.

Toad looked at me and almost laughed. I felt embarrassed. He could make idealism seem the most ridiculous thing in the world.

Our general agreement with the contractors was due to expire on June first, and Toad, hoping to negotiate a new agreement without the pressure of a deadline, had arranged a series of talks between the union principals and the representatives of the Contractors Association. We would get acquainted, each side would feel the other out, all the talk would be off the record. It seemed like a good idea to me, and Bragg reluctantly consented.

We began meeting with them, one week at Toad's headquarters in Oakland, the next week at the union hall in San Francisco. Occasionally, we ate lunch in a group and worked through the afternoon. It was an informal arrangement; there was no agenda, no stenographer, men on both sides arrived late, left early, made phone calls, took messages, kept other appointments. There was no feeling of crisis, and we seemed to get along. There was, after all, much in common. The contractors had all been union men. They talked like us; we understood them. Toad had known the men on their side personally for years. A stranger, seeing us at that first restaurant lunch in Oakland, would never have guessed that our group of mostly short beefy men represented opposing sides of anything.

There was one big difference. At some point in his life, each man on the contractors' side had decided to give up his job and assume, in its place, a business interest. In order to acquire good clothes, a better home, a new car, money in the bank, he had accepted certain values of the business community. He had to. Wages became overhead; work, a commodity; fooling around, wasteful grab-ass. He became a boss.

Baxter Bragg, in his rumpled workingman's clothes and his shaggy personal appearance, was an unpleasant reminder of this choice. He was a union officer, yet he remained rank and file. No one had ever succeeded in doing that before. Bragg owned nothing, and he owed nothing. Everything about him was a rejection of the whole idea of being a boss. Anybody's boss. Yet here he was, sitting where they sat, eating what they ate, treated as an equal. Right from the start, he made them uneasy. A trouble-maker in strange clothes and long hair, dirty-looking, a beatnik or a hippie, a fruit maybe, or a Commie. The kind of person they wouldn't let in their homes. At that first luncheon, I could see their eyes stray down the table, past dark suit after dark suit, stopping at the one blue denim workshirt and bright-red bandanna, looking away, then sneaking back; or they'd avoid looking at his end of the table entirely, so aware of him that they pretended not to be. It added a tension to the table that wasn't noticeable when we were talking work: job rules, hiring practices, seniority, peripheral matters where we arrived at a quick understanding; but it rose like fever when the business talk stopped and the conversation grew personal, and everything became tight when it should have been loose, with coughing, dropped forks, nervous laughter, and fast, anxious glances. It was in one of those deserted pauses that I saw Andy Donovan, President of the Contractors Association, a tall, lean, ruddy man in his seventies who had spent forty years at negotiating tables, had seen and dealt with some of the most obstinate and hot-headed men imaginable without losing either his temper or a major dispute, turn, a napkin tucked under his chin, and stare at Bragg in open bafflement. Bragg caught him at it and grinned back, that terrible, clenched-teeth grin, as if to say, "I'm at least as good as you are," and tucked his own napkin under his own chin in exactly the same manner, embarrassing Donovan, so that he turned away and blushed, the oldest man I've ever seen blush.

After the luncheon, our side caucussed in Toad's office, where he sat behind his desk, which never has anything on it. Bragg, Silk, and I sat across from him on his leather couch, while Toad explained what to expect, and advised us how to handle ourselves.

"You may not like these people," he warned us. "But remember, you didn't choose them and they didn't choose you. We're all stuck with each other, no matter what happens. We depend on the same work. Even if everything breaks down, we still have to settle with the same men."

He paused, emphasizing his point. He didn't raise his voice. He didn't have to. It rumbled so deeply that I felt it as much as heard it, like the concussion of ship's guns when I was in the Navy.

"Remember, what you say goes beyond the room. You aren't just speaking for yourself in there."

We weren't sitting down to settle every question between the union and the contractors. That was impossible. It was more important to agree on a few principles than on the application of the principles to all sorts of imaginary cases. You discuss general problems and don't argue about the terms of the agreement. Co-operation is the goal. Try to sympathize with their side, get them to understand yours; then it's easy to modify the agreement later.

Toad had been there, and he knew. All the years of coddling, haggling, tedium, and pressure had hardened into something valuable. A philosophy, I suppose, though he'd never call it that: do what you can, and waste no time on what you're unable to change. If he cared little about the work of the men he represented, he knew all there was to know about his own. At first, Toad was pleased with the way the talks were going. There'd been no threats or insults, and Bragg seemed to be accepting the framework of a normal labor-management relationship. But there was this personal thing between their side and him that never seemed to settle itself, a fear and resentment that wouldn't come out in the open, and wouldn't go away. As the negotiations moved to the bread-and-butter issues—wages, pensions, control of welfare funds—it grew stronger.

George Harris, the spokesman for their side, was a sharp-tongued, embittered little man with a wet smile and hard, angry eyes. He had tried to start his own contracting business, failed, and retreated to working full time for the Association, only to discover that the man in the top job was apparently going to keep it forever. He felt cheated, and he was determined not to be cheated again. He disliked the union, and he hated Bragg.

Donovan, the old man, kept Harris ruthlessly under his thumb, making him do most of the talking, interrupting him bluntly whenever he wanted to speak himself. His face was smooth and shiny as wax fruit, except for the skin at his mouth and chin, drawn flat and tight around a black, ragged pipe which he puffed so intently that at times I thought he would bite through its stem. Once, when he'd opened up a little over lunch, reminiscing about the old days when men had to work their asses off for four dollars a day and union membership could cost you your job, I began to warm toward him, and Bragg slipped me a note: "SCAB-HERDER."

69

He never looked quite the same to me again.

Milt Demetrios was the other man on the contractors' side, a numb, dark man with thick black hair, pock-marked skin, and a nose that appeared to have been broken four or five times. He was slow, a frowning listener whose contribution to the talks consisted of a gruff, skeptical laugh, frequently repeated.

"Haw, haw. Bullshit!"

But he was the city's largest contractor, and he hadn't become that simply by bellowing. He usually came late and left early, without bothering to announce that he was leaving.

There were two other men, named Cobb and Loomis, who appeared from time to time for the contractors, but these three were the regulars. Their attitude toward the talks seemed to be that we were meeting to discuss the terms of the contract, not the work or the men who did it. The area of disagreement, if it existed at all, was surely very small, and there was no problem we couldn't work out among ourselves, amicably. We would arrive at a joint solution, which each side would take back to its membership and persuade them to accept. It was an attitude Toad shared: that we were all fellow professionals, whose goal was to get things settled as quickly and cleanly as possible.

Bragg wouldn't let them get away with it. He would not let them separate the negotiations from the work. He interrupted. He asked questions. He admitted he didn't understand certain points. What about men working overtime and being paid straight time for it, he wanted to know. Or working on speculation and not being paid at all. What about contractors skipping health and welfare contributions? The contractors would groan and sigh, exchange pained, knowing glances, and give him vague, evasive answers. Which he asked them to explain.

70

They couldn't get used to him. There was nothing familiar about the man. Instead of sitting calmly at the table while other men spoke, Bragg would slip off his boots and pad around the conference room in his socks. Or sit on a corner of the table. Sometimes, when one of us was reading from a wage study or some other dull report, he'd go to sleep. Waking to the silence when the report was finished, he'd leave the room and return with his hair wet. Once, when Harris quoted from a table of absenteeism statistics, Bragg walked over and stood next to him, staring over his shoulder as Harris read, stumbling and fuming, then coolly asked to see the paper himself when Harris was through. He was unembarrassable. Emotionally, he wore you out.

Gradually, subtly, he began to influence both the discussions with the contractors and those within our own union caucus. Unconsciously, both we and they began addressing our remarks to him. You couldn't help it. If you tried to avoid doing it, you only sounded worse. We were all so overly aware of his reactions that we would speak to the room, but keep looking toward Bragg. He accepted this evenly, looked directly back, and, with as simple a gesture as the tilt of his head or the expression on his face, commented on our remarks even as we were talking. Without shouting or threatening or pounding the table, but by the sheer force of his personality, always firmly pressing his own demands, he assumed the dominant role on our committee.

The initial proposal, by the time it was presented, was his proposal. No one else seemed so certain about what we should ask. Bragg himself read the terms, standing in the small meeting room that adjoins Toad's office: across-the-board increases in wages and fringe benefits for bricklayers, carpenters, cement finishers, hod carriers, ironworkers, laborers, plasterers, lathers, and painters, averaging

71

eighty cents an hour over a three-year period; a jointly controlled pension fund; restrictions on automatic equipment, a permanent grievance committee, a holiday fund. I could feel the temperature rise across the table. They stared at him as he read, radiating hatred. Harris held his head with his hand, as if it ached. The old man *did* bite through his pipe. I saw him take it out of his mouth and stare at it. Demetrios' blue jaw dropped. Toad noncommittally examined the grain of the table.

"You can't be serious," said Harris in a dry, choked voice, his face white. "You want *everything*."

Bragg looked at him, and this time he didn't smile.

"That's right," he said.

He could be blacklisted. He could be beaten up. He could be killed. But he couldn't be denied.

7

Rose calls me, as promised, apologetic and concerned.

All is chaos at Sally's: police interviews, telegrams, phone calls, letters to be acknowledged, money, insurance, callers dropping by at all hours, no privacy, the strain of being nice to people and consoling Sally in the black loneliness when they have gone; she knew I'd understand.

It's easy to persuade her to take a night off; I have a gift for expressing neglect. She invites me to meet her for dinner at her house.

I drive directly there from work, call Hoxie, and tell him I'm not coming home. There are frozen dinners and Pepsi in the refrigerator, and Doug knows how to work the stove; he has nothing to worry about.

He blows up. What do I think he is, a baby sitter? He calls me stupid and crazy and demands to know where I am, but I won't tell him. He rages, haunted by visions of the powerhouse. I listen with delight. Then he says something that rings in my ear long after I've hung up on him.

"Whoever's with you is running the same risk you are. They won't leave witnesses."

"Who was that?" Rose asks from the kitchen.

"Just a guy." I know that I should leave, and know just as well that I will stay.

I sit at the kitchen table and watch her fix dinner, a pot bubbling, a pan crackling, steaming her hair up in little wisps, Rose rediscovering the simple pleasures of her own home, her own things. I've always wanted her, some times more than others; now I feel a remorse so deep it aches.

I ask her about Sally, and Rose takes a deep, weary breath. She says Sally is now a martyr's widow, a special kind of woman. It means that though she's lost her husband, he's still here for other people. "She has to listen to people talk about her husband and then sleep in their bed, alone."

There is a career in being a martyr's widow, Rose says, causes a woman can lend her husband's name to, committees she can serve on, jobs that are created for her; and Sally is ambitious.

"They want her to be a delegate to the convention."

"Who does, Lenny Silk?"

"Some of the men from the union. There's one man with a scarred face."

"Eisan. Tell her to forget it. Tell her Joan of Arc was killed."

"She feels someone should carry on his work."

His work. As if there'd been a plan, an announced goal.

"Sometimes I think he got what he really wanted."

"Joe!"

"Martyrdom. A legend. A dramatic death. People will be talking about him long after you and I are gone. Not the truth, probably, but they'll be talking about him. I think he wanted that more than anything."

After dinner I go outside and pick a couple of logs from a pile stacked against Rose's garage. White oak that I'd cut

74

myself from a big tree knocked down in a windstorm in the city park more than a year before. With a rusty ax I find on her garage wall, I splinter off some thin pieces for kindling, and think of Sally Bragg: a provocative girl, flirtatious, a tease. She stands right up next to you when you talk, looks you in the eye, touches your tie, your sleeve; the kind of woman who is always being proposed to by the wrong man. The thought of the trouble she could cause in union politics makes me shudder.

I gather the firewood into an armload, take it inside, and, using most of the Sunday paper, start a fire. Rose comes in, brushing her hair into place with her hand. We turn off the lights and sit together on the couch, staring into the fireplace.

"What's going to happen, Joe?"

"I don't know. I think I'm doing things the way I always have. There are problems, I try to solve them. I do my job. It's just that everybody expects you to declare yourself now, because of Bragg. I never did see it completely the way he did. It was like there was a monster that he had to go out and fight every day, and someone had to win, and someone had to die; as though the battle itself was everything and what you were fighting about was unimportant in the end. It isn't in me to care that much. I get to wondering what I'll have for dinner, or feeling my back ache, or thinking about us in bed. I'm lazy. Work is something I get done so I can relax. Not Bragg. I don't think he knew what it meant to be satisfied."

That was the way it had been with him; but it wasn't all of it.

"He did give things a purpose. He made you feel that putting a stamp on a letter was somehow helping to change the world. I miss him for that."

I kiss her, and feel the fire's warmth on her cheek, her neck, her hair. She lies back, across my lap. I try to undo her clothing, but she's wearing a girdle that might as well be a safe.

"I'll go get ready," she whispers, and walks away toward the bathroom.

Be yourself, I tell myself, and imagine Bragg and Sally, buck naked and impulsive as kids, rolling on the floor before the fire.

About two in the morning, I awake in Rose's bedroom, soaked with sweat, my arms around a pillow that feels as heavy as a stone. I am convinced that I am going to die; I don't know why, but it suddenly seems certain. I leave Rose sleeping in her warm bed, put on my clothes, go out to the front room, and sit in the fire's flameless afterglow.

Bragg's killers are going to get away with it. Retributive justice does not apply to labor leaders. How many times over the years have union men been shot and lynched and bombed and beaten to death? Wesley Everest, castrated and hanged by the American Legion in Centralia; Frank Little, lynched by the citizens of Butte, Montana; a bomb attempt on Walter Reuther; unsolved murders on the Jersey docks. Few trials, fewer convictions. In silent consent, the community turns its back; the death of a labor leader is the death of an outlaw.

Bragg had realized that going in, and used it. An outlaw's death entitles you to an outlaw's life: wild clothes, cocky swagger, the indiscriminate use of insult, freedom. Respectability is valued only by the guilty. He had pushed it to its end, and his. Fair enough, it was his choice; but what about the people he took with him? Well, that's labor for you, the citizens would say. Strong-arm tactics. Threats. Intimidation. Violence. No use grieving. Can't stop 'em all. If you can't stand the heat, stay out of the kitchen. And let the world become a kitchen.

Rose comes out of her bedroom, walking slowly, groggy

76

with sleep, her hair long, down around her neck, nightgown clinging to her nipples and her hips, and sits on the couch next to me, bending her legs under her like a girl.

"What's wrong, Joe?"

I want to contain my fear, to bear it alone and be a man; and can't. My skin turns cold beneath my clothes.

"Somebody is trying to kill me."

With the palm of her hand she touches her cheek softly, as if to assure herself she is awake.

"I'm under police guard. There was a phone call, a threat. And there are two men, I've seen them. I think they're the ones who shot Bragg."

Even as I say these things, I feel strangely distant from them, like somebody else talking about a Joe Burke who is already dead.

"Oh Joe," she says, staring at me and beyond me, withdrawing despite herself, as though murder were a contagious disease.

"Rose, let's get married."

She turns away, unwilling to listen.

"You'll be taken care of in case anything happens. I have insurance, and a union pension, and there's the house. And Doug would have somebody. He's not as independent as he thinks. If nothing happens, we'll only have done what we planned to do anyway. We can drive to Reno in the morning."

She shakes her head.

"No, Joe. Not like this. I'm sorry."

"Maybe you'd rather forget the whole thing."

She turns back, angry. "You know that isn't true. It's just that we've waited so long, for everything to be right, that I couldn't do it now, for this. It's getting married for death."

We sit there until the fireplace goes black and the room turns cold.

"All right," I tell her. "We'll wait. Doug leaves for school in September, and all this will be over by then."

We go back to bed. It's only right. An outlaw should have a mistress, not a wife.

8

"I told him it would come to this, didn't I?"

Toad Fuller carried his large, heavy suitcase into our room at the Golden Hills Motor Hotel, swung it up onto the bed I wasn't sitting on, and snapped it open.

"You heard me warn him," he reminded me, "and the son of a bitch went ahead anyway."

The negotiations with the contractors had deadlocked. They wouldn't meet our demands, we wouldn't give in to theirs, and the existing agreement was about to expire. Both sides suddenly found themselves in the crisis they had been trying to avoid.

We had agreed to rent a set of rooms in the same hotel, union and contractors splitting the bill, and begin continuous negotiations. Bragg and Silk were sharing one double room, Toad and I another. I had checked in first, opened our room, and left my overnight bag on a chair. Now I sat watching Toad unpack, hanging extra clothes in the closet on his own folding hangers to preserve the pants crease, filling the dresser drawers with changes of underwear, rolled socks, and starched white shirts, taking all the space on top of the dresser for his electric razor, alarm clock, shoeshine kit, aspirin, bennies, transistor radio, electric vibrator, and a flask of whisky. When everything was in place, he looked at the arrangement with satisfaction and closed his suitcase.

"I was doing this before he came, and I'll be doing it after he's gone."

He had become so obsessed with Bragg that he assumed everyone else was always thinking about him, too.

"I didn't know he was going."

"He will be. You get a few things you want, you get ideas. He's ambitious, though he denies it. He's thinking National office already, and he'll never get it. You have to be born into the Cannon family for that, or marry in. I had a few ideas myself. So he'll quit, like he did that other union, or he'll push too hard and they'll get rid of him; or maybe he'll forget this radicalism, though every time he wins a beef there's less chance of that. He can't sustain it, just being against. He'll burn himself out. Things will go back to normal. We'll be back with the same old situation, only it won't seem so bad any more."

He walked into the bathroom, turned on the bath water, tried the shower and the faucets, and flushed the toilet.

"Not bad," he said when he came out.

He sat in front of the TV, turned it on, and started fiddling with the color picture. He'd turn the set to one channel, tune it, change channels, and start over, indifferent to what was on, examining the workings of the television as a piece of hardware.

"I'll tell you something about him," he said, still staring at the set. "Wherever he goes, whatever he does, he's gonna have problems, because he invents them for himself. If you want them, too, you're welcome to them. Personally, I've got enough of my own."

He dropped his pants, took off his tie and shirt, and

80

struggled out of his underwear. I couldn't help staring at his tattoo, a huge American eagle glaring fiercely from his chest, clutching arrows and an olive branch, all in purple ink, trimmed with red, and a scroll below. Toad walked into the bathroom, taking short steps with his skinny legs, like a huge, featherless bird. As he passed me, I could read the inscription on the scroll: DEATH BEFORE DISHONOR.

The hotel is new, a plastic-paneled box just off a freeway exit in downtown San Francisco, only four stories, but spread over half a block of cleared slum. The place does a lot of union business, and the management reserves a number of rooms just for meetings. When officials from the National come to town, they usually stay there, and it's rumored that our union owns a piece of it. I know there was no question of us staying anywhere else.

I slept badly in the unfamiliar room, got up early in the morning, and dressed while Toad sawed away in the other bed, lying on his back. Even in sleep he looked troubled and angry; when he shifted positions, the bedframe creaked like a ship. Whatever demons pursued him, at least they didn't keep him awake. I didn't want to shake him, and I didn't want to wait, so I walked out to the hotel coffee shop to have breakfast. Silk was there, sitting alone at a table, wearing an Italian suit with a little coat and tight pants, like a bellhop's uniform. He gave me a big hello and I sat down with him. He was all tied up about the negotiations, openly nervous, knowing he was in over his head, smiling at me, wanting me to affirm his doubts with mine.

"How long do you think we'll be here?" he asked me, his eyes shooting all around the room.

I told him that these things had been known to go on for a week, and that Toad had come with a full suitcase.

"A week!" he said out loud, in despair.

So you miss a few dates, I said to him, and have to eat a few restaurant meals. You can make it up later.

That wasn't what bothered him. "I've got to live with him for a week?" Rooming with Bragg was apparently no easier than anything else about Bragg.

"He isn't human," said Silk, ignoring his food. "He stays up half the night reading or watching TV. He doesn't wear underwear, and he brought only the clothes on his back. He sleeps bare-ass, on a mattress on the floor, with just a blanket over him, like an Indian!"

It surprised me, yet it was the way I should have expected Bragg to react to a boxy, plastic, soundproofed, air-conditioned modern hotel. He would be himself, wherever or whatever.

"What's wrong with comfort, for Chrissake?" said Silk, incredulous.

At exactly nine o'clock the smiling, optimistic reservations manager unlocked the door of one of the meeting rooms and turned up the lights. We filed in, their side and ours, men moving stiffly in unfamiliar surroundings, silently nodding to one another, laying attaché cases and clipboards and bulging plastic envelopes on the table while the reservations man droned on about where all the switches were and who we should call for service. Harris carried a file folder thick with papers, holding it with both hands. The old man, Donovan, looked pale and short of sleep, and he lowered himself into a chair carefully. The room was white-walled and windowless, with a narrow table of highly polished wood, lined by chrome-and-black-leather chairs. There was a note pad and an ashtray with the hotel's name on it in front of each chair and several cups filled with sharpened pencils. On one wall was a small painting, a scenic view of San Francisco, the city and the bay; and at one end of the table, a tape machine.

The room was chilly from uncirculated air, and the manager, as he was leaving, told us that if we left the door open, it would warm up inside. Harris set his file folder on the table in front of him importantly. Silk fussed with the tape machine, counting into the microphone, playing the tape back and adjusting the volume while Milt Demetrios watched, scowling with concern. The old man glanced across the table at Bragg, turned away, then jerked his eyes back. Bragg had added to his regular costume a pair of wrap-around sunglasses.

The pressure was up on both sides. Everybody knew that the contract was about to expire, and Bragg had announced that without a new contract his local wouldn't work. For every rank-and-file union man and every union-hating contractor, years of unfaced problems and unresolved grievances had fused into one raw, ugly chance to get even. Screw the bastards, stick 'em good. Let them strike—it'll clear the air. We faced the cold consequences: loss of wages, men out of work, using up their savings, on our side; lost contracts, shrunken profits, the sure failure of some small operators, on theirs. I could read the doubt in the faces on both sides of the table. We were all seated. The room was quiet. The tape was running. Harris looked sharply at Bragg.

"You ready?" he said.

"You bet your ass we're ready."

Harris scratched his nose with his finger, unbuttoned his coat, and began reviewing our demands in a whiny, complaining voice, claiming that what we were asking was excessive, that we were demanding too much in wages and too many fringes, and that we wanted too big a say in things like the welfare fund. It was all too costly, wildly impractical. He had a copy of the presidential wage guidelines in his file folder, and he quoted from them, reading through little half-moon glasses, pointing out that

83

our demands exceeded the government's limits and saying that that proved they were inflationary. His voice grew righteous and moralistic. His scolding tone suggested that we were wrong not in what we demanded, but in making demands at all. We were out of line with the contractors, our own union leadership, even the government. Wrong, wrong, wrong. It seemed more natural to Harris than his earlier pose of friendship, more like the man he really was, an employer without employees, whose only job was bargaining, getting the most in exchange for the least. He presented their newest proposal patronizingly, implying that he knew what was best for us, even when we didn't. It was almost identical to the pattern contract suggested by the National, and was a long way from what we wanted.

There was a restless quiet when he'd finished. Men on both sides of the table spoke quietly to each other; chairs were moved back or moved closer; Silk self-consciously lit a cigar. Toad rested his huge arms on the table and started talking, gruff but conciliatory, about how we all knew the main interest of both sides was avoiding a strike and how there had traditionally been a partnership between the contractors and the union, and he'd hate to see that turn into a labor-management war. The old man nodded. Toad, for one, thought that Harris's last offer had been a good one, and he wouldn't be ashamed to go back to the union with a contract based on it. He thought our side ought to caucus and discuss it.

The talk lapsed, and the whooshing sound of the air conditioning hung in the room. The attention fell to Bragg, as it always seemed to; he sat leaning back on the hind legs of his chair, his body lazy and his face expressionless, his boots crossed on the table. The fluorescent light in the room was so flickery-bright that his sunglasses didn't seem like such a nonsensical idea any more. Suddenly he swept his feet from the table, tensed in his chair, and began talking in an injured, angry voice. Maybe we were

84

asking a lot of the contractors, he said, but it was only what was owed us. They would have to pay the bills now that they'd skipped in the past. The payments were overdue. Besides, look what the union was giving. A three-year contract, guaranteeing not to strike. We *had* to get what we wanted now: we were signing away our only weapon. As for inflation, he said, with a contemptuous look toward Harris's file folder, he'd start worrying about that as soon as the butcher did.

Now it was just their side that was stung into quiet: motionless, heads cocked, waiting. The deeper we got, the closer we came to the reality of a strike, the clearer it became that Bragg wasn't bluffing.

"Don't you trust us?" the old man asked him, innocent and hurt.

"I don't trust anybody," Bragg told him coldly.

At lunch in the coffee shop, the two committees sat at separate tables with no conversation between them. Just muttering and angry glances. The hotel guests watched us curiously, staring at this strange group of coarse men who dressed clean with one man who looked dirty. My stomach was in knots; I could hardly get any food down. While we ate, Toad kept coaching us in a low, urgent voice, almost mumbling, so that we had to huddle over our plates to hear him.

"What the contract *says* isn't important. We got to reach an understanding. We can modify the terms later."

"Three years later," Bragg said in a loud, sarcastic voice that drew looks from the other table.

Toad stared at him angrily, then silently finished his steak.

In the afternoon, the room grew stuffy and hot, despite the air conditioning, or maybe because of it. We took off our coats and slung them over the empty chairs; the ashtrays filled up with cigar and cigarette butts, and the odor of stale smoke hung in the air, overpowering the ventilation. There was crumpled note paper scattered here and there, and bent cardboard coffee cups. The men began to look worn and rumpled. We raised our voices, interrupted one another; sometimes we shouted. I could imagine the hotel guests, crouching in their rooms, waiting for the sound of punches and breaking furniture. It got pretty rough.

Harris went on pushing for an agreement that would avoid a strike and keep everybody working, with the details of the contract to be settled later. Toad was willing to go along, but Bragg wouldn't give in. It was as if the problem was Bragg's attitude, not the issues. Harris had his tie off, as well as his coat; his file folder was sweat-marked, and the corners of the papers inside were curled from handling.

"If we have to spell out everything, we'll be here till Christmas!" Harris shouted.

By late evening I was so tired that I could no longer concentrate on the men in the room as individuals. My attention wandered to their features, to noses, Bragg's prominent horn, Harris's sore-looking red beezer, the old man's, with weedy hair growing out of the nostrils; then I'd start over with ears.

The old man was nodding. Several times he dozed off and woke up minutes later, looking startled and pretending to have missed nothing. Harris was straining, pushing harder and harder as the hours wore on, until his voice grew shrill and hoarse. Once, he flew into a fit of coughing so violent that he had to leave the room. Demetrios looked blank and bored, and he needed a shave badly. Toad had pulled the tails of his shirt up comfortably out of his pants. The rest of us looked as grubby as Bragg did.

All the arguments were repeated so often that everything had merged into a thick, muddled hum, in which only one thing became clear: what was expected was an understanding, not on paper, but between men. Bragg had bobbed up unexpectedly from the ranks of the union, had attacked men the negotiators now represented, threatened them with a strike and insulted them by his manner and dress. Even now, Harris looked at him with open hatred. Yet they would accept him, if he would simply become their accomplice.

It was the same here as out on the jobs. The same old game with the same rules. A simple extension of the small-time chiseling between a job foreman and a union business agent, among men protected by secrecy, hardened to any indignities done to other men and their work, dedicated only to survival. They were inviting Bragg to become a part of it, and he didn't want to. And that was the worst insult of all.

At one o'clock in the morning, the night manager came by, complained about the noise we were making, and asked us to let the maids in to clean up the room. Harris, his voice a choked whisper now, admitted that we weren't making any progress, and suggested we adjourn and reconvene at noon. Perhaps we'd feel differently then. The idea of sleep sounded so inviting I felt instantly drowsy.

But Bragg balked. "I'm not going to feel any different."

"Oh, come on," Toad pleaded wearily down the table.

Bragg ignored him, and spoke directly to Harris. "You going to have anything new tomorrow?"

"Probably not," rasped Harris, coldly irritated.

"Me neither," said Bragg.

They sat staring at each other for a moment, the rest of us looking at them. We began to realize what was happening. The talks were ending. Both sides had admitted it. There would be no agreement, no contract, and probably a strike.

"We're all tired," said Toad emptily. "We'll get some rest and go at it fresh in the morning."

Harris was standing, straightening up his papers angrily. Bragg was up, too, stretching out his arms, cool but watchful. Silk rewound the tape on the machine and removed the reel. Gently, Harris shook the old man awake.

"Let's go, Andy," he told him. "It's over." Sleepily obedient, Donovan stood, straightening his clothes.

"Look here," Toad pleaded to everybody, "we can't break it off so soon."

They were past listening to him.

"We'll expect to hear from you," said Harris, opening the door. Demetrios was standing with him, straightening his tie.

"No," said Bragg, determined to have the last word. "We'll expect to hear from *you*."

The old man looked puzzled. He must have thought everything had been settled. Harris shrugged and walked out. Demetrios followed him. The old man stared at us, at Toad, at me, at Bragg. Two women in green uniforms pushed past him with rags and a vacuum cleaner. With a jolt of awareness he realized what had happened, and I could tell by his eyes that he wished it hadn't. A third woman was trying to shove a cart loaded with brushes and sponges and cleaning cloths into the room. Excuse me, will you, mister, she said. Donovan hesitated a moment, looking fearful and drained and bleakly sad. With his lips moving silently, he followed the others.

9

Sunday. I drag myself out of bed early, intending to fix
the kitchen lights, which shorted out last night while I was
cooking dinner, go to the garage and get my repair box
from the storeroom, along with a coil of electrical wire, a
roll of friction tape, and a roll of black plastic electrician's
tape, take it all inside and lay everything out on the kitchen
counter. I unscrew the plastic switch facing on the wall,
remove the switch, and examine the wiring: the insulation is shot, so old and brittle it falls off at a touch. It was
lucky we hadn't had a fire. I go outside and turn off the
main switch, come back with a crowbar and a hammer,
and start tearing out the wall paneling. By the time Doug
gets up, the kitchen is a mess: splintered wood, bits of
wire, tools and electrical parts all over the floor. I explain
to him what I'm doing, diagram a simple circuit for him,
and he gets interested, playing with the switch, handing
me tools, removing part of the paneling for me.

It's more of a job than I should have attempted myself;
the smart thing would have been to call a contractor, but
the way I'm feeling about contractors, I'd rather not. It

feels good to be doing something I understand, working with Doug, him squatting barefoot in his Levi's and T shirt, watching me show off, his hair hanging down almost as long as Bragg's. It keeps him around. Normally, he takes off as early as possible on a weekend day to rush to some drive-in where he and his buddies give some poor carhop a hard time. But today he stays. I show him how to tie a splice, stripping off the insulation with the cutting edge of the pliers, bending the copper strands away from the steel, tying a square knot and wrapping the copper strands back over, then winding the two kinds of tape over it so tight there's barely a bulge. Doug's impressed, and he asks me where I'd learned it.

"In the Navy. I was an electrician's mate."

It's as if I told him I was an admiral.

Doug takes after his mother; he has Angela's black hair and brown eyes and the same long lashes. And he's moody the way she was. The Dark Lonelies, she used to call them, hours of silent, staring reproach that grew into days, then a permanent, inconsolable gloom. The baby would have been her copy. The unfocusing eyes were the same color, and she was born with hair enough to tie bows in. Marked from the difficult delivery, but the marks would have faded. . . .

By the middle of the afternoon, we've worked our way out to the garage, me standing on a stepladder, reaching overhead; Doug handing up the pliers and cutting strips of tape, his portable radio blaring rock tunes and announcing the time of day every ten minutes. My head is in the ceiling; I can't see anything but wire, beams, and laths.

It was a circulatory problem that transfusions were supposed to correct. Today, I guess, they save the ones like that. But we lost her before we ever brought her home, and Ange drew that mood about her like a black shawl that had been tucked away carefully in some mothball-smelling drawer, and moved from hospital, to rest home, to sanitarium, to grave, on a secret, suicidal schedule of her own. She must seem, in memory, to Doug more like a grandmother than a mother, lying gaunt and pale, never smiling, while he had to learn to make his bed and eat my cooking.

I don't know how many times he calls me over the radio noise before I look down.

"What is it?"

He's staring out toward the front of the garage, a roll of tape in each hand. I climb down the ladder. Out in the driveway is a tall man, just a shadow against the glare coming off the cars, and back a bit, so I can't see all of him. He steps forward into full daylight, and I see his tapered slacks, fancy plaid sports coat, white turtleneck, and a necklace of blue beads. I'm halfway out of the garage before I see his face: Eisan. I say hello to him, trying hard to look at him while forgetting the face itself, the way you'd look at anybody. His hair is brushed into place perfectly; maybe he figures that and his clothes compensate for his face, make him just another man and not a horror.

"I've got something I want to talk to you about," he says, dead serious. I look around. There doesn't seem to be anybody with him. Across the street, John Olmstead is staring, letting his garden hose water the sidewalk. Next door, the front-window curtains part, and Peg McCabe snoops out. I wave to John, and he turns quickly back to his watering.

I don't like their nosiness, but I want Eisan to know that they're there.

"Okay," I say to Eisan, and lean against Doug's car in the driveway. He sees I'm not going to invite him inside, and that puts him off a little, but not enough to leave. He sticks his hands in his coat pockets and looks down for a moment. Then he stares right at me.

91

"Fuller's asking the National to put your local under trusteeship," he says, glad to give me the news. "He sent a letter to Cannon with a list of charges."

He pauses. Doug has walked out to the doorway of the garage, and is watching. I tell him it's okay, and he goes back into the musical dark. Eisan waits till Doug is gone before he continues.

"You're charged with violating the Brotherhood Constitution, withholding assessments, planning to hire your own business agent, and undermining the Area Committee."

I swallow hard. It's just exaggerated enough to be true.

"How do you know?" I ask distrustfully.

"I saw the letter," he says, daring me not to believe him. He leans against my car, the way I'm leaning against Doug's, and crosses his arms, satisfied.

"How long have you been reading Toad's mail?"

"Somebody showed it to me," he says slyly. "Another friend of Bragg's." As though that automatically made us all part of a plot. "They're out to get you, just like they got him."

He's loose and drifting; without Bragg, he's nobody. He needs another Bragg.

"What are you going to do about it?" It's almost a demand.

"That's my business," I tell him, and he backs off a little.

The question of assessments had come up during the strike. When the National refused to back us, Bragg quit assessing the men National dues. Our local had voted to do the same. We had never resumed making the payments. They'd been too high all along for what we'd been getting, and the National refused to discuss lowering them.

Eisan is looking down, disappointedly picking at the

worn paint on my car. The news hasn't had the effect he expected. His mood has changed, and he's openly depressed. "Look, you've got to do something." He almost begs. "You're the only one left," he admits. "Silk is weak and stubborn. He has no convictions of his own. Max Volt doesn't know what's going on, and he's too old. Fuller and the National and the Contractors want to change it all back the way it used to be, and you're the only one with enough clout to stop them."

There's a lot going on behind that mask. He misses nothing.

"I'm not Bragg; I never could be."

"You went along with him," he says. "He got you things you couldn't have got yourself. You're obligated."

Maybe it's true, but I resent him for saying so. Maybe I had depended on Bragg, but not as much as he had. At least I got my job on my own. There's an attitude of moral superiority about Eisan that bothers me. Toad and the National aren't telling me what to do. He is.

I ask him some questions about the letter. A person whose name he won't reveal to me had showed it to him, and in it Toad has said that if I was permitted to carry out the actions I was planning, his job would cease to exist. Eisan says he's telling me because he thinks it's time I get off my ass and do something, because even if I don't realize it, I'm in bad trouble.

I've had enough. I tell him I'm working on the wiring, and have to get it finished before dark. He stands up, away from the car.

"People want to know what you're going to do. What should I tell them?"

"Tell them I'll make up my own mind, the way I always do."

He hangs his head and laughs bitterly.

"What's so funny?"

93

He looks up. "That's the one thing Bragg said you could never do."

I feel those words so, I know it shows; know that Eisan sees it. He turns and walks away, light and easy, pleased with himself. He'd come here having to prove himself to me, and he's leaving me having to prove myself to him. One up. I can hear Bragg's voice say it. I watch Eisan's car, a black Corvette, rumble away aggressively, then I walk back into the garage. Doug is gone, and so is his radio. Another loss. I put the pliers in my back pocket, pick up the rolls of tape, and climb back up the stepladder.

The sky is glowing red when I turn the main switch back on. The kitchen lights go on and the alarm on the stove begins to buzz. At least there are some things I can still do. I walk inside and clean up the kitchen; my back aches and my hands are black and scored from handling wire. I drink a beer and take a shower. Hoxie turns up, annoyingly cheerful, thirsting for duty, and Doug comes home shortly after.

The kitchen wall now looks as though a shell hit it, and I suppose I'll have to call somebody out to repair the hole and match the paint. Looking at it, I keep thinking of Eisan, wondering how much of what he said was the truth, and what his motives really are. I consider calling Toad and asking him about the letter directly, set the telephone on the kitchen counter, lift the receiver, then push it aside. I don't have the nerve to accuse the man of attacking me in his own mail.

What Bragg said about me is true. Even now, I feel wounded by it, irritated and angry at him, a corpse. Surely he had known me better than I ever knew him, better even than I know myself. He saw into me. He saw into everybody. He revealed to us all the way we really are. No wonder people hated him.

94

10

The evening after Bragg's local voted to strike, I sat in my office, typing out a statement to read at our own strike meeting, stewing over it, trying to combine an explanation of the contractors' position and ours, a promise of gain and a request for sacrifice, all in one short speech that would somehow stir the men to mobilize. I'd write half a page, read it over, tear it out of the typewriter, and start over, while Potter prowled about my office in squeaky, rubber-soled shoes.

Bragg's men were in fever. They had voted nine to one or ten to one to strike, better than unanimous because no one could say it had been rigged. Now they were out, sitting at home probably, or hanging around the union hall, or circling quietly outside the interrupted jobs with picket signs. I knew the vote wouldn't be so lopsided with us; our local is divided almost evenly between older, more conservative men, concerned mainly with job security, and militant kids who want a stronger union. There was a good chance that a strike motion wouldn't pass at all. According to Toad, the contractors' attitude was hardening; they would welcome a short strike that failed. It would mean the end of Bragg and force us back to work at the old contract rates. A losing vote here could do it.

I felt Potter reading over my shoulder; I was opening my mouth to tell him to clear out when he turned away suddenly, walked to the window, and looked through the blinds.

"What in Christ's name is *this*?" he said.

A Greyhound bus had pulled into our parking lot and stopped, motor throbbing; the door was open and men were stepping off, bunching up beside the bus as though for mutual protection, hands in their pockets, talking quietly to one another. There must have been fifty of them, some of whom I recognized as members of Bragg's local: balding old-timers with a burdened, family look; big journeymen with moist, beery eyes; a little beige man with an elegant goatee; Grimes; Buxton. Bragg himself got off last, and the driver pulled the bus off to a far corner of the lot and parked. Men from our local were standing around watching, pointing out Bragg to one another. I could see our men speak his name as he moved among his own men, shaggy head bobbing, coaxing them out of the bunch, urging them to circulate. A few conversations began. Bragg's men started offering handshakes, introducing themselves and talking, fanning out toward the building, splitting our men into small groups of two or three. Two men started arguing without any real heat; a few others laughed amiably; but the attitude of most of the men seemed to be a quiet surprise at finding themselves in such a situation at all. Everything turned around Bragg. He was everywhere; you couldn't miss him as he walked from group to group, making introductions, pointing out a lone man for another man to talk to, answering questions, jabbing a finger into a man's chest, flashing a candidate's automatic grin.

"It's a goon squad!" Potter said indignantly.

The nearest goon looked to be about fifty, stood perhaps

five foot three, was fat, wore a hat and horn-rimmed glasses, and was armed with a newspaper. I told Potter we ought to go outside and take our chances, and reluctantly he came along, not really wanting to be part of anything like this, but not wanting even more to be excluded.

Outside, the men had clustered into a few large groups, Bragg's men and ours mixed, standing two and three deep, listening while one or two men talked.

"We'll stay off the jobs till grass grows over them," I overheard a big horse-faced man telling a circle of about twenty men.

"And we'll eat the grass before we scab," his buddy, a little guy with gold teeth and a big nose, added in a scratchy voice.

"When you're sixty years old, they're through with you," I heard an old man complain shrilly. "They might as well take you out and shoot you, like a horse. What we need is a pension." I was surprised to see that he was from our local and not Bragg's.

As we walked through the crowd, men on the edges of the different groups would look my way, their eyes full of questions, until they saw I wasn't going to interfere, and they'd turn back to whoever was doing the talking. I could feel Potter grow tense beside me. "This is coercion," he said to me under his breath as we walked among the groups. When in truth it went far deeper. There was a common mood among these men that you could see in the attentive way they stood and listened, and the intense way in which they talked, a feeling that Bragg had inspired or sensed when no one else had, a herd urge like the migration of fish or the flight of birds.

We came upon him, standing in a circle of perhaps a dozen men, in a corner where one wing of our building joins another, with a quieter group than the others, listening to Bragg answer questions in a voice unusually calm

97

for him. What about the National, someone asked him. Would they help us? No, Bragg answered. They hadn't approved the strike. Probably they would oppose it, side with the contractors, even exert pressure on the locals to settle.

"Let's face it," he told them. "The leadership of this union is antilabor. You pay union dues to the National for years, and when you need them they aren't there. We asked them for help, and they laughed at us."

At this there was a visible release among the men listening. They were looking at each other now, shaking their heads and nodding. Somebody had finally admitted it. Somebody who mattered.

"What do you say, Joe?" Bragg called to me, out on the edge of the circle. "Are you with us?"

The men looked my way, and those standing between Bragg and me backed off, so that we were suddenly face to face.

"I'm not against you," I said, resisting.

The men were gathering behind him now. "It's getting dark out here," he said.

And I knew that the decision had been made, that everything necessary had been said, because Bragg had made my speech for me; and I let the last of my memorized words slip from my mind.

"Why don't you come inside?" I said.

He thanked me, grinning, and I felt the whole crowd relax. Bragg came over and put his arm around me in that approving way of his, and we walked into the union hall together, the others crowding after, full of noise and strike fever: three hundred warriors in sports clothes, going into battle in an old, old war.

The next day we had joined them. I spent the morning driving from job to job, watching men from our local walking back and forth in front of unfinished houses and stores, looking sheepish and lonely, three or four men at a time carrying placards on sticks or wearing blue sashes with PICKET in white, outside the places where they had been working only the day before, while people dressed for business or shopping drove by with curious, disapproving glances. Labor, out on the street. Airing grievances publicly. Inconveniencing everybody. Pushing up the cost of living. The passing people looked away quickly and hurried about what they were doing. I handed out stacks of leaflets to the picket captains, explaining our side of the strike, and tried to make the pickets feel a little less isolated, talking in the odd quiet of idle machinery, establishing the rules. No booze. No goosing women. No mouthing off. No rough stuff. No weapons. No threats. If a foreman shows up alone, let him through; he probably just wants to lock up; but if he has a gang with him, stop them quietly but firmly, block the entrance, and call the local. You'll get reinforcements. It felt strange to say these things, and even stranger to be planning the actions they implied; yet oddly exciting, because it made the rest of the world outsiders.

Each morning at eight o'clock, Potter or I opened our building. There would be half a dozen men standing around waiting in the parking lot, and they'd follow us inside to the auditorium, where card tables and folding chairs had been set up, sit down, and start reading the newspapers. Soon others joined them, reporting in by habit, as if for work, neatly dressed in weekend clothes and looking uneasy. Men who had been working on the same jobs would gather together, start complaining what a bastard their foreman had been and tell private jokes; card games would begin, men playing pitch or a game called Oh Shit because it was so frustrating to lose, playing joylessly, making work of it, more men watching than holding cards; a few men sitting off by themselves silently reading trade manuals or library books; two monitors standing at the door, eyeballing everybody to see that no one was there who didn't belong. In the afternoon, a fresh shift of pickets would go out and men who'd been on the jobs would come in, wind-blown and anxious to talk, filling in the card games and reporting what they'd seen. The transistor radios would all go on if there was a ball game, or Wayne Henneberry would play his guitar, the air would fill with smoke, the floor with butts, and the chairs with discarded newspaper pages. By six o'clock, the hall would be littered and empty, and the janitors would be dragged in, complaining, to clean up. By eight, the men would be back, the evening shift of pickets going out, wearing parkas and scarves and overcoats and mittens; the serious card games would resume, and the television would be turned on. At midnight, there were always a few men left, card players stolidly insisting on one more hand, an old-timer asleep in front of the Late Show, and I'd have to flick the lights on and off to drive them out so I could close the building and turn the lock on one more day of the strike.

Other locals were joining us. The strike was spreading, shutting construction down so widely that in whole counties, San Mateo, Monterey, Alameda, Napa, not a single compressor ripped the air, not a mixer mixed, not a single hammer was being banged against a nail; the only thing moving on any construction job was a slow line of men with picket signs.

Wherever the issue was in doubt, Bragg appeared, giving a fiery speech or swarming with a busload of his men into a union meeting, sometimes invited, sometimes not, standing in the back of the hall with his arms folded to watch the debate, or waiting out in front for the local to vote; at times even turning up out on the jobs to persuade men to put down their tools and join the strike, while an angry foreman watched. Intimidation, the contractors screamed, and appealed to the men by letter. Bragg's men were armed, they said; they carried lengths of bicycle chain, pipe, guns. Men had been threatened and beaten, and this would not go unpunished. Which gave rise to worse rumors: that the contractors intended to bring in goons of their own; that the word was out in the San Francisco Tenderloin that strong-arms were wanted; that there was a price on Bragg's head. As the strikes widened, the stakes grew: more equipment lay idle, lumber was warping, paint settling out, time lost. Bragg had struck at last to the heart of the contractors' concern. He was costing them money.

He bathed in their hatred as if it were sunlight. The idea that he had enemies who were openly condemning him seemed to please him. He took no offense. They gave him no quarter, he would give them none. Nothing they accused him of, no name they called him, was capable now of angering him.

The contractors communicated with us now only through Toad, put-upon and harassed, dragging himself to our Strike Committee sessions every Monday, Wednesday, and Friday evening with the same proposal. The way Toad told it, the contractors weren't going to budge. Though the strike was spreading, they saw this as working in their favor: the more locals that went out on strike, the greater would be the financial burden on the union, so that a large strike without National support would be harder to sustain than a small one. Which was all too true. We were hard up for money almost immediately. The National controlled most of the union funds, and they had denied us access to them. So we grubbed and scrounged. I had cleaned out our local's checking account, used up our petty cash, and was diverting rental payments from the tenants in our building into the strike fund. We issued food certificates of up to twenty-five dollars each week, which men used to buy groceries, the grocers then billing us. But for most families, this wasn't nearly enough. Men were beginning to miss mortgage payments or fall behind in their rent. Those who could, borrowed. Others had to dig into their savings to pay large bills and utilities. Many of the wives were taking in sewing and ironing. And a few men were working on the sly, despite warnings not to scab; but this was on a small scale and didn't involve crossing any picket lines.

"The longer you wait," Toad warned us again and again, "the tougher they're going to be."

Mondays were the worst. For some reason, the end of the weekend and the thought of everybody else going back to work drove morale to its lowest among the men on Monday mornings. I could hear them standing around out by their cars, griping about the way the strike was being led. Pickets would report sick. Men would go off by themselves, and the crowd around the hall thinned out. I'd walk around and talk to as many men as I could, wheedling and teasing, telling them to be patient, to stand up for their rights and we'd win, trying to hide my own doubts, knowing that if we somehow got through Monday, we'd last the week. I'm sure the contractors understood this; and that was why, on the strike's third Monday, Harris told Toad that they wanted to meet with us and talk.

That afternoon, Toad drove us all out to the contractors' hall, Leo Silvestri, from the Napa local, riding up in the front seat with him, while Bragg, Silk, and I were squeezed into the back. Toad was almost giddy with relief at the thought of the strike ending, talking a lot and laughing in a nervous, jerky way.

"Come over this afternoon and talk, he told me," Toad said, passing a bread truck uncomfortably close. "Just like that, no conditions. Will we ever! I told him. What time?"

He was so pleased that the rest of us were smiling in sympathy, except for Bragg, sitting next to me, staring glumly out the window.

"You figure it's a good sign," said Silvestri, "them coming to us?" He was a tired, gentle man with a tanned bald head, a black mustache with gray in it, and big, dark, hopeful eyes.

"You've got to see it that way. Hell, they *walked out* on us, last time. It's almost an apology. What probably happened was, they took a vote this morning, decided to raise the offer, and want to settle right now and get it over with."

We stopped for a red light next to a half-completed apartment building where five pickets from Bragg's local shuffled slowly by with signs.

"I'll be glad to see the end of that," said Toad. "Poor bastards." The light changed, somebody behind us honked, and Toad lurched the car forward. "Be a long time before they earn what they lost," he said.

We parked about half a block from the contractors' offices, a whole upper floor of an old building whose bottom floor is leased out to a market. We had walked about halfway there when Bragg, who was wearing a flaming-red ski sweater, peeled off this sweater and ran back to put it in Toad's car.

"Look at him," said Toad, teasingly, as Bragg reached through a side window to open the car door. "He looks like he's stealing it."

We walked up a narrow stairway to a small lobby with a high ceiling, dark wood-paneled walls, brown linoleum floor, a leather couch with two matching chairs, three large potted plants, and a sour library smell. There was a large dark door with a small knob in one corner of the lobby, and next to it a small window where an old woman with a long, narrow nose and a green eyeshade sat at a telephone switchboard. Toad walked over and announced himself, and she nodded and rang.

"It's like a museum," said Bragg, looking at the pictures

103

on the wall, framed photographs that must have been thirty to fifty years old, groups of men all wearing derby hats, a bearded public official cutting a ribbon, a gang of workmen standing in front of a "new" building with vaults and cornices; a contractors' picnic.

"I bet the old man's in this one," said Bragg, pulling the picnic photograph off the wall roughly to examine it.

"Mister Fuller," said the switchboard lady in a whiny voice, "Mister Harris will see you now."

All five of us started for the door. "Just Mister Fuller, please," she said sternly, looking with alarm at Bragg. Toad, who appeared puzzled, went inside alone.

Bragg sat noisily on the couch, studying the picture. Silk took a chair. Silvestri stood stroking his mustache, while I walked around looking at the pictures on the walls.

"Hey, here he is," said Bragg, and we gathered around him to look at the photograph. A picnic table in some long-ago park, maybe twenty men stiffly standing or sitting, and one of them Andy Donovan, tall, gawky, and vulnerable. The strict mouth and ardent eyes that were so impressive in the old Donovan looked preposterous in the young.

"Looks like he pissed his pants," said Silvestri.

We all laughed, and the woman with the eyeshade shook her head.

"Get a copy made of this," said Bragg, handing the photograph to Silk. "Put it inside your coat."

"Let's see if there are any more," said Bragg. But before he could get up, the door opened and Toad came out looking disappointed and embarrassed.

"What is it?" Bragg shouted at him. "Have they forgotten how to talk?"

"They want to talk," said Toad, walking over to us slowly. "But not to you. The rest of us are okay with them, but not him. They won't negotiate with you," he said to Bragg.

"The hell with them," I said. Silvestri and Silk agreed.

Toad nodded faintly. "They want to talk contract, and they're willing to increase their offer."

"What do *you* say?" Bragg asked him, standing.

Toad thought for a moment. "There's this personal thing now that's only going to make it worse. I think we can arrive at a better contract if you're not present."

I felt uncomfortable, and was aware of the woman listening. I looked over at her window and stared at her until she turned away.

"And break the strike," Bragg said.

"*End* the strike," Toad insisted.

Toad thought again, watching Bragg. "What difference does it make if you're not there, so long as you win?"

Bragg's face went cold with anger. "The union decides who represents the union."

There was nothing more to say. We just stood there awkwardly, aware of the woman watching. Finally Toad turned to her.

"Tell Mister Harris I'll call him."

It was the last thing he said to anybody until he let me out at my car.

11

Lieutenant Ganley, from the San Francisco Homicide Bureau, is an older man than I would have expected, heavy, slow-moving, and polite, apparently important in his line of work, because Hoxie is falling all over himself trying to impress him when he comes by the house at dinnertime, taking Ganley's hat from him, telling him eagerly about the phone call and the two men in the car while Ganley, looking like he knows it all, silently gives me, Doug, and the house the once-over. He tells Hoxie he wants to speak with me alone, and it's an order.

We go into the living room and sit down, while Doug and Hoxie finish dinner and start on the dishes. Ganley wears a quiet pin-stripe suit and a shirt that has been carefully mended around the cuffs and collar; he looks like the kind of man who cares so much about his job that he's almost indifferent to what it pays him, and in this he reminds me of Bragg. He hands me a stack of small photographs, police mug shots, and asks me to look through them to see if I recognize anyone: old, hard-eyed cons, a falsely cocky kid, a stunned Latin-looking man, a glowering black man, head on, in profile, numbered. A nun could be photographed that way and come out looking like an ax murderess. While I study the pictures, Ganley questions me in a voice so soft that I have to strain at times to hear him; he doesn't raise his voice or even vary it from question to question. He asks about people: Bragg, Toad, Silk, Harris, Tom Cannon; and then in that same soft, polite voice he aims one directly into me.

"Do you own a shotgun, Mister Burke?"

Making me so uneasy that I actually feel guilty.

"No. That is—yes. I don't. I did, but I gave it to my son."

While he looks at me with cold green eyes. "May I see it, please?"

Feeling nervous and watched, I go and get the gun, stuck back in a corner of Doug's closet in a pile of old sports equipment. I bring it out to Ganley, who takes it in his big, freckled hands, breaks it open, looks into the breach, and squints down the barrel.

"Has this been fired recently?"

"I don't know," I say, angry at myself for being flustered. "My son takes it out once in a while and shoots at tin cans."

"Needs cleaning," he says, with just a hint of accusation in his voice. I tell him that Doug doesn't take very good care of the gun, and that as far as I know there isn't even any ammunition in the house. He sits on the couch, snaps the gun shut, and sets it on the floor, barrel up, against his leg; he intends taking it with him. He asks me where I was on the night that Bragg was killed, and again my answer sounds flustered and guilty. I was with Rose, at her house; we'd had dinner and watched an old movie on TV, and nobody else had seen us. I couldn't remember the name of the movie, except that I thought Kirk Douglas was in it. Ganley writes down Rose's address and phone number, and says that he'll be talking to her.

"Did you get along with Mister Bragg?" he asks me in that soft voice again. I tell him that yes, we'd been friends.

"Just through your work, or did you see each other socially?"

"It started out as business, and grew into a social thing, but the work was part of that, too. He never really got away from the union."

He wants to know how often Bragg and I saw each other, and what other people were present when we did.

"Did just you and he see each other socially, or his wife and your . . ."

"Friend," I finish for him sourly. I can see Ganley's wife, at home, tirelessly mending his shirts; four kids in parochial-school uniforms, while Daddy has to be out talking to fornicating union bosses.

"Now," he says, becoming less polite and more authoritative, "you and he were on the same side in a labor-management war?"

I don't like the implication that Bragg would have killed somebody if he hadn't been killed himself, and I tell Ganley so. That wasn't the way it was at all. He asks me to explain. The real beef was within the union itself, I tell him, between union labor and union management. Bragg felt the men *were* the union, and he ran his local that way, with democratic representation and majority rule. And the National hated him because he made union democracy work.

"So he was the leader of the men representing the anti-management point of view?"

"That's right." I feel better now, satisfied with myself for setting things straight.

"And who was next, after him?" Ganley asks me.

"Well, I don't know. There were several men in Bragg's local—Leonard Silk, Paul Eisan . . ."

"Silk." He leans forward now. "Would he have taken Bragg's place as the leader of this movement?"

108

"No," I tell him flatly.

"Eisan?"

"No."

"How about you?"

And I realize that he's been waiting to ask that question all the time. That's why he's delayed seeing me. He's talked to the others, to Silk and Eisan, and probably Toad and Sally Bragg, and from what they've told him, he's put together a line of investigation to follow, that I was Bragg's natural successor as the leader of a union revolt, and therefore had a motive to kill him.

My mouth goes dry. "No. Not me. I don't want to be a high-powered labor leader."

"That's what I've heard," he says in a suddenly hard and cynical voice. He's pure cop now, all suspicion, with a motive and a weapon and a suspect. And I can see what's coming next. I'll be taken in for questioning, led down the front walk, handcuffed, with Ganley beside me carrying the shotgun, while the neighbors watch through their curtains. Instead, Ganley backs off and relaxes, and his voice becomes soft and polite again; he has tested me as much as he chooses and wants to move to a different subject.

"You say a threat has been made on your life?"

"Yes." I feel a slight relief. "The day after Bragg was shot." I tell him about the phone call, and bring Doug in to repeat exactly what was said, and Ganley listens, watching Doug closely until he seems convinced he isn't lying, then nodding. I tell him about the two men in the car, and Hoxie comes in, a dish towel in his hand, to verify it. Both of them sound like liars, and that makes me feel better. It must be Ganley's technique to make people act guilty; he treats you as if you are. Therefore, he must have his own yardstick for measuring the truth, and the more cool and self-possessed you are, the tighter your alibi, the likelier it would be that you are lying. Maybe I haven't done so badly after all.

"I'd like to take this along," Ganley says, standing with the gun. He turns to Doug. "Got any shells, son?"

Doug says yes, he has some twenty-aught buck shells, and my jaw drops. Ganley hadn't believed me when I told him there wasn't any ammunition in the house. Has he believed anything?

Guiltily, Doug goes into his bedroom and comes out with a large plastic bag containing maybe a dozen loose red shotgun shells and a couple of shell boxes. Ganley looks through the bag, takes out two shells, and puts them in his coat pocket, then tosses the bag back to Doug.

"May I have the pictures?" Ganley asks me, so softly that for a moment I don't grasp what he's talking about. Then I realize I'm still holding his stack of photographs. I hand them back to him. They'd meant nothing. He'd only used them to distract me while he asked me his questions. Not one of those men is really a suspect. And I am.

"You'll hear from us in a day or so," he says, putting the pictures into his bulging pocket, even and noncommittal. I search his face for some sign of judgment and find none. Hoxie brings him his hat, and Ganley thanks me and goes down the front walk, heavy and impassive. He's holding the shotgun in one hand, through a handkerchief; but at least it's dark out, and he isn't taking me with him.

Doug and I go into the kitchen and sit at the counter, and Hoxie takes a Pepsi out of the refrigerator, opens it, and sits down with us.

"He's a cool sumbitch, isn't he?" Hoxie says proudly. I nod ruefully. "Made some great pinches," Hoxie adds in open admiration.

"Hoxie, is it true that shotgun pellets can't be traced to an individual gun because there's no rifling in shotgun barrels?"

He frowns, thinking. "I guess that'd be so."

"And is twenty-aught buckshot fairly common?"

"Twenty-aught? Oh, yeah. In deer season, you can buy it in supermarkets up around Willits and Ukiah."

"So the pellets that killed Bragg could match Doug's."

"Naw." Hoxie puts the Pepsi bottle to his lips before the thought stops him. He sets the bottle down. "Yeahhh," he says, with a nodding stare.

Doug squirms with anxiety. "They don't think *you* did it!"

"Somebody did it who has a shotgun," and I held up one finger; "who knew where Bragg would be that night," and I held up another finger; "and who can't prove that he was somewhere else." And I point all three fingers at myself.

12

By the strike's fourth week, conditions within the union had grown desperate. Everyone was short of money. Men began appearing at our union hall wearing old work clothes, or the same deteriorating sports outfits day after day, skipping haircuts and laundry and ironing, until they looked like an army of Baxter Braggs. Those who had kept busy at home, painting and fixing, abandoned their projects and came to the hall to hang around, bored and restless, waiting for the strike to end. Some sent their families off to live with relatives and, in loneliness, loitered at the union hall all day. The weather had turned warm, and the men would gather in the parking lot, standing around in the shade of the trees, smoking and spitting and talking loud, exchanging gossip and strike rumors, watching someone rev up a car or motorcycle engine, taunting and testing one another in plain view of the people who live in the neighborhood, who looked out at the men in disgust. The strike which had tied them so closely together now strained those same ties. Men from the same shop, who'd discovered they shared a common dislike for a boss, often found that they shared nothing else, and began drifting into groups not bound by work: old men and young; white men and black; sharing confidences, laughing privately, looking at the other groups with growing distrust. There was some drinking; joints of pot were being freely passed among the young white men, and every two hours a squad car passed by slowly, while a couple of city cops took a long, critical look at the building and the crowd of men outside it. At last, toward the end of the day, the men would disperse, slowly and noisily, starting cars and calling back and forth, looking guilty and tired from not having done any work, heading home to face an evening newspaper that repeatedly complains that unions have the public at their mercy.

While the men waited, idle, outside the building, inside we worked frantically, calling and dispatching pickets, answering questions, hearing out pleas for money and part-time work and occasionally even for food; telephones rang constantly, typewriters clacked, people shifted about impatiently as they waited to be interviewed, or simply sat with listless stares, looking physically beaten; Dorothy argued with them, trusting no one; Beverlee broke down once a day in sympathetic sobs. At times it seemed that the office would burst from the concentration of so much life and energy. It was with no small measure of guilt that I left some evenings for strike meetings while it was all still going on: people sitting at desks, interviewing or being interviewed, talking on the telephones, pleading, waiting; our office lights burning into the night, while the rest of the building was dark.

Because Bragg's local was the logical nerve center of the strike, our strategy sessions were held at the San Francisco Trades Union Building. So three nights a week, having listened to personal problems all day, I'd get into my car, drive across the bridge, and fight for a parking place in the city, to talk union problems half the night.

On Monday evening of that fourth week, Toad came to the meeting looking more confident than I'd seen him since before the contract talks began. He'd been visiting the outlying locals, beyond the city and the suburbs, and he was greeting everybody with the assured attitude of a man who knows he has information that people are anxious to hear, helping himself to the swivel chair behind the desk in Bragg's tiny office, refusing to answer questions, holding it all back importantly until Silk, Bragg, Silvestri, and I were all settled, quiet, and looking at him attentively.

His news met his own grave forecasts. In the outlying locals, the strike was destroying the union organization, just as he had said it would. The locals were stripped of funds, membership was dropping, morale was poor. Men were in danger of losing cars, furniture, homes. They wanted to go back to work, and the local officers were ready to pull out and settle on the employers' terms.

"You seem pretty sure of that," said Bragg. He was standing leaning against his office wall, his arms folded.

"I am," said Toad, unmoved. "They've had it."

"Things are tough for everybody," Bragg said bitterly. "What did they expect?"

"You got to understand," said Toad. "They got open shop up there. Work is starting again, union or no union. They got to go back to work or lose their jobs."

Bragg dropped his hands, as though pushing something down. "All right. We'll send a delegation up to talk to them."

"No," Toad insisted, with a sudden, savage bluntness. "They don't want you."

Bragg stared at Toad as if he didn't understand.

"They told me to tell you not to come," Toad explained. "They don't want any more trouble."

114

If it was true, if Bragg had pushed the men as far as they would go, if even he couldn't hold them out any longer, the strike would crumble. But more than that, Bragg had already cut himself off from the contractors and the National. If the rank and file gave up on him, he would be finished. No one seemed to be looking at anyone else. Nobody spoke, until I felt someone had to.

"Suppose we let one or two locals go back?" I offered. "Out of hardship."

"The others will want to go back, too," Toad said with a shrug. "What do we say to them?"

I had no answer, but they all waited. Unopposed, Toad continued.

"There's still a firm offer. I think we should reconsider."

I heard a click behind me and turned. The office door had closed, and Bragg was gone. Inside the room, there was a shift of feeling. Silk let out a long, deep breath. Toad slipped off a shoe. Silvestri took out a pack of cigarettes, offered one to Toad; they shared a light. They were smiling at each other with the certain relief of men freed from uncomfortable scrutiny.

They were changing sides already. If there was going to be a defeat, let Bragg take it. The strike was his idea anyway.

"There's a general meeting here Friday," Silk volunteered in a wary, soliciting voice. "They could vote on it then."

I felt trapped. Excusing myself, I got up and went out the door after Bragg.

I found him sitting in the darkened hiring hall, in one of a row of attached seats, leaning forward, elbows on his knees, hair hanging down the side of his face, looking at a floor he couldn't see.

"You okay?" I said.

He didn't answer, so I sat down a couple of seats away.

The seat was uncomfortably hard. After a few moments, Bragg began to speak.

"I was just thinking," he said. "This is the first society in history whose most reactionary element is labor." He sounded wounded and rejected, voicing a final, painful conclusion. "What's the use, trying to convince them it should be otherwise?"

I told him that I was sure it was worth doing.

"Why?" he challenged me. "What good does it do?"

To my surprise, thoughts that had been puzzling me for weeks and months suddenly fell into place and, in the dark, I found words for them. I told him I was convinced that conflicting feelings exist within the same union, the same local, even within the same man; that at different times the same men could be greedy and self-sacrificing, cynical and idealistic, honest and corrupt, kind and cruel, intelligent and stupid, inspired and lazy. The way men act in a group, I said, depends almost entirely on which of these feelings prevail, and therefore on what is expected of men, and the manner in which they are led.

Bragg sat with his head bowed. I think it was the first time he ever really listened to anything I said.

Then he began speaking in a disarmed, confiding voice.

"Every night when I go home, I pick up the phone and somebody is calling me names, you dirty son of a bitch, you dirty rotten Communist, we're going to kill you, we're going to blow up your house, we're going to gang-bang your wife. They drive past the house and yell and throw beer cans and bottles." His voice fell until it was nearly a murmur. "Now, they're even calling in the daytime, in the morning when they know I'm out. They get Sally on the phone and call her names until they have her in tears. And that has me scared, because I don't know what I'll do."

He stopped, on the verge of tears himself. I had never

116

known him to talk so openly about himself, to leave himself so vulnerable. Then, as though collecting everything, he sat erect in the seat and breathed deeply.

"No one wants to end this more than I do," he said grimly.

The light from the hallway was cut off. I turned. The others were standing in the auditorium doorway, clinging to the light as though afraid of the dark. We sat for a moment, until it became apparent that they were waiting for us. Then Bragg stood and walked directly toward them. I followed him, squinting, into the hall. Toad was standing, ready to leave, his shoes on, his coat over his arm. Silk and Silvestri were standing behind him with new expressions of firmness.

"We want to put it to a vote," Toad announced curtly. "Friday."

Bragg walked past him, looking at the floor, then barged through Silk and Silvestri, who looked bewildered. He continued down the hall, toward the stairway leading out of the building. We stood staring after him. The moment when his guard had dropped was over. About halfway down the hall, he stopped and threw Toad one icy word of recognition.

"Strikebreaker."

On Wednesday morning a crowd of men as large as the one we'd had the night of the strike vote gathered in our parking lot, where they waited agitatedly for news to break. Through the window I could see them standing in large groups again, talking and moving about, looking toward my office expectantly. Everyone seemed to sense that there had been a disagreement of some kind, a break, disunity in the union.

"What happened over there the other night?" Potter said, coldly inquisitive.

117

"I can't explain it to you," I said, embarrassed by how little I really knew. Four times the previous day I had called Bragg's office, and each time I was told he was out, they didn't know where, just going around talking to the men out picketing the jobs. I had no better luck with Toad; he was out of town, gone for the day, might not be back tomorrow.

"Well, are we still on strike or not?" Potter persisted.

"Don't worry," I told him. "If anything happens, I'll let you know."

Ignoring him, I watched the men. They stood poised; a balance had been reached between their desire to get what they wanted and their fear of being out of work.

While I was watching, a car pulled into the lot and edged boldly into the crowd, forcing men to step irritably out of the way, with injured shouts at the driver. Surrounded, he got out, a red-haired man with a white-on-white shirt and tie and a shiny, metallic-looking suit, and began talking to the men, who drew in around him to listen. After a while, he began asking them questions, and hands gestured toward my office. He turned and looked right at my window, then made his way around his car and through the crowd, and crossed the lot toward the building.

He introduced himself as Harry Walsh, a paint salesman from Sacramento, who had just announced to everybody outside that the strike had been settled there and that the men were already back at work.

"Thought I'd get the jump on the competition down here," he told Potter and me with a twisted grin. "But your boys outside say it isn't over yet."

I felt Potter give me an accusing look.

Enjoying the stir he'd caused, Walsh told us that he wasn't familiar with the details of the settlement except that, in his case, it permitted the unrestricted use of rollers, sprayers, and other automatic equipment. The employers' terms.

"Toad Fuller come up yesterday," Walsh said admiringly, "and the whole thing was settled last night. Guess it'll be over here any day now."

Potter told him that Bragg's local was having a general meeting on Friday.

"Well, that's it then," Walsh said confidently. "Good thing. A long strike like this doesn't do anybody any good except the radicals."

I asked him if anybody else had gone back.

"Yes," he said. "They're back in Yolo County, Solano and Sonoma, and Contra Costa votes tomorrow. They'll go. That's Fuller's local."

Nosily, he asked what our plans were, and I told him that we'd see what Bragg did first.

"You labor guys," he scolded coyly. "You sure stick together."

"Do we ever," I said, with an irony he ignored.

On Friday evening, there wasn't a single place to park on any of the streets or alleys around Bragg's building. Everything was taken. Cars had been pulled into driveways and driven up onto the sidewalk, and, everywhere I looked, men in twos and threes were walking purposefully toward the meeting, aware that something was up. Giving in, I left my car blocks away in a gas-station lot and joined them.

A crowd of men had collected on the front steps of the building, where they stood watching the rest of us arrive, an audience already, eager for a show to start, most of them wearing union buttons or badges.

"Where's your button, brother?" someone shouted at me as I went inside the front door. More men were standing inside, strung out along the hallway and bunched at both ends of the stairs, talking sullenly, nodding to friends and staring at strangers, impatient and curious, with something of a lynch mob's anger simmering below the surface.

I found Lenny Silk and Max Volt arguing by the open stage door. "Where is he?" Max was saying. "You're the program chairman, you're supposed to know."

"I haven't seen him since Monday," Silk pleaded. "I called his house; there was no answer."

"I don't want to begin without him," Volt fretted, looking around. Eisan was standing with the Safety Committee, watching, and I'd seen Grimes and Buxton out on the front steps. But there was no sign of Bragg anywhere. "Hello, Joe," Max said to me, preoccupied. Glancing at his watch, he resignedly suggested that we go inside.

We walked through the dark into the glare of the stage. Toad and Silvestri were already there, sitting at the trestle table. We said hello to one another, and I sat down next to Leo, while Max walked out to the edge of the stage to talk to the men working with the sound equipment. Toad looked nervous, and he kept shooting hard glances out at the audience, which as yet took up only about a quarter of the seats, but was so restless and noisy that it sounded bigger. The lights were up full, and as many men were standing and walking around as were sitting, with that same impatient curiosity I'd sensed on the stairs and in the hallway. Suddenly there was a large noise, a booming shout, with yells and whistles, coming from outside, so loud that it drowned the auditorium's rattling chatter. Everyone looked up. The noise was rolling inside toward us, echoing up the stairs and down the hallway, growing louder until it burst through the back entrance of the auditorium and Bragg plunged in, riding it, wearing his familiar uniform, walking with his old, cocky stride, grinning his fierce grin, Eisan and the Safety Committee,

120

Grimes and Buxton following him, smiling with relief. The men in the audience were shouting, too, now, yelling and applauding as Bragg passed them heading toward the stage, while those outside flocked in the back door after him, filling the seats and standing in the back, still applauding, so that the auditorium reverberated with their noise, continuing while Bragg climbed up on the stage, grinned at all of us, and said something we couldn't hear. Turning, he faced the men and held his palms out for quiet. The men shouted even louder. Toad sat studying them as if positions were reversed and they, not we, were on the stage. Silvestri whispered something to Silk. Volt stood back from the podium, afraid to ask the men to be quiet, waiting instead until they wanted to be. Then Bragg threw up his hands in an exasperated gesture and sat down at the table with the rest of us. Only then did the noise dwindle, not to a drained silence, but to its former restless whir.

Cautiously, Volt stepped up to the podium and read a few familiar, nagging announcements. No smoking in the auditorium, try to keep the place picked up, fold the seats when you leave, so the janitors can sweep. He cleared his throat. The meeting was to be an open strike-strategy session. The Negotiating Committee had decided to hold a discussion of the purpose and direction of the strike. There was to be a report from Brother Bragg, Local President, and from Brother Toad Fuller, Area Representative, concerning the strike and certain negotiations now in progress. At this, Bragg gave Toad an inquiring look that wasn't returned. A vote on the strike itself would follow, Volt concluded.

"And now, Brothers, it's my pleasure to introduce our distinguished President, Brother Baxter Bragg."

There was an anticipatory silence as Bragg got up and walked to the podium, leafing through a handful of three-

121

by-five index cards. His shortness surprised me for a moment—he was shorter than Volt as they passed—but when he reached the podium I no longer noticed it. He stood erect, with his chest stuck out, his long hair, mustache, and costume making him seem at home under the lights.

"I have some strike news," he began, his voice harshly loud through the microphone as he turned through his cards, "somewhere." Reading, he continued, "Local Eighty, Contra Costa County, has voted to return to work and accept the terms as offered by the contractors."

"Boo-oo!" someone bellowed from the rear of the auditorium.

Bragg seemed not to notice. "Local Eighty-six, Sacramento, Local One Twenty-seven, Solano County, and Local Forty-four, Yolo County, have accepted the same terms," he continued.

"Boo-oo!" echoed a few more voices.

"That's the *good* news," said Bragg, at last, in reply. And some of the men laughed nervously.

He put his notes down where he could read them, gripped the podium with both hands, looked out over the audience, his hair dangling, and shifted into a sympathetic mood.

"These last few days, I must have spoken with nearly a hundred of you. Some of you here at the hall, hanging around, waiting, watching card games or reading newspapers. Others out on the line, walking back and forth over the same ground, standing at night around a garbage can with a fire in it that's supposed to keep you warm, but doesn't. I wanted to find out how you feel privately about what's been going on with this strike and this union, and now I think I know."

"He's been electioneering all week," Silvestri whispered to me.

Bragg's voice grew more assured. "I know you've all got

a million things on your minds. You're tired of being out of work. You're worried about your jobs, you're running out of money, and some of you have people sick. You're wondering if this situation is ever going to end, and if what you get is going to be worth what you've sacrificed."

The voice hardened now, and became dry. "I don't know when it's going to end," he admitted. "It's in your hands after all. This isn't a goddam corporation. I *do* know that I haven't seen an offer yet that I wouldn't be ashamed to accept. But you're the ones who vote the local back to work, so it's up to you.

"I also know that there are people in this union who feel the strike has gone on long enough, that the men have suffered enough, so it's okay to go back to work for a bad contract, a sellout contract, a *sweetheart* contract."

The word hung in the air as he paused. Toad, listening, made a face.

"I'm not one of them," said Bragg, to shouts and enthusiastic applause.

He paused, and the listeners returned to a nervous, stirring half-quiet.

"This local has come a long way in a short time," Bragg resumed. "We cleaned some deadwood out of office and got some good men in. We merged two locals that were patsies into one with real muscle. We enforced the safety regulations on the jobs and reduced the chances of getting hurt. We mounted a strike that shut down a whole industry, and shook the contractors the way they've never been shaken before . . ."

Interrupted by shouts and whistles, he waited them out.

"A strike that bound us together like nothing else ever has. Not wearing buttons or badges or shouting slogans or throwing testimonial dinners. We're brothers."

There was satisfied applause at this, the first of the night that wasn't mixed with shouting.

Bragg squinted in disapproval, and a hard edge came

into his voice. "But there are those among us who would sell their brothers down the river."

"No! No!" the men started in again.

"It's true," said Bragg. "There are those in this union —on our union payroll—who want to see us lose this strike."

"Boo-oo!"

He was working the crowd into a kind of fever which he kept catching back himself, their heat feeding his. He was in a sweat from it now, his hair limp and tangled, his speech clotted. He coughed and spat.

"They say they believe in union democracy. So we take them at their word, and they hate us for it.

"They say they believe in collective bargaining, yet they're trying to break their own union's strike.

"They say they believe in human dignity, and then deal a man's livelihood away when he isn't looking.

"What kind of leadership is that?" He was looking closely at the men now, studying them. "Leadership by *scabs*." He held the word before them like a knife. "By *sick, feeble-minded, sellout artists!*"

The audience let out a stunned grunt.

"By *political cowards*, who've made a career out of keeping this union weak. Who've lied and lied until they even believe their own bullshit!"

A man sitting halfway back in the audience jumped up and shook his fist at the stage, shouting something that couldn't be heard. Unsatisfied, he sat down, still fuming.

"They'll get you back to work," Bragg said, shaking a finger at the men, "and bust your union doing it. They'll get you a wage increase that's nothing but a payoff. They'll get you a contract, but it'll be a sweetheart contract. These high-class *pimps* will lead you into the *whorehouse* of *illusion!*"

"No! No!" came one huge, indignant roar.

124

"And if you follow them," Bragg began against the noise, and then had to repeat himself. "If you follow them, you'll be finking on yourselves, and you'll be getting exactly the kind of *weak, chicken-fed, labor-faking* leadership you deserve." His words beat the audience back into half-silence. "Personally, I wouldn't follow men like that out of a burning building."

He paused importantly and picked up the last of his cards, holding it with both hands.

"Or, as Thoreau said, 'I'm a man first, and subject later.' "

Abruptly, he turned from the podium and walked toward the table. The audience exploded with whistles, applause, and yells. Men were standing up clapping. Others were yelling, waving their arms, making angry shadows on the wall. Picket signs appeared, wigwagging. Crumpled handbills began dropping on the stage; one bounced on the table and landed in my lap. Volt looked at Bragg, who ignored him and sat down. Toad peered out at the audience, shielding his eyes with his hand against the light. Volt walked up to the podium and stood in Bragg's place, opening and closing his mouth soundlessly against the crowd's sullen roar. Bragg wouldn't lift a hand. He simply sat, watching the crowd, measuring the effect of his words. Volt, giving up, returned to the table. There was a drumming noise that must have been the stamping of feet, shouts that collided, canceling each other out, boos, and whistling. It was deafening. On stage, you couldn't shout at the man next to you and be heard.

Then, without a sign, Toad got up and walked heavily to the podium, firm, annoyed, his face a scowl of deep distaste. The audience rose to it. This was what they'd come for. They shouted at him. A ball of paper struck his forehead.

"Fink!"

"Strikebreaker!"

He stared at them, waiting. A boy in the first row ran up to the edge of the stage and waved a picket sign in Toad's face. The crowd cheered. Toad took a step forward, reaching out first as if to grab the sign, then motioning to the boy to sit down. Surprisingly, he did. Up close, Toad still possessed that glowering authority that kept him from being humiliated. They yelled at him, but only from a distance. And with that last bit of respect, the crowd lost its momentum. He was going to wait. They weren't going to push it any further. And he knew it. The shouts became scattered. In the audience, men began looking at each other. Some of them sat down. The paper stopped flying. The noise subsided, until I was gradually aware of another, smoother sound: Toad's deep, stomachy voice, flooding the loud-speakers.

"I haven't come here to explain myself to anybody," he began.

Far back in the hall, angry replies were made which couldn't be understood on stage.

"I don't have to," Toad continued in a scolding tone. "The facts speak for themselves. Those locals were in bad trouble, in danger of going under, and I took what action was necessary to save them. I'd do it again."

"Boo-oo!"

"Sellout!"

Almost all the men were sitting now. The lights made Toad's skin an odd orange color, and he was leaning forward to reach the microphone, which was too low for him, so that his ass stuck out under his coat in back. It was an odd posture, a mixture of power and vulnerability, which suggested that the slightest stumble would send him crashing.

"I'm a union man; don't make any mistake about that. I've been elected to office six times." Pulling up his sleeve,

126

he displayed a wrist watch on a gold band. "I wear a watch that the men of my own local chipped in and bought me."

"Payoff!" a lone voice yelled.

Toad ignored it. "I've opposed this strike from the start, because it's the worst thing that ever happened to this union."

The victim wasn't giving in or trying to slip away. He was fighting back, and the crowd began muttering in frustration.

"It's cost you money you'll never get back. It's poisoned the union's relations with the contractors, maybe permanently." Still facing the audience, he pointed back, toward Bragg. "The truth is, he doesn't *want* a settlement. He wants a *surrender*."

The crowd cheered derisively. Toad made a sulking face and waited till the cheering stopped.

"And a surrender is exactly what you're going to get. Not the contractors. They're not going hungry. They're not missing rent. If they need money, they can borrow it. Why should they give in?"

The noise was stretching thin now; the men were beginning to listen.

"It'll be *your* surrender," he said, pointing at them. "Unless you come to your senses like the other locals. We got a good offer, a damn good offer, a good increase in wages and fringes. Other locals are back at work for these wages and fringes right now. And you could be back Monday, if you'll only use your heads."

There was a long silence. Then, off to one side of the audience, a little man with a disproportionately long face stood up and bellowed through cupped hands, in a voice like a ship's whistle:

"Good night, sweetheart."

And the tension of the crowd snapped in laughter.

127

"Good night, sweetheart!"

Like a huge release of breath. The men were up again, shoving each other and laughing. They took out handkerchiefs and waved them. They blew kisses toward the stage. The little man with the big voice was singing.

"Good night, sweet-heart, la-da-da-de-DAHH-dah . . ."

The picket signs bobbed up again, the murmuring, and the scattered, angry shouts.

Toad stood rigid, watching. And in a cluster of men standing at the back of the hall, a new cry began.

"Throw him out!"

Eisan and the Safety Committee, maimed and unforgiving; Buxton, wearing sunglasses in blind, black hate; and Grimes, smiling at the thought of violence. They began chanting.

"Throw him out! Throw him out!"

Men turned toward the back of the hall to watch, picked up the chant, and faced forward. It spread.

"Throw him out! Throw him out!"

Until the entire audience was standing, facing the stage with one dense, gleeful shout.

"THROW HIM OUT! THROW HIM OUT!"

From the back of the hall, they started walking forward, Eisan, Grimes, Buxton, and the others, the men applauding as they passed. Men edged their way out to the center aisle to join them, yelling encouragement and shaking their fists. They were perhaps a dozen strong by the time they reached the edge of the stage.

"THROW HIM OUT!"

Breaking through, Buxton leaped up on the stage and grabbed Toad's arm. Grimes, following, grabbed the other arm. Toad angrily shook both off. But they wouldn't leave. Now other men began jumping up after them, bunching around Toad. He shot a quick, anxious glance back toward the table. Volt attempted to intervene, but Grimes shoved him out of the way. Grimes and Buxton started to take hold of his arms again, but Toad put up his hands first and stopped them. They stepped back, and he left the podium by himself, walked to the edge of the stage, and climbed down clumsily. The crowd cheered and whistled. He started up the center aisle, and the men who had climbed up on the stage climbed down after him. The audience yelled and threw papers. Somebody threw a picket sign at his head and missed. A man leaped into the aisle in front of him and yelled in his face:

"We'll remember you, you fink son of a bitch!"

Someone spat on his coat.

Volt was yelling into the microphone, pleading for order, but nobody was listening.

Head erect in his final humiliation, lumbering along with his odd, mincing walk, Toad made his way up the crowded aisle toward the back of the hall, accompanied by Bragg's men, yet alone. They escorted him out the back door, out of the building, and down the street to his car.

While the only man who could have stopped it sat watching, without a word.

13

Even now, when I think back to the night of that meeting, my face grows hot and my mouth acquires a dead, coppery taste. I hear the jeering voices and see Toad, white and trembling slightly, escorted past the rows of twisted faces, while Bragg sits, arms folded and feet crossed, calmly watching the cold fear of that vast pool of men boil up in hatred. The scene returns as nightmare, and I awake nearly strangled by a sheet and with an acid coat of phlegm in my throat; and in the morning, after a full eight hours in bed, I am numb and feverish and nearly exhausted as I leave the house for work.

I try to read my office mail and can't concentrate. The words swim before me. Potter says a contractor is requesting a specialist, an elevator constructor, and wants to know where he can find one. Nothing seems important; I can't make myself care. While Potter paces, griping, my phone rings, and I grab it mechanically.

"Joe! What on earth is going on?" an outraged woman's voice demands of me. "I keep hearing all these rumors, but no one tells me anything. What's *happening*?"

"Sally?" I ask cautiously.

"Yes! Who did you think I was?"

Potter is staring out the office window, looking abused and annoyed. I cover the phone and tell him I'll talk to him later. He throws up his hands impatiently and stalks out.

Sally is still complaining. ". . . why they haven't got them yet. They said they were going to put *four* inspectors on the case and they only put *one*. They haven't arrested *anybody* . . . all this in the paper about gang-style executions . . . I don't think they know *who* did it. They're going to let them get away."

Gradually, I become alert; Sally's voice seems to cut across not only distance, but time. It is a voice as full of changes as a church organ, rising and falling, strident, then faint, that assures her maximum attention no matter what she says.

"Now wait a minute," I interrupt. "There's a forty-thousand-dollar reward. You can't tell me people aren't going to talk for forty thousand dollars. And the police *are* working on it. They questioned me the other day."

"Why don't they arrest Toad Fuller then?" she says indignantly. "It's so obvious."

"He was in Salt Lake City, at a banquet, with twenty witnesses."

"That's just the sort of thing someone would use for an alibi."

"He was there. I know people who saw him."

There's a reluctant quiet at the other end of the wire. I turn in my chair so I can see out the window.

"The police check all these things, that's what takes time. They can't make an arrest without evidence. But they have leads."

I start to tell her about Hoxie, and decide not to. Instead

131

I ask her how she's feeling. She's alone, she says; Rose has been wonderful but now she's gone.

"We'd both like to see you," I try to console her.

"I'd like to see *you*. I need to talk to somebody. Will you take me to lunch?"

"Of course," I say, staggered.

"When?"

I look at my watch; it's nearly eleven o'clock. "How about today?" I ask, confident she'll decline.

"I need time to get dressed," she says to herself.

Then she commands: "Pick me up."

"All right. Sure. I'll come by for you in about an hour." I try politely to make it seem like lunch is my idea.

At quarter to twelve, baffled, I leave to drive into the city. A lunch date with Bragg's widow. I feel faithful and blasphemous at the same time, a willful puppet. My palms are sweating and my body's chilled. All the way across the bridge, I half hope for an accident, a flat, some excuse to telephone Sally and beg off, but I make it through the light midday traffic in easy time, and I'm soon in the Mission District, looking for Bragg's street.

Their flat is in a noisy dead-end alley whose entrance is flanked by a gas station and a machine shop. I park on the cross street in front of the machine shop, and head down a sidewalk littered with the hulks of cars. The air shakes with metallic hammering and smells of exhaust and gasoline. I pass a row of sagging Victorian houses with peeling paint and torn window shades. Their address is on the last house.

Sally answers the doorbell's echoing ring, and takes both my hands in hers. "Joe, it's so good to see you!" She leads me inside as though we're walking onto a dance floor. "I was so *brusque* with you at Baxter's services."

I mumble something about the demands of funerals, and we stand looking at each other smilingly. Then she gives my hands a parting squeeze and sits down on the couch. She's wearing a black suit that is supposed to make her look matronly, but her blond hair is long and loose, hanging straight, falling into her eyes as she sits; when she brushes it away with her hand her skirt rides up and a lot of young leg shows.

"You look fine," I say, sitting in a chair opposite her with what I hope is an innocent smile.

"Do I?" She brightens. "I feel like an old hag. I wouldn't even have got dressed today if you weren't taking me to lunch. I'd spend the whole day in my housecoat."

The room is dark, the light and sound from outside muted. I can see shelves of books, Bragg's chair with the cushion still dented from him, his oversized photograph staring at me from the wall, daring me to tamper with his memory.

"I feel so *cut off*," Sally says, pouting. "Baxter used to talk about the union all the time, and now I don't hear anything. They're always busy when I call."

She looks at me expectantly. I tell her that's the way it is in the union, that the simple day-to-day detail of the work can take up all your time. She doesn't believe me.

"Lenny Silk—he's such a phony. Always looking after you when there are people around, and as soon as no one's watching—boom!—he's gone. And Max—a union treasurer with an eighth-grade education."

I'm silent at the size of her displeasure, realizing how easily it could include me.

She softens. "You were the only one he felt close to, Joe. He respected you because you'd been to college. He knew that you were more intelligent than the others, and more compassionate."

I stare at the worn carpet, my ears burning. Sensing the

133

contempt in her flattery, knowing I will have to vomit up every word, I silently, shamelessly swallow it.

Her voice grows firm. "They think they can just go on as if nothing happened. I can't believe people could forget something so cruel . . . so *terrible*. That's why I want to help you." Her eyes burn with determination, and I feel uncomfortable at the way I must look in them.

Her voice becomes a mixture of offer and command. "I'll come to any meeting that you want me to. I'll make speeches. I'll write letters. I'll walk the picket line."

A cheap flat in a run-down neighborhood. No kids. All he'd left her was what he'd made of the union. She brushes her hair away again, a girl's gesture, with a thin, pale hand.

"I'm not going to let his whole life's work be thrown away," she warns.

As we drive downtown, she talks, sitting beside me in my car, holding a cigarette between two dainty, upright fingers, wearing giant sunglasses on a midget nose, spinning webs. What is needed is a single democratic government for all the Bay Area construction locals, a super-local patterned after Baxter's. It could start with a meeting to which the leaders of all the locals would be invited. It would be impossible to get them all to come, of course, and the group would be under attack from the National, but if they are asked in the right way by the right people, enough will be there. Out of this will grow our own regional government, which will be strong enough to break away from the National if they refuse to give in to our demands. If they don't give in, and maybe even if they do, we can contact Baxter's friends in locals across the country and launch a full-scale revolt that will topple the whole structure.

134

The girl next door, I remember someone saying, is made of steel.

She insists on going to Dominic's, a plush, cluttered, whispery restaurant on the edge of the Tenderloin, kept nearly as dark as a theater. It's a local hangout for union officials, and we're no sooner seated blindly in a cushioned booth and handed menus than they begin coming over to our table.

"Joe Petrolli from the Steamfitters, Missus Bragg. I knew your husband from way back. Thirty years I been in the union, I never knew a more dedicated man."

"I recognize your face," Sally says. "You were at his memorial service, weren't you?"

I look his way but can't see much in the darkness.

"That's right! How did you remember me?"

"Baxter used to talk about you."

"Well, I'll be damned. He did? I'll be damned. He was a great man, your husband. He could bring out the best in people because he always give his best himself. Missus Bragg, I'm going to give you one of my business cards, and if there's anything, anything, I can do for you, you let me know. Joe Petrolli from the Steamfitters."

My eyes have adjusted to the dim light, and I can see a short, burly man with a black mustache and hair that begins halfway back on his head, shifting his weight nervously from one foot to the other. Sally thanks him sweetly and he turns and leaves.

Another man walks up to our table, a thin, intense young man with wide, surprised eyes and a patchy beard.

"George Cassia, Missus Bragg," he says, taking her hand. "From the *Construction Workers Free Press*. I'd like to talk with you about your husband. We want to print the total story, including the parts that the Establishment papers have left out. The whole fascist murder."

135

Sally agrees, and he slides avidly into the booth, bumping against me.

"Would you say your husband was a true revolutionist?" he begins.

"I don't know," Sally ponders. "He had a deep belief in people, in what they could *do*. He could inspire them, win their enthusiasm. . . ."

"And their *unflinching support*," he suggests admiringly.

He questions her for nearly an hour, monopolizing the conversation while we eat. He takes no notes, claiming he has total recall. He has his ideas, and Bragg must suit them. Militant, progressive labor leader slain by conspiracy of bureaucratic and reactionary officialdom. He finishes by asking Sally what the future course of the union will be.

"I don't know," Sally pleads, but Cassia waits hungrily, wanting more, something she can give him that can be carved in stone. "I think—" she fumbles for words—"no, I *know* that what Baxter believed in was important, though he was just a dreamer to some people. . . ." She pauses, still groping, then seizes on the words for what she feels, and all the steel flows out of her voice, leaving a husky grief almost too soft to hear.

"They killed him, but they didn't kill his dream."

Cassia is moved, and he sits nodding to himself until he realizes that he is as close to the core of her memory of him as he dares come, and he thanks us both and leaves. Sally has a stunned, glazed look, and to try to stop her from crying I reach over and take her small, hard fist in my hand.

We leave the restaurant, and she puts her sunglasses in her purse, opens the window on her side of the car, and looks out at the passing city. The day has gone as she'd hoped. People have recognized her; they care. She's been intelligent and touching; she's had her way. Triumphant, she glows. She thanks me for taking her to lunch and admits she'd chosen a union hangout because she wanted to be noticed. Her shrewdness seems to dissolve in her joy, and she doesn't mention union politics all the way home.

When we get to her street, I park by the gas station, and as we walk by the machine shop, all the hammering stops. I can see the faces inside, watching. One of the men winks at me. Sally seems suddenly small and alone and badly in need of protection, the weakness and vulnerability underlying all her plans revealed; I offer her my arm, and she takes it, and I walk her to her flat, waiting while she unlocks the door. She steps inside, taking both my hands again and thanking me, like a submissive prisoner being led into a cell, and suddenly I'm inside, too, holding her and kissing her hair, her forehead, her cheek, her mouth; we stand in each other's arms, breathing heavily, warm, rocking slightly, staring at each other with mutual surprise.

"Oh, Joe," she says to my suit coat. I kiss her again. She smells of flowers and tastes faintly of salad dressing; her body feels firm, almost muscular, yet slender.

Once more, I kiss her.

"I could love you, Joe," she whispers, her eyes closed. Erect, I drive myself against her and we hold each other tightly.

"You better go," she says faintly.

I look up past the curtain of her hair and into Bragg's unforgiving eyes, staring at me from the wall like a religious figure whose gaze follows you all around a room. Sally looks at me, then turns to where I've been looking. Her arms drop and we move away from each other. She straightens her hair with her hand. I button my coat. Suddenly polite, we glance away, look back, smile. I tell her

137

good-by and back stiffly into the hallway, turn away, and then turn back. She has become a blur.

"Joe," she says, holding the door half-open. "Don't forget. About the union."

I nod and plunge into the light and noise of the street, aching and dazed, spinning somewhere between elation and remorse. By the time I've reached my car, I already doubt the reality of what has happened.

14

The Saturday morning after Bragg's meeting, I went with Rose to the Flea Market, an abandoned chain store in the Madrone Shopping Center that has been converted into a bazaar, where anyone who wants to can come and sell whatever can be palmed off as handcrafted or antique: old toys, fireplace irons, paintings, gilt flowers, old beer signs, Easter eggs with a scene inside, feather dusters, bead necklaces, wood carvings, preserves, billfolds, shoulder bags, soap. The market was jammed with customers: eager girls in short dresses, squealing with discovery and holding items up to show one another, young men with faces of hair and steel-rimmed glasses, suburban women, mentally redecorating, kids running in the aisles, reluctant-looking husbands. Rose bought a beaded curtain, a reed mat, and some dyed feathers which even I knew were overpriced. I paid. It was worth it. My mind was off the union and the strike.

Walking out, teasing Rose about what she'd bought, I passed a man and a fat woman in the doorway, trying to persuade three bickering children to go inside. The man said my name and I looked at him. George Harris.

"Boy," he said, smiling at me knowingly, "when you guys are through with somebody, you don't waste any time letting him know, do you?"

He was wearing a cheery Tyrolean hat that was too small for his sweating head, and it made his eyes bulge.

"Come on, George," his wife said, dragging the children inside.

"You go ahead," he told her. "I'll catch up with you."

Rose and I stepped out onto the sidewalk and Harris followed us. "Yes sir, that must have been some meeting you had last night," he said. I introduced Rose to him; he tipped his hat, and then ignored her.

"I never thought it would come to this, did you?"

I mumbled something that sounded to him like agreement.

"I got a picket line in front of my own office," he continued. "Can't even go out for a sandwich without being called a union buster. How do you think that makes me feel? I used to be a steward."

Rose took her packages from me, excused herself, and said she'd wait for me in the car. Harris tipped his hat again as she left.

"What a mess," he resumed dolefully. "The jobs are there. The money's waiting. Work for the asking and we can't touch it. We're losing, you're losing. Like a couple of kids socking each other to see who can stand it the longest."

People were walking around us, entering and leaving the building. I stepped off the sidewalk into the shade of a fir tree growing in a redwood pot. Harris offered me a cigarette and then lit one himself.

"What it is, is a total breakdown of communications," he continued. "I have no love for Baxter Bragg, but that doesn't mean I can't sit down and talk with him. Hell, I understand what he's up against. I know what it's like to work under a man with outmoded ideas. Not that I don't admire Andy. He's a giant. But the world moves too fast. You can't stand still. The times have passed him by." He looked at me. "Like Toad."

One of his children, an adolescent girl already taller than her father, came out of the Flea Market and yelled at him to come inside.

"In a minute," he called, and waved her back. He returned to me, and a certain stress came into his voice. "With Toad, though, it's even worse. A man gets thrown out of his own union's meeting, I figure he's come to the end of the line, don't you?"

I nodded, and looked around, feeling as though I had shouted.

"It's inevitable," Harris said reassuringly. "The old leadership has to give way to the new, on both sides."

His look embarrassed me, making me feel we were conspirators.

"I don't think we'll ever have a better chance to settle this than right now," he said, his face growing even more serious.

"On what terms?" I said.

"It's open. Any time. Any place. With Toad or without him."

"It would have to be a three-year contract," I insisted.

"Whatever."

The girl came out of the market again and yelled, this time almost screeching. "Daa-dy!"

He winced at the sound of her voice and yelled back. "All right!"

I told him I'd talk to Bragg, and we shook hands. He drifted back toward the store, being bossed, wanting to be a boss.

Rose had been watching from the car. "What a rude man," she said. "What did he want?"

"I think he wants to end the strike," I said, and, saying

141

it, realized that it was so. End the strike. On our terms. We'd won. Suddenly, the day seemed short of time. I had to get to Bragg with this. I asked Rose if she'd mind if I took her home early. Of course not, she said, disappointed. I backed out of the parking space and roared the car forward, peeling out like Doug. We'd gone less than a block when Rose remembered she had more shopping to do. I offered to wait, she insisted I shouldn't, and I let her out at the Swedish bakery.

I had never had a faster ride into the city. It was Saturday morning; there was practically no traffic, and no police. Rose must still have been selecting sweet rolls when I drove off the freeway exit near the Trades Union Building.

A big white semitruck and trailer had been pulled into the center of the local's parking lot, and men were standing in line up a flight of metal steps and through a door in the back of the van. SAFETY-SHOE MOBILE, it said in green on the side. Bragg was standing beside the steps when I pulled up next to the van.

"I have to talk to you," I called to him, trying not to seem too excited with all the men watching.

"Just a minute," Bragg said. A shoe clerk had come out of the back door of the van and was standing beside Bragg, crew-cut, wearing a short-sleeved shirt, carrying one of those sliding rulers they measure feet with.

"You said half of them would pay cash," he complained. "So far I haven't seen a nickel."

"Don't worry," Bragg told him. "The union's good for it."

"It better be," the shoeman said distrustfully. "You didn't tell me you were on strike, either."

"That's how we wore out the shoes," Bragg said, walking around my car and opening the door. "Walking picket lines."

The clerk stared at him angrily for a moment, then

142

turned to go back inside his van. I headed the car over toward a far corner of the lot.

"New shoes," said Bragg. "Keep them going for a while. They think it means they're all going back to work."

I stopped at the flat brick wall of the building.

"I just saw George Harris," I said. "I bumped into him completely by accident, coming out of a store over in Madrone. He says he wants to talk. Any time. Any place. No conditions. With Toad or without him."

Bragg closed his eyes.

"I think he means it," I said.

"Thank God," Bragg said softly. "We're flat-on-our-ass broke."

On Monday morning, we filed into a conference room at Foster Wilkins' law offices, Bragg, myself, Lenny Silk, and Leo Silvestri taking chairs below a solid wall of brown lawbooks that looked forever unopened, Wilkins sitting at the center of their side across the gleaming table, Harris and Demetrios taking chairs next to him, and Donovan off to one side, looking at Bragg as though he were a jungle animal.

Wilkins began by standing and carefully reading a prepared statement that seemed pried through his thin lips. His tone was conciliatory, but firm, and as coldly genteel as the bare wooden walls and the even rows of books around him. In the best interests of all parties concerned, and due to growing economic pressures on both sides, the contractors were prepared to open discussion without restrictions as to terms in the hope of reaching the earliest possible settlement.

Before he could even sit down, Bragg was reading his reply, not bothering to stand, as Wilkins had, but instead quoting from a dog-eared three-by-five index card propped on his stomach as he sat in a slouch with the contemptuous air of a motorcycle rider or an attendant in a parking lot where they screech tires and dent fenders a lot. His terms were the same as those he had originally demanded. Across-the-board increases in wages and fringes averaging eighty cents an hour over a three-year period; a jointly controlled pension fund; restrictions on automatic equipment, a permanent grievance committee, a holiday fund. Surrender.

Across the table, there was the awe-struck silence of an audience that has been unexpectedly presented with what it considers obscene. Then Demetrios, who had seemed to be merely an onlooker in the past, preoccupied with his own business and impatient with the tedium of negotiations, turned to Wilkins.

"Come on, let's get it over with," he said gruffly. It was an order. Things were out of the hands of the professionals on their side now; the businessmen were taking over. Forget the principles involved; it was time to pay up.

Wilkins swallowed. When he spoke, his voice was dry, on the verge of cracking. "We feel these terms are acceptable as the basis for a new contract."

By noon, we had worked out a rough draft that was ready for the lawyers, and Harris made a short speech about how he hoped that union-management relations would continue in the amicable manner that had characterized them in the past.

"How soon can I get my men back?" Demetrios interrupted him.

"They have to vote on this," Bragg told him. "Wednesday?"

"Okay," he said. Getting up, he shook Bragg's hand, mine, Silk's, and Silvestri's—unsmiling, businesslike—and left. The door was open behind him, and we were all left looking at each other, uneasy victors facing grudging losers, sharing nothing but the end of boredom and common dealing and perhaps some sense of guilt over what had happened to Toad, no one wanting to say the wrong words, words that could be brooded over afterward like scars, our side resisting the urge to gloat that was swelling in my chest like a bubble.

Bragg gave in first; but then, he was the proudest. Turning to the old man, who hadn't let out a peep all morning, he grinned at him savagely.

"See you in three years," he said.

15

This record, which has been accumulating night by night, I am now keeping by day, even by the hour; for I know now that what is coming to me may come at any time, in any place.

This morning, arriving at the office late, I find Dorothy and Beverlee waiting impatiently in the hallway, coats on, holding brown-bag lunches, purses, and their morning newspapers. We keep a key on the molding beside the doorway so whoever arrives first can unlock the office door. They've tried the key, Dorothy says, and it doesn't seem to fit. I try my key, and it doesn't work, either. The key looks all right, nothing is broken or bent. It matches the key from the molding. Kneeling, I check the lock. A shiny new lock is in its place, with streaks of putty around it, installed overnight. Who would do that, Dorothy says. I tell them both to wait while I go find the janitor. I start walking down the hallway toward his room when Dorothy calls me back. Two men, both short but one stocky as a gorilla, have come down the hallway from the opposite direction, in from the side, and have stopped at our office, where they stand talking with the girls. The big one wears a black-and-white lumber jacket that makes him look like a huge optical illusion, while the little man has glasses, short red hair, and a trim red goatee.

"These are the men who changed the lock," Dorothy says, introducing them with a frown. Both men look at me with eyes like bayonets.

The big one clears his throat. "This local has been placed under National trusteeship, as of last night." His voice is oddly officious, and what he says sounds memorized. "You people can all go home now, and you'll get a letter explaining the details shortly."

I stand gaping at him, trying to pick his face from among the hundreds I've seen at union banquets and conventions. He has a double chin and a polite manner that don't fit his lumber-jack clothes.

"Just a minute," I tell him. "There has to be a list of charges first, and a trial, and a probationary period."

"They been waived," the little one says, and steps forward tauntingly. His short hair, trim beard, and glasses give him the reserved look of a professor, yet he's all swaggering schoolboy belligerence. The two of them seem dressed up, playing parts, phony.

"They can't be," I say back to him. "It's in the constitution."

"That's tough shit," he says.

The big one takes out a key of his own and unlocks the door. "You people run along now," he says. He opens the door and starts into our office as if it's his, switching on the lights, pushing in the catch on the doorknob to lock the door again after him, his indifferent back toward us. Dorothy and Beverlee look at me, expecting me to say something, do something, and I realize that if that office door closes on me now it's closing on me forever, that it's all over, the good and the bad, and inside me some membrane that has been swelling with fear bursts, and I run blindly at his back and jump him from behind. Oom, he goes, and staggers under me into the office, so big I can't knock him down. He shakes himself, bear-strong, trying to throw me off, and I hang on, clawing for a hold at his jowly face; he turns around and turns again, spinning, and I cling to him, my face against the giant checks of his jacket with its tobacco smell. The girls are running down the hallway screaming, lunches and purses and newspapers scattering over the floor. The little guy is trying to grab me from behind and pull me off as I duck and dodge, and we bump into the counter, then carom off the wall on the other side. I try to tear his nose and gouge his eyes, and he falls backward on the floor, half landing on me. I roll out from under him, the little man kicking me twice in the back with sharp shoes, the big one grabbing at me with huge arms, his breath sour in my face. I get up, flushed and panting, and they're panting, too, the little one wheezing slightly. It's the only sound in the room, now smelling of our sweat. Crouching, they both face me, arms loose and dangling, excited and frightened, glaring hate at me between apprehensive looks around. I feel every ounce of extra weight that's on me. The little one stamps a foot toward me, and I swing on him, one solid shot that hits him in the side of the face, sends his glasses flying, and gives him an abrupt, drowsy expression. Then the big one pile-drives into my stomach, knocking the wind out of me with a loud uh, like a huge cough, and I go back against the counter, and the shelf cracks me in the kidneys. Nimble as an ape, he vaults the counter, grabs my arms and pins them behind me, so that I'm bent backward, my head on one side of the counter and my feet on the other. I can't get at him and I can't get loose.

"Okay," he says with a sickening, second-wind calmness to the little guy. "Take him."

148

The little one jams his broken glasses into his coat pocket and comes at me, mean and squinting. He reaches for my face, and I jerk my head back, keeping away; but he's got my necktie. I kick at him and miss, and the other one tightens his hold on my arm so it's like I'm caught in machinery. There's no give to him at all. I try to yell and there's no voice: the little guy is tightening the knot in my necktie, forcing it up against my Adam's apple, cutting words and sound and breath from my throat. I try to turn my neck and, where the tie is, it burns. My heart is pounding. The little guy is staring at my throat, with his red goatee quivering and a vein popping out on his forehead. Tighter. Like a drawstring on a bag. I gasp and get no air, only the taste of blood. I'm strangling. I can feel my eyes bulge. My face is hot. The tie is like wire. I can't swallow. Tighter. I shake my head but he hangs on. My tongue is huge; my head is going to burst. No air. A flash of black. Then voices. Dorothy and Beverlee run in screaming: they're killing him, they're killing him. People are pushing and swearing, knocking into each other. Suddenly I'm flat on the floor on my back, my neck throbbing, feet kicking and running around me. I recognize a man from the local grappling with the big man: it's Clarence Equals, with a big red welt already showing on his forehead. I try to move, but I can barely breathe, so I just lie on the floor, getting stepped on, my head back against the counter.

Get a doctor, the women are shouting, get a doctor. The door slams and there are footsteps, running. They're getting away! Get a doctor, get a doctor!

"Let me through." It's Doctor Loeb, bursting in so authoritatively that people let themselves be shoved back inside. They clear a path; Loeb kneels beside me, looks at my neck, and starts working with the necktie. More people are in the doorway, staring. What happened? Beverlee is crying. The doctor takes medical scissors out of his starched white jacket and cuts the tie. Look at his face, someone says, it's PURPLE. The doctor feels all around my Adam's apple, poking here and there with his finger. He asks can I swallow, and I can, but with the worst sore throat of my life. My stomach feels as though I'm going to vomit, and my throat as if it will never pass. Loeb helps me into a sitting position, takes off my coat, and unbuttons my shirt. My kidneys ache. He leans my head back and examines my neck. OOH, someone says, disgusted. Get back, says Loeb. Give this man some air. Dorothy hands me a glass of water. It feels like ground glass, going down. More people come running from outside. What happened? They tried to kill him. Two men. Got away. "I'm going to call the police," Dorothy says, taking back the glass. I hold her arm.

"Locksmith." My voice is a painful rasp. "Call a locksmith."

"All right, go away," Loeb says irritably, waving everybody out. "He's all right. Go away now, PLEASE." He gets most of them out and closes the door. I get up on rubber legs and sit in one of the waiting chairs across from the counter. Loeb sits down next to me and looks at the neck again. "That's a bad burn. You're going to have some beautiful bruises."

"Locksmith."

"All right, all right. Take it easy."

I begin to shake all over, cold to death. Loeb is staring at me, his hands in his lap. "You're in shock. I'm going to give you a sedative and have someone drive you home."

I shake my head, chafing my neck so my eyes water, and get up, swaying. Sit down, Loeb orders. Do as I say. I stagger away from him, around the counter, through the door, into my office, around my desk, and sink so heavily in the swivel chair that it almost catapults me backward. Loeb charges inside after me, and I grab the arms of the chair and glare at him.

"All right," he says, pointing a finger, "you sit there—just sit."

Equals bursts in, breathing hard; with him is Mike Sullivan, a thick-featured hod carrier with blood trickling from his fat lower lip.

"Them fuckers had a Jimmy pickup right out front, big as you please. Got clean away." Equals lets out a long, low whistle. "Boy, you ought to see your neck!"

Dorothy brings in another glass of water. I take a drink from the glass, and it's a little easier to swallow than the first. Loeb watches me swallow, then feels around my Adam's apple again, and looks into my mouth. "I don't think there's any damage to the trachea or larynx, don't think you need X rays. You're going to be hoarse for a couple of days, though, and you'll have trouble swallowing." He's still angry at the interruption, the confusion, my disobedience. "Were they friends of yours?" he asks sarcastically.

I don't even try to shake my head this time, just close my eyes.

"I'll go get some salve to put on it," he says, standing. "I'm not bandaging the neck, because I want the air to get at it. If it gets any worse, you let me know, and I'll look at it again tomorrow." He stares at me with disapproval. "If I haven't moved out of here by then." He sweeps out. Through the doorway, I can see Beverlee bending over, gathering up the papers scattered on the floor. A chair has been knocked over and a coat rack is stabbed into one of the pictures on the wall.

I look down and find it isn't so painful to move in that direction; the neck only chafes when I move it from side to side. I notice I'm still holding the tie, all black and thin and twisted, the knot a hard, wrinkled nut of hate, and I throw it into the wastebasket, where it lies like a dead snake.

"Your shirt's torn," says Dorothy. And sure enough,

151

there are buttons missing and blood on the shirt front, and suddenly I can feel the goons' hands all over it, so I start to take it off.

"Do you have another shirt?" says Dorothy. I'm already pulling my arms out of the sleeves. With the shirt off, I can touch my neck all over, and it feels ballooned up and warm and throbbing with soreness. "Bev!" Dorothy yells. "Find a shirt!" And she takes away the old one. It's coming back to her. Dorothy is a campus activist from Berkeley, 1948 vintage, a precinct worker for Henry Wallace who gave up when Wallace did, married a man from Boalt Hall who became a lawyer, moved to Madrone, had two kids, who kept her busy until both had entered school, and suddenly felt cut off; so she'd come looking for a job, nothing routine, something committed, progressive, engaged: labor. I had interviewed her. A big-boned placidly determined woman who chain-smokes, feels intellectually superior to secretarial work, and does it fast, uncomplainingly, and in huge quantities to prove it. A bargain. I have come to depend on her, so that in fact the union now needs her more than she needs the job, which as far as Dorothy is concerned was the case all along. And now, involvement. She has been whisked back twenty years and is once again defending her card table full of leaflets at Sather Gate against bullying red-baiters or dumb jocks.

She comes back in carrying my shirt, soaked with water and rolled into a ball, wraps it cool and soothing around my neck, and, for the first time, the throbbing stops.

"The locksmith's on his way," she says, the unruffled campus-trained professional. "And the police. One of the tenants called them." The last she adds with disapproval.

Equals, seeing that he's in the way now, says that he and Sullivan are leaving, but that they'll wait outside in case they're needed. They leave and Dorothy closes my office door.

Holding the wet shirt around my neck with one hand, I lean forward in the chair and close my eyes. I can see both men, feel the big one holding me while the little one works at my throat with his horrible detachment. What if I had been alone? I begin to realize how close we have come, at the very least, to being taken over. Once inside, they could have done anything they liked with the personnel files, the correspondence, the books, the local funds.

"Dorothy," I croak, measuring the effort against the raw feeling it makes in my throat. "Call the bank. Don't let anyone close our account."

She runs out heavily, passing Beverlee, coming in. Beverlee hasn't been able to find a shirt, so she's borrowed an old blue denim work shirt from the janitor. It's more of a rag than anything, faded and stained with paint, but I put it on and button it up, and the collar feels limp and soft around my neck.

Through the window I see Equals and Sullivan telling three other men outside what has happened, Equals grabbing where Sullivan's tie would be if he wore one and pantomiming what happened to me, pointing inside the building, at himself, to where the truck had been, the men shaking their heads angrily in response. We're rebels now. They tried to take over and we shut them out.

The locksmith arrives, a confused-looking man in blue overalls and a dark-blue coat-sweater, carrying a green metal toolbox, his hair sticking up as if he had just got out of bed.

"Change the lock. On the front door," I tell him feebly. He goes away and comes right back and says there's a lock on there already, a brand-new one, perfectly good.

"Change it!" I yell, tasting blood, and he heads back out to go to work. The doctor returns with a small, flat jar of ointment, takes a look at the wet shirt, leaves the ointment on my desk, and goes away without a word, as though tell-

153

ing me that if I want to cure myself, I can go ahead, for all he cares, but that he won't help me next time. And I began to wonder if they'll be back. Perhaps with a court order. Maybe it's me who's broken the law. The National always seems to have it on their side; they have their hands on every string and every lever. But we're here. We hold the office and control the men, and if control is what they want, they'll have to come and take it.

Potter comes running in, late for work, looking flustered and guilty over what he's missed, saying he should have been here, apparently expecting me to chew him out. Instead, I ask him to go out in the field for me, and I begin writing out a list of calls for him to make. He's relieved, surprised, and then delighted, squirming with eagerness, yet trying to keep himself from lighting up as he watches me write down the jobs, forcing himself to be serious in a serious situation that has turned into an opportunity for him. He's acting business agent. He studies the list eagerly, slips it into his coat pocket along with the keys to my car, and walks out, thanking me, inadvertently rubbing his hands together.

The locksmith brings in two new yellow keys and lays them on my desk. The lock is installed; the previous change, he says, had been a sloppy job, done by amateurs. I tell him we want to install a bolt and chain, a strong one, figuring that if they come again and one of us is here, that may be enough to keep them out, and he rummages through his toolbox until he comes up with something the dull color of fake wrought iron, and I nod approval.

My throat is feeling no worse than an ordinary sore throat now, and I put the wet shirt on my window sill to dry. Taking the ointment, I get up and walk down the hall past people on union business staring at me curiously, and faces looking guardedly from open office doors, and go into the men's room, where I examine my neck in the

154

mirror. There's a red, raw band nearly all the way around it, like a rope burn, with black and purple marks the size of finger tips on either side. I rub the ointment on gently until my whole neck is glistening with it. Turning, I lift my shirt and look at my back, but there are no marks. I let the shirt fall and stare at myself wearing it, faded-blue denim, like I wore every day for years, installing switches and light fixtures and doorbells, air conditioning and heating, repetitive work that seemed to lead nowhere, with no women around and lunch just something in waxed paper, yet, in all, more satisfying than anything I've done since because of the simple, lost pleasure of being able to look at a physical object and know I made it work.

Feeling uneasy with myself, I rinse my face with cold water, comb my hair, and go back into my office. The Madrone police have arrived, and Hoxie is one of them, coolly businesslike in deference to his sergeant, a fat-faced man with black, slicked-back hair and little pig's eyes. Dorothy is proudly recounting what has happened while they listen, frowning and nodding with concern.

"You recognize either of these men?" the sergeant asks me. I shake my head.

"How about their car?" says Hoxie, hopefully.

"A truck," I say, and they look surprised at the gravelly sound of my voice. "They had a pickup truck. And no hats," I add, anticipating his next question.

"Did they show you any authority?" the sergeant asks. "Court order or a telegram?"

"They just tried to take over," Dorothy answers for me. "And when Mister Burke objected, the little one told him tough shit."

Both cops look down, embarrassed. The sergeant hitches his belt down comfortably under his stomach and says that he thinks he better report this to San Francisco Homicide. He'd like to leave Hoxie with me right now, he says, but he can't spare him. I tell him sure, I understand, and Hoxie looks relieved. The sergeant promises to have a prowl car drive by every hour to keep a check on things, and I tell him that sounds fine. Hoxie promises he'll be over early tonight. What did the man do with his evenings before he met me?

With a parting warning about calling more promptly when we need help, the police leave to go question some of the other people in the building. We spend the next hour or so settling the remaining confusion in the office; I go through the morning mail, and have Dorothy make some phone calls that I should have made earlier. Beverlee brings in my lunch, a cardboard cup of fruit drink as thick as a milk shake from a health-food store. I've taken just one sip, cleaning the last bloody taste from my mouth, when the phone rings.

"Well, what did I tell you?"

It's Eisan, sounding pleased and justified by what has happened, and his pleasure quickly turns to enthusiasm.

"Listen, you haven't got a thing to worry about. We're with you. If they want to play rough, we can play rougher."

My heart sinks. "Thanks," I say, touching my neck.

"What's the matter with your voice?"

"They almost strangled me," I say, fishing a little for sympathy.

"Jesus, that's too bad. It'd be good if you could make a speech right now."

At first I think he's kidding, but there isn't any laughter.

"I'll tell you what," he says, after thinking a bit. "You write an open letter to the rank and file, and we'll put the whole story in the *Free Press* and print your letter in the middle of the front page. This is too good a chance to miss."

I sit thinking how an appetite for power lets people feed

on anything, flesh, blood, misery, excrement, and I realize that it doesn't matter now, that it has been my mistake to consider myself outside a tragedy that I have been caught up in all along.

"All right. What do you want me to say?"

"That the struggle for honest, aggressive, democratic trade-unionism goes on. That we won't give up, because they can't make us quit. That what Bragg started can't be stopped. Look, you want me to have somebody write it out for you?"

"Yes. Go ahead. Write anything you like."

I hang up feeling dazed yet cleansed, having somehow relieved myself of terror and anguish simply by making a judgment and speaking a sentence, and wash down the thought with the last of my fruit-drink lunch.

For most of the morning several men have been sitting in the outer office, leaning forward expectantly or standing each time I have come out, waiting quietly to see me on union business, while, absorbed in my own problems, I have completely neglected theirs. Feeling irrationally angry at them for having this advantage over me, I ask Dorothy to start sending them in.

The first man, a bald-headed electrician with fingernail scratches on his pate, has had a row with his wife, is leaving town, and wants a transfer card to a construction local in another city. I sign a card for him and hand it to him with the remainder blank, so he can write in his own name and any city or date he chooses. His resentment at being given such brief treatment after so long a wait is lost in the satisfaction of getting an open job ticket, good anywhere.

I have worse luck with the next man, a crooked-faced roofer who talks out of the side of his mouth. He wants a job for his cousin. I tell him we aren't admitting any new members right now, and he flares up and demands to know why the hell somebody didn't tell him that two hours ago. I start to explain but he won't accept it, complaining about the dues he's paid over the years and the little he's asked in return, until I despair of it, give in, ask his cousin's name, and promise him I'll see what I can do. Hating myself, I warn him not to tell anybody about this, and he accepts the compromise with a glower. He swaggers out, passing Dorothy as she stands in the doorway. The men from Bragg's local are here, she says. I look at her, but she doesn't seem puzzled or alarmed. I get up, feeling a panic I'm ashamed to acknowledge, and walk stiffly into the outer office. Grimes and Buxton are standing together at the gate in the counter, grim and stiff with purpose.

Grimes stares at my blue denim work shirt and nods faintly, while Buxton, his sunglasses off, searches my eyes with his.

"We work for you now, right?" he says softly.

Drained of innocence, I nod. Buxton turns, drags a chair over beside the counter gate, and sits, his long legs extended, a finger thoughtfully stroking his goatee. Grimes walks over to the office door, lifts a foot up behind him and leans on it against the wall beside the door, and folds his arms. The rest of us exchange brief looks and return to work.

16

The conclusion of the strike meant the resumption of work, not only for the rank and file of our local, but for local management as well. Once again we were in the business of matching men and jobs, but on a larger and busier scale than ever before. In addition to existing crews that had to be returned to interrupted work, those projects whose start had been delayed by the strike were now rushed ahead. On top of this, the contractors, as though frantic at the prospect of rising labor costs, were filing contracts for new jobs almost daily, without regard for our ability to absorb their requests. Our office became a beehive, with men lining up at the dispatch window at seven o'clock each morning so Potter and I could interview them, taking turns collecting their union books, asking each man about his job category and qualifications, then making an assignment which, as often as not, the man would question, hoping to find something better until he was convinced that, by comparison, he was better off with either one job or the other, and agree to report for work. While we were assigning the men, Dorothy, Beverlee, and Ruth, a new girl Dorothy had hired temporarily from a secretarial service, would type away furiously, preparing the necessary papers from the information in the men's books, tearing the forms from the typewriter as they were completed, stuffing the finished forms, every one a different size and color, into each man's book, until the man's status, medical coverage, life insurance, and pension and welfare plan were completely documented, the girl shouting the number of the book until the man claimed it, jamming book and forms into his hand while rattling off hurried instructions on how he should get to his new job, then rushing away from one dazed man to process the next.

It was hectic, aggravating work, it lasted a full three hours every morning, and we never did grow accustomed to it. By ten o'clock, the office was invariably littered with paper and empty of workmen except for a bewildered or dissatisfied straggler or two, the rest of us standing around feeling foolish and grumbling about having to run around the way we did. Everything would stop for a few minutes then, while the tempo of the office changed and we poured ourselves coffee from a percolator kept on an electric hot plate in the outer office and waited for our nerves to calm.

After coffee I'd turn the dispatch window back over to Potter, go into my office, and start calling out to the jobs, checking to see if the referrals we'd sent out had arrived. There were frequent mix-ups; men reported to the wrong job, or didn't show up at all, preferring to wait until the afternoon or the following day before starting work, and I'd try to track them down by telling one of the girls to call the men at home. Occasionally a man we'd sent out would run into a foreman or a contractor he didn't like and walk off the job rather than take it; or, just about as often, one of our men would be considered unsuitable, and the employer would call back, refusing to hire him. Since there were plenty of openings, I didn't argue much with the men or the contractors about these situations; it was such a simple matter to arrange something else.

Promptly at noon, I'd leave to go out in the field, picking up a delicatessen sandwich and eating as I drove, feeling relief at being alone and beyond reach of the telephone and outside the suffocating routine of office work. Yet I was every bit as busy. The accelerated work schedule had created not only new jobs but also new stewards and new foremen, which meant increased confusion about who should be doing what and how men ought to be paid for different tasks, and a corresponding increase in grievances. In addition to this, everybody on the employers' side seemed to be pressing me to go out and recruit new men. At almost every stop I would be asked, can't you send us more men, can't you send us better men, can't you send us a specialist? I opposed throwing open the local to a large number of new men, knowing full employment was too good a situation to last; but I did try to meet the demand for specialists like tile-setters and sheet-metal workers by having them work half a day on one job and half a day on another, a move which, though it satisfied no one, seemed to pacify nearly everybody. The stewards I urged to try to work out grievances before bringing them to me, stressing the importance of keeping the enforcement of the new contract terms consistent. But the beefs kept coming, and almost every working day at quitting time I would be still out making a call, lingering on some job while the construction men, the steward, and finally even the foreman went home, leaving me to drive back to the empty office, contemplating the fact that while the men were now making more money than they ever had before and had a contract guaranteeing regular wage increases for the next three years—a contract the employers were using as an excuse to raise the amount of their estimates —the union officials who had negotiated that contract were now working longer hours than ever for salaries that hadn't gone up a cent.

One evening I returned to the darkened office, my list of unfinished calls in my hand, and found an airmail special-delivery letter on my desk with the National Brotherhood's Washington headquarters printed on it as the return address. I turned on my desk lamp and opened the envelope; inside was another envelope, on stationery like the first, addressed to me with PERSONAL AND CONFIDENTIAL rubber-stamped on it thick and black. Inside the envelope was a formal letter ordering me to appear in two days at a hearing held by the National at the Golden Hills Motor Hotel, "investigating certain charges brought against Brother Baxter Bragg concerning violations of the Brotherhood Constitution, Articles XVII and XXII." The letter was signed by Martin Morrison, General Counsel for the Brotherhood, and it was postmarked just the day before it arrived.

I turned on the lights in the outer office so I could look at the copy of the constitution framed on the wall. Article XXII concerns the right of members of one local to visit another local, and must apply to Bragg's bus trips to locals like ours. Article XVII refers to "conduct unbecoming a union officer," and could apply to almost anything. I read the letter over several times, and each time it disturbed me. From attempting to ignore Bragg, the National had swung all the way over to confronting him face to face, a situation that I was sure he welcomed. But it had been done with an abruptness that could only be deliberate. They wanted to take him by surprise, and they wanted it to be done in secret. I sat in my office a long time, thinking about it, before I turned out the lights and went home.

● ● ●

On the morning I was scheduled to appear, the first thing I noticed when I got to the Golden Hills was a crowd of people, scores of them, lined up outside for half a block in both directions, men and even a few women and children, shuffling past each other in two long columns, carrying placards. I parked my car in a side alley and got out, carrying a green binder with some meeting minutes and union correspondence that I thought I should bring along, and headed toward the hotel's front entrance. The building was completely surrounded by pickets, and their placards all had angry, hand-lettered messages: DOWN WITH UNION-BUSTING! WE DEMAND OPEN HEARING! THIS TRIAL IS RIGGED! It was Bragg's rank and file, this time looking as though they were on an outing, skylarking, laughing and talking, and wagging their signs around, some bringing part of the family along for the fun, while cars slowed on the street and pedestrians stopped on the sidewalk to stare in astonishment at what must have been three hundred people noisily picketing a meeting of their own union.

I put my head down and had started to cross the picket line in front of the main entrance when a woman yelled my name.

"Joe Burke! Don't go in there!"

I stopped, and so did several of the pickets immediately around me. Sally Bragg was charging toward me, carrying a picket sign which said, in red, GET YOUR HANDS OFF OUR THROAT!

"Joe," she said in a scolding tone, "you can't go in there. We're boycotting them."

"Is he in there?" I asked her.

"You're darn right he is."

"Then I'm going in, too," I said. But I could see by the faces around me that to try to bull in anyway would only create a hassle.

Sally walked up to me, determined and exhilarated, looking like a song girl at a college football game with her short dress and pretty legs. "This whole thing is a farce," she said, holding her sign with one hand while she held her hair in place with the other. "They've got no right to try him, and even if they did they can't do it in secret."

I told her that, on the contrary, they could try him for just about anything they pleased under the heading of unbecoming conduct, and that if they were doing it in secret he needed every friend he could get in there.

While we were talking, Eisan and another ghoul from the Safety Committee walked over from elsewhere on the line and stood listening.

"I've been ordered to appear at this hearing," I said to her, but loud enough for the others. "And if I don't, I've disobeyed an order and that means they can try me, too."

The two men looked at me sullenly.

"If these charges are going to be beaten, or dismissed, it's got to be done in there," I said. Then I started bluffing. "I've got some evidence that's going to be useful to him, if I can just get inside with it."

They could have offered to take the binder inside for me, but none of them seemed to think of that. Sally looked convinced, and after huddling briefly with Eisan and the other man she told the pickets to let me through.

"He's with us," she called cheerfully as I slunk, to scattered applause, into the hotel lobby. Inside, Bragg's people were everywhere, hanging around the news counter and the desk, drinking Cokes in the soda fountain, lining the corridor where the meeting rooms were, talking, smoking, leaning on their signs, listening to transistor radios. About two-thirds of the way down the first-floor corridor, a red plush rope was stretched between two brass stands, cutting off the remainder of the rooms. Bragg's people were clustered on one side of the rope, and on the other side

164

was an out-and-out torpedo, a swarthy block of a man about medium height with a fixed sneer for an expression and terrible, placid eyes in which any human, flickering flame had been doused for good. He made Grimes and Buxton, standing at the front of Bragg's group, look harmless, like boys. Behind him was a row of four chairs, and Leo Silvestri sat in one of them with his hands folded.

"I'm supposed to be in there," I said to the torpedo, nodding at the room number on the door behind him as I handed him the letter. He took the letter in his huge broken-knuckled hands, glanced at it, then opened the door just a little and spoke to somebody inside as bits of smoke drifted out and someone in the hearing said, in an angry voice, "If you don't like the way the union's being run, why don't you go somewhere else?" The torpedo shut the door, walked over, opened the rope, and handed me my letter. In a frighteningly mild voice, he told me to sit down.

Silvestri tried to look ingratiating. "How did you get through the picket line?" he said. I told him. He admitted he'd let himself be turned away, and then had sneaked in a service entrance. That was at nine o'clock. It was now almost ten-thirty.

"Bragg's been making a statement for over an hour," Silvestri said. I stretched out my legs and started leafing through my binder. I couldn't afford to lose a morning, and here I was, waiting.

Down at the other end of the corridor, somebody started singing, and the song moved toward us in a chorus, "We shall overcome," as others picked it up, locking their arms and swaying back and forth against the wall. The torpedo endured it for several moments, then, in a flash of rage, he singled out a woman in the crowd and pointed at her.

"You!" he said savagely. "Cut it out! Stop singing!"

The song died in her throat and gradually faded away

down the corridor until we were all in an exaggerated stillness which allowed some of the voices to carry from inside the room.

"We tried it your way," I could hear Bragg's raw voice crying, "we tried being patient, and it didn't get anything done. So now we're trying our own way."

Like the song, his voice faded. But then it came back.

"I'm ugly to you," Bragg was saying, "because I remind you of every compromise you've made and every promise you've failed to keep. You talk about things changing. I change them. And I'll do whatever I have to, to do it."

His voice faded again, until after a few minutes the room sounded as quiet as the corridor. Then the door opened wide, letting out a rush of smoke and conversation, and a bald-headed man with a sharp nose ducked just that much of himself outside. Behind him, people were standing in the room, taking a break.

"Leo Silvestri?" he said politely, and Leo stood in reply.

"Come in," he said with a wave, his politeness turning quickly to impatience. Silvestri looked at me with raised eyebrows, walked inside, and the door was closed after him.

Alone now, I started reading the material in the binder, since I couldn't hear a word from inside. I had brought along the minutes of our first strike meeting, and as I studied the flat condensation of what had occurred, the details of that evening came back to me: Bragg's men pouring out of the bus, our men meeting them in the parking lot, the small groups listening in the twilight, and the strange herd urge that they all had seemed to feel.

Suddenly another noise came toward me down the corridor, this time an angry sound of boos and shouts and people calling names: "Fink!" "Scab!" They picked up their signs and waved them. Between the lines of people on each side of the hallway, Toad was walking with his

166

head down, a uniformed hotel security guard on each side. Toad's face was grim, but not angry; he appeared to accept the abuse he was receiving now as his personal cross. The torpedo let Toad through the rope, the security cops remaining on the other side, and he sat down next to me as the noise in the hallway faded once again. I felt uncomfortable about sitting there with him, and guilty for feeling that way. I didn't know what to say to him. The shouting had brought back everything that had happened at Bragg's local, and I knew how sensitive Toad was to what people thought about him.

"How've you been?" he attempted.

"Busy," I said, closing my binder and sitting with it in my lap. "We always seem to end up at the same hotel," I said.

"What?" said Toad.

"We always . . ." I began again; but then the door opened and Silvestri came out, looking defeated. When he saw Toad, the last bit of hope went out of his face.

"Max Volt?" the bald-headed man said, looking at Toad and me. "Is Max Volt here?" There was no answer. Apparently Max hadn't made it past the pickets. "Joe Burke?" he asked. I got up, and my stomach turned over as I walked inside.

The room was shallow, but wide; it overlooked the swimming pool, so that the glare from outside came bursting through the undraped picture window and made everybody between it and me a shadow. A row of shadows was sitting on one side of a shadow table. Two other shadows sat apart from them at the table's end, and I recognized one of them, in profile, as Bragg.

"Just take this chair," a calm voice said to me from the center of the table. "We'll be talking to you in a minute."

I groped until I found the chair, sat down, and tried to

167

make out the faces across the table. The man who had just spoken to me was sitting low in his chair. He had a wide face and wore glasses, and he was conferring with the bald man who had called me into the room, who was now standing, bending over beside the first man's chair. Sitting next to him on one side was a man in a short-sleeved shirt, with crew-cut hair, chewing a cigar. And on the other side, a man wearing a suit and vest, who had a pear-shaped face with full cheeks and pouting lips that gave him a bored, petulant look. It was a look I recognized because I felt it every day from our office wall: Tom Cannon. He said nothing, but stared at me, drumming his fingers on the table.

The room was quiet, but it was the moody quiet of an interrupted family quarrel. The bald man sat down next to Cannon and half turned in his chair to face me at an angle. He told me to raise my right hand and repeat an oath after him, which I did.

"You're Joseph Burke, President of Local Two Fifty-two, Madrone County," he read, in an accusing tone.

"President and Business Agent," I said, feeling an urge to correct him.

"You were also a member of the strike committee for the Bay Area Construction Workers?"

"Yes, I was."

"And on the night of April twenty-second did you attend a strike meeting at the San Francisco Trades Union Building?"

"Yes."

"Tell us briefly what took place at this meeting."

I tried to summarize what had happened that night, how the hall had been crowded with men whose feelings were running high over the strike, who had come to decide whether we should give up or continue, and that Bragg had made a speech and the men had got all excited.

168

As I talked, I couldn't notice anyone reacting to what I said; there was only a sniffle now and then and the whispery sound of papers being shuffled. It was like speaking into a closet, and my voice became flat, a monotone.

"In this speech," the bald-headed man interrupted, "did Mister Bragg not call a brother officer of this union certain derogatory names, such as 'scab' and 'sellout artist'?" He spoke the words with unfamiliarity and distaste.

"I believe he said something to that effect, but he didn't mention anybody in particular."

"He didn't mention anybody in particular, but he MEANT somebody in particular, didn't he?"

"I don't know," I said. "How can I answer that?"

"Did he not say—" he paused, picked up a paper, and began reading—"that 'there are those among us on our own union payroll who want to sell us down the river'?"

"Something like that."

"Something like that. Very well. You're a union officer, on the union payroll. Did he mean you?"

"No, I don't think so."

"How about—" he paused to read again—"Leo Silvestri. Did he mean him?"

"No."

"Max Volt? Leonard Silk?"

"No."

"Toad Fuller," he said, not asking.

I felt myself cough nervously. "Yes, he may have meant Toad Fuller."

"All right," he said, now pleased. His voice sounded younger than he looked. "Now after Mister Bragg had made these insulting and derogatory remarks about Mister Fuller, what happened?"

"There was some yelling, and then Toad made a speech."

"Mister Fuller made a speech. And what did he say?"

169

"He wanted us to accept the contractors' offer and go back to work."

"Did he call anybody any names?"

"No, he didn't."

"Did he finish his speech or was he interrupted?"

"He was interrupted."

"By whom?"

"By everybody. They were all yelling at him. They wanted to throw him out."

"They were aroused at him?"

"Yes."

"By what Mister Bragg had called him in his speech?"

"Yes, that. And also by the fact that he was telling them to give up the strike."

He paused, leaning his elbow on the table and turning slowly through his papers.

"Mister Fuller was, in fact, thrown out then, wasn't he?"

"Yes."

"By a gang of men, some of whom are probably part of the crowd around the building now."

"Objection!" the man at the end of the table with Bragg bawled. "You are dealing with a generalized area outside the known periphery of fact. We have no way of determining which individuals are folded into the multitude outside and which are not. The public confrontation of which this is a continuing manifestation is the result of an existing conflict, complicated by game-playing."

Before a board representing a union management which did its best to keep a single black hand from touching a pick or shovel, Bragg had chosen, as his counsel, a black lawyer with an insulting flowery manner. It must have been infuriating to the men across the table, and it was obviously bothering the speaker for their side, the bald-headed young man, who I had decided must be an assistant to the General Counsel.

170

"All right," the young man said irritably, returning to me. "Tell us, what was your reaction to seeing a union officer thrown out of a meeting, you being a union officer yourself?"

"I was surprised," I said, "and I guess I was frightened."

"You were frightened and surprised. And what was Brother Bragg's reaction?"

"He just sat there."

"He didn't try to stop it?"

"No."

"He didn't call the union sergeant at arms or the meeting monitors to restore order?"

"They were the ones who were throwing Toad out," I said.

Bragg laughed softly at the end of the table, and the bald-headed man watched me for a moment before he resumed.

"Tell me, do you think Brother Bragg was surprised by all this, too? Or do you suppose that maybe he engineered it all deliberately so he could have Brother Fuller thrown out?"

"Objection!" cried Bragg's lawyer. "You are asking for a conceptual overview into which no specifics are inset."

"Just answer the first part," the man with the calm voice at the center of the table intervened.

"Do you think that Bragg was surprised?" the young one repeated.

"Yes, I do," I said.

A silence fell, in which I could feel myself being studied by the men across the table. The young man got up and came over to the center of the table and conferred with the General Counsel again, speaking behind his hand. The General Counsel took off his glasses, cleaned them with a handkerchief, and put them back on, looking at me while he listened to the young man. Cannon stared, drumming his fingers. From outside, the sound of individual voices

171

leaked into the room. "What's going on now?" "Nothing." "Just the guy from Madrone." And across the table, faces looking.

The young man returned to his chair, opened a folder, and looked through it briefly.

"Going back to an earlier date now, on the night your local voted to join the strike. Is it true that a gang of Bragg's men showed up at that meeting?"

"Yes."

"Had you invited them to come?"

"No."

"Did they come in cars?"

"No, they were in a bus."

"So a busload of men from another union local pulled up outside your office. Did they have guns with them? Or knives?"

"Not to my knowledge."

"And what was your reaction to this invasion?"

"I knew it was a custom in some Bay Area union locals that a delegation might go from one local to another to lobby for a position, but I'd never seen it done before."

"You didn't feel that the men in your local were being intimidated by this 'delegation' of men?" The way he asked the question convicted me of stupidity.

"No. There were maybe fifty of them, and over two hundred of us. Nobody was threatening anybody. We all just stood around and talked and asked questions. They wanted to talk about the strike and so did we, that was all. I don't think anybody did anything he didn't want to."

The General Counsel scratched his chin. "When you took your strike vote," he said in his calm voice, "was it a secret ballot or a show of hands?"

"A show of hands," I said, opening the binder. "I have the minutes of the meeting here, if you'd like to see them." I started to slide the binder across the table, but Cannon stood up and with an angry sweep of his fat hand knocked it onto the floor.

"What kind of union officer are you, anyway?" he yelled at me with whiplash contempt. "Can't you control your own men?" His cheeks red and shaking, he pointed a finger at Bragg. "You let him run your local for you! You ought to be ashamed of yourself!"

My stomach turned over again. My face was burning. What the hell did he know about my local? In a year, all we ever got from him were bills for assessments and a lousy Christmas card. He'd even cost us half a day of my time to bring me here. I felt angry but not humiliated, and, in a strange way, reassured; with that sweep of his hand, Cannon had also swept away the legal puppet show of the hearing, and we were down to the ugly reality of a vicious man fighting tooth and claw for what he was convinced was his. I wasn't picking the binder up, and the other men across the table looked embarrassed. I leaned over toward him and spoke in a voice almost as loud as he had.

"The day my men don't like the way I'm running things, I'll turn my job over to somebody else."

Eyes narrowed, jowls working, his mouth a pout, he sat down, looking at me, knowing that what I'd said about my job he couldn't say about his.

"Wuh-wuh-what if *I* don't like the way you're running things?" he said, stammering in his rage.

Suddenly, he *was* a child, Old Tom Cannon's son with a vest and manicured nails, spoiled, shouting, and scared. And I felt contemptuous of him.

"I work for them," I said. "They elected me. Not you. And not him."

He stared at me, breathing hard. I was certain he was going to fire me in a tongue-tied, stammering fit. And I didn't care. It wasn't worth it. Let him try to find someone else who could deal with the men and the contractors and put up with his abuse on top of it. But he turned to his General Counsel and took it out on him, speaking out of the side of his mouth, the way you'd talk to a delivery boy.

"Who else is out there?"

"Fuller," said the Counsel, his voice no longer calm, but anxious.

"Send him in. And ma-make sure this one keeps his nose clean."

He didn't say it to me directly, so I didn't have to reply. But as I picked up the binder, I gave him a slow look I knew he'd remember, so he'd know I hadn't cringed. Then I got up and walked to the door, brushing by Toad, white-faced, walking in.

In the corridor, they all looked to see who was coming: Buxton and Grimes, the torpedo, the lines of people leaning out from the walls. I walked through them with my head down, sure that Cannon's voice had carried through the wall.

"Who is it? Bragg?" a voice down at the other end asked.

"No, it's just the Madrone guy," somebody answered.

"What's his name?"

"Burke."

"Hey, Burke!" A kid with a lot of hair, like Bragg, grabbed my sleeve. "How'd you make out?"

"All right," I said, my stomach churning. And shook loose.

When I reached the lobby, I hesitated. Sally would be waiting outside, wanting to know what was going on, and I couldn't simply brush by her as I had the others. Instead, I slunk into a small dark bar behind a partition of tinted glass in a corner of the lobby, and ordered a Bromo-Seltzer from a pudgy, rancorous bartender.

"I wish they'd arrest those creeps," he said, nodding toward the crowd outside, "and put me in with 'em." He handed me my drink and displayed a soft, white fist.

I sat on a bar stool, listening, watching the people in the lobby through the glass.

"Just give me some tomatoes," the bartender pleaded, "so I can let 'em have it."

Directly across from the barroom doorway, two teenage girls were standing, waiting, both wearing miniskirts, one taking quick little puffs from a cigarette, the other shifting back and forth, leaning on one leg, then the other. Through the blind of the glass, I watched them, fascinated. They stood on tiptoe and looked down the hall. The girl with the cigarette put it out and lit another. The other girl fussed with her hair and straightened her dress. They didn't talk to each other, and their eyes had a glazed, faraway look, both girls apparently in a trance of profound sexual excitement. While I was watching them, there was a shout, and everybody stepped forward, away from the walls, looking down toward the end of the hall. The girls started jumping up and down, clapping their hands and screaming in anticipation, so that even the people shouting around them turned and looked. The crowd gathered in closer, everybody pressed against each other, the shouts and screams growing louder. Then Bragg came, bobbing along slowly because of all the people, grinning and waving in his nervous, jerky fashion; with him was his lawyer, with both arms raised in a victory sign. "It's over! The hearing's recessed!" he kept repeating dazedly, still not fully believing it himself. "It's all over!"

On either side of him, Grimes and Buxton worked with the crowd, trying to force them back; but the people reached over them to yell at Bragg, talk to him, pound his back, his shoulders, his arms, the two girls each with an arm out, trying to touch him, their eyes wide and their

175

mouths open. Suddenly the smaller of the two burst under Buxton's guard, threw her arms around Bragg, and kissed his hairy face, hanging on to him so hard that her feet were off the ground, while Bragg stopped in unresisting surprise, his arms outstretched. The girl let go, playfully tousled Bragg's hair, and scampered back into the crowd before anyone could touch her. Bragg stood blinking as the men around him ordered everybody back accusingly, then guided him quickly out of the lobby, the crowd closing in after them and ebbing away through the main entrance, dragging all manner of noise with it, leaving a sediment of paper cups and newspapers and cigarette butts on the wall-to-wall carpet.

Still watching where the girls had been, I drank the rest of my Bromo-Seltzer, while the bartender stood staring.

"Be some panties rinsed out tonight," he said in an oily, suggestive voice that made me marvel at his powers of observation.

I was still looking into the lobby when the others came bustling down the corridor, the hearing officers, the torpedo, and Toad, all in a bunch around Tom Cannon, walking fast and not talking to each other, carrying coats and hats and briefcases. I saw Toad and would have called to him, but something in Cannon's face stopped me. The boredom and petulance had all flown out of it, replaced now by a glare so fierce in its driven intensity, so awesome in its hunger, that I pulled my head back instinctively in the already-dark bar, so embarrassed was I at the thought of being seen seeing it, a face that gave him away like the stammer at the height of his rage, a face at odds with itself, pampered and deprived, caring and pretending not to care, weak and forceful, because it made a statement even as it tried not to.

He is loved, it said, and I am not.

17

The first few days, I couldn't drag a razor over the skin of my neck, so I didn't bother to shave at all; after that, I began to trim the hair a little until now it's fairly even, reddish-brown with streaks of gray. It's strange the way people respond to it. They notice, but they don't say anything; and nobody laughs, which was the reaction I had always expected if I ever tried to grow a beard.

This morning, as I walk up to the doorway of the office, I nearly collided with Glenn Small, a huge bulldozer operator, coming out. Glenn and I have known each other since I was an apprentice, and as I put my hands on his chest to keep him from walking on over me, I smile at him as if to say hello. And draw a blank. He looks at me, excuses himself, and, ducking away, starts down the hallway until I call his name and he stops.

"Joe?" he says, frowning. And when I nod, slaps the side of his head with his hand, offering me the other hand to shake.

Inside, Dorothy and Beverlee and Potter all give me the same quick stare at first, checking to see if it's still there;

once they know it is, they act as if it isn't. The morning is cloudy, so the lights are on, and as I walk into my office I meet my reflection in the window and it stops me as if it's someone else and me at the same time. There's a strangeness to it, a sense of having the drop on people that makes me feel . . . strong.

For a long time I sit staring at the office walls and furniture as though everything is new and I'm new in it. Then I pick up the phone and start calling out to the jobs.

It's quieter around the office now. There's less chatter among the girls, and the members coming in to pay their dues or to see about work tend to their business quickly without arguing or squabbling, while Grimes and Buxton sit beside the counter, looking everybody over.

What made me do it, take on the goons and try to fight them off, when I've always told myself that I don't care? I could have let them take over, and I would have been off the hook. Forced out. I could have gone back to being the electrician I've always said I want to be. I feel my entire life has changed. Being persecuted means I'm taken seriously. Nothing seems unimportant now, and in the smallest task there is some satisfaction. The details of my job, which used to annoy and frustrate me until I'd fall into numb routine, trouble me no longer; and the sense of patient waiting, which had occupied me so long that it seemed to have become the tone of life itself, is gone. Savage urges charge through my mind: buying a gun, pulling the local out and challenging the National, holding Sally Bragg and kissing her until she whispers filthy words to me. Sometimes I feel I can do anything. I am no longer sure I can entirely trust myself.

In the afternoon, Grimes and Buxton decide they want to ride out with me on my calls, and I tell them sure, okay. It's uncomfortable for everybody in the office with them waiting around, watching, anyway. So we pile into my brown Dodge, Grimes driving, leaning sideways so far his back is up against the door, one tattooed hand on the wheel, following cars closely and cutting in and out; Buxton beside him, stretching in front of the radio, pressing the push buttons one by one to his dissatisfaction until he uses the knob to tune in the soul station whose warmth he desires, while I ride in back, in my car that isn't mine any more.

At the first job, a restaurant where they are redoing the interior and roughing in new equipment, we arrive like Murder Incorporated, Buxton unfolding out, wearing shades, his face cold, rigid, a mask; Grimes slamming the door and setting out in a lopsided walk like a wolf's lope, with a bulge beneath his coat that I'm convinced is a gun. All work stops. The men lay down their tools, the foreman freezes. Everyone must expect us, yet still we're a surprise.

We stand talking, the foreman, the steward, and I. A cement-finisher has walked off the job, complaining that the foreman was working him too hard. The steward, a thin, impatient man who stands beside me as we talk, eager for me to take sides, says the man should be hired back. The foreman, facing us, doesn't want to do it. The truth is, well, the man was, well, lazy. He has to bend and twist to say it, his eyes moving back and forth from the steward to me, under an aluminum hard hat jammed low on his head.

The foreman glances off to one side where Grimes is throwing rocks at a can while Buxton bongo-drums on a box, suggesting deeper trouble. I can feel power, like current, rush around my legs.

"I think you ought to take him back."

The foreman looks at me, surprised; maybe it's just dawned on him that out here he represents one man, the contractor, while I represent more than two hundred; then he nods and turns away, hands on hips, and kicks a scrap of lumber into a corner of the building's gutted shell.

I lead the steward, grinning with satisfaction, over by the portable toilet.

"You tell that finisher, for me, that he's got to start putting out—or *I'll* fire him. Understand?"

"Of course," he says, turning serious. "Absolutely."

"And don't be in such a god-damn hurry to bring every beef to me."

We leave, and there's no handshaking or small talk, nobody waving or yelling while we walk back to the car; just an exchange of stares, and distance, and the wind.

Riding in the car, Grimes and Buxton look at me and smile at each other approvingly. I've found an approach, a way of being, a point of view that gives me answers, so that what I should say and do comes easily and naturally to me now. On the surface, it's swift and smooth. Yet I know I can be dragged under. As Grimes runs the car through a flashing red traffic light, I feel its warning is aimed directly at a part of me that wants to turn it all around. STOP. STOP, YOU ARE BEING SWALLOWED UP.

It's too late. Too much has been done for me to undo.

Tonight, as I'm washing the dinner dishes, the doorbell rings, and Hoxie peers out the spy hole and opens the door. It's Ganley, bringing back my shotgun; and while I'm relieved to see he's no longer interested in it, I wish he had waited until after dark before walking up my front walk with it under his arm. He comes inside, and I can tell right off the beard bothers him. He keeps looking at it, trying to figure out what it means. I suppose if you're a cop, an alert one, you get used to looking at people that way, in pieces, at what people do with their hands when they talk, the condition of their shoes, that kind of thing. It must become a habit, trying to pick out the things about

180

a person that give him away. I know Hoxie doesn't do it. But he's still a patrolman, and easier to be with.

Ganley asks me about the trouble at the office, and I tell him what happened there, how the goons claimed they were from the National and started taking over, that we fought them off, and no, I didn't recognize them from anywhere. And all the time he's looking at me, bothered: he's read me as one thing and now I've gone and done another, and crossed him. I go back to the kitchen and finish the dishes, talking with my back to him, while Hoxie eavesdrops, studying his technique. Finally Ganley's curiosity is too much for him.

"Are you on vacation now?" he asks me.

"No, I'm still at work."

"Your neck, is that okay?"

"Fine."

"People say anything to you about the way you look?"

"Not a word."

"I always wonder what it would be like, wearing one of those." He makes a feeling sign with his hand under his chin.

It's the first time he's ever asked me a question that sounds like he didn't memorize it ahead of time.

"Different," I say. "It shakes people up. You ought to grow one."

"Me? They'd shoot me."

"Small world."

As soon as Ganley leaves, Hoxie is sprawling in front of the TV, open-mouthed.

"You've got too much sense to try and run while I'm holding a gun on you," a gruff voice from the television says.

I walk back into the kitchen and sit down at the counter. From outside, Doug's car, pulling away, sounds like an airplane taking off.

181

As Doug, Hoxie, and Ganley have left, a part of me takes leave. I sit alone in the kitchen but wonder distantly about Bragg, the goons, the union, until my thoughts stop, as they seem to do most every night now, on the slim young figure of Sally Bragg, scheming and vulnerable. I think about her walk, the way she stands, the soft way she looks when her eyes are closed; and I feel a rush of desire that makes swallowing difficult and—even though I am alone—embarrasses me.

18

The letter from the National arrived on a Wednesday morning nearly three weeks after the hearing officers had left town. Everybody had assumed the charges against Bragg had been dropped, and when he called me and told me about the letter he was furious, threatening to file countercharges against Cannon and Toad or even to pull his local out of the Brotherhood. I urged him to wait until we had talked it over before doing anything, and promised to stop by his office as soon as I could.

That afternoon, instead of going out on my calls, I drove into San Francisco and headed straight for Bragg's local. I found him in the hallway outside his office, talking to the men loitering there, showing them the letter.

"Look at this. Guilty! They leave town and send me a letter. What kind of trial is that?"

I read the letter over another man's shoulder. Bragg had been found guilty of intimidating other locals and of conduct unbecoming a union officer. He had been placed on probation by the General Executive Board, with the warning that the charges could be reactivated at any time.

"They can't do that, tell me I'm guilty by mail. I have the right to confront my accusers, don't I?"

The men scowled and mumbled and handed the letter back to him, helpless to do more than share his rage. Still indignant, Bragg handed the letter to me.

"Martin Morrison! He was a good labor lawyer. Fought right-to-work, defended those ironworkers accused in that bombing. How can he sit at a trial he knows is rigged, and send me a letter like this?"

Something made him bring his hand up and rub the back of his neck.

"Cannon. It's Cannon who does it. He numbs them, so they can go along with it and not feel anything."

I walked with him into his cramped, cluttered office, and we both sat down. Then he got up nervously and looked out the window.

"He numbs them," he said, thinking. "And me, I'm just the reverse."

"An irritant," I said.

"An irritant." He was delighted at the accuracy of it. "That's me, an irritant. Beautiful."

He sat down behind his desk again, smiling to himself, took a pencil out of the desk drawer, and printed the word "IRRITANT" on the back of the letter. He put his feet up on the desk, relaxing a little, and pointed the folded letter at me.

"There's a way to beat this. All I have to do is find it."

"Why?" I asked him. "It's just a gesture. If they really intended doing anything, they wouldn't be warning you about it."

He frowned at me. "I learned something a long time ago. Anything anyone does to me, I can do to him, only more."

A tall, muscular-looking woman in a black skirt and sweater brought in some union papers, which Bragg

184

looked at, then referred to Lenny Silk. The secretary left, and Bragg picked up the letter and read it again.

"What do you think?" he said. "Should I sue?"

"You mean take them to court? What for?"

"Oh, libel, defaming my character . . ." He laughed to himself. "No, on second thought, better forget that."

I felt obliged to suggest something. "What if you complain to the AFL-CIO or the Labor Department?"

Bragg waved the suggestion away. "Those people listen to you until you go away, and then they don't do anything."

"Congress?"

"It's an election year."

He put his hands behind his head and leaned back in his chair. I pushed my chair back and stretched my legs, feeling we'd be here for a while, stymied.

"An irritant," Bragg repeated, smiling. "I had a mustache when I was eleven years old. Eleven. Everybody thought I was a little old man. In school they never let me be bathroom monitor. I've been an outsider ever since. I rode with it, that's all. I have a mustache? Okay, then I'm going to have a MUSTACHE, thick and droopy, a real sleeve-wiper. Hair? Let it grow. Cops stopped me, treated me like a hood. Okay, I'll be one. In the union, I'm automatically a radical, no matter what I say. You see? I could have fought it, but I didn't. I followed my natural inclinations, and now I have a function in life: I scare people. Besides, I enjoy it."

There was a timid knock on the door frame, and Max Volt appeared, holding some pink forms and what looked to be the floor plan of a building.

He smiled apologetically and excused himself for busting in, explaining that he was reserving hotel space for the union convention.

He walked up to Bragg's desk, spread the floor plan out

185

on top of the loose papers there, and the two men studied it.

"I don't want my room anywhere near Cannon's," Bragg said.

They peered at the plan, considering various rooms and discarding them. This one was next to the pool, that one had a private sun deck for Sally, this one over here was close to the meeting room. Suddenly Bragg stopped, looked up from the plan, stared straight ahead.

"That's it," he said softly. "The convention. We'll bring it to the convention."

He lifted the floor plan and found the letter again. "We'll bring them out in the open and settle it, once and for all."

Volt was waiting with one of the pink forms. "Will you want the suite near the meeting room, then?"

"What?" Bragg said absently. "Yeah, yeah. Go ahead."

Bragg took a large lined tablet out of a desk drawer and picked up his pencil. "How do I get to make a speech at the convention?"

"It's probably up to the chairman," I said.

It didn't discourage him. "I'll have to get around and talk to as many of the delegates as I can. . . ."

He was writing furiously, listing things to do, scrawling out phrases to say, underlining words and using double and triple exclamation marks.

Finishing his form, Volt read from it. "You'll have a double room at the Disneyland Lodge, beginning the night of the twenty-first, through the twenty-fourth." He started to leave, taking the floor plan with him.

"Remember," Bragg said to him, seeming to snap out of a trance, "no bed. Just a mattress on the floor."

I hadn't been planning to go to the convention. I'd been a delegate to union conventions before, and had regretted

186

it, feeling that all I'd done was waste time, drink too much, and hang around feeling lonely. It always seemed to me that everything important was decided in advance, and that the real reason the delegates were gathered was to approve and applaud the Cannons. There were always parties and tours, and I always seemed to get stuck with people with whom I had nothing in common. Then there was Rose: everybody else brought a wife or a secretary along, but Rose refused to go. It was just too embarrassing to her, being away from home with a man who wasn't her husband, meeting all those people, suffering through all those awkward introductions. It didn't seem to bother anybody else—you were always running into a delegate with a hooker or someone else's wife—but it bothered Rose. So going to the convention meant, for me, going by myself, being with everybody yet completely alone.

But when the twenty-first day of the month arrived, there I was, wearing a blue badge with my name on it, standing in line in a hotel lobby, exchanging waves and handshakes with people I knew and didn't know, waiting to register as they walked in couples in and out and across the lobby, wearing sports clothes, alpaca sweaters, polo shirts, sun dresses, pastel slacks, looking unfamiliar in them, like customers still in a store trying them on. When I reached the head of the line, the desk clerk seemed overly formal, dressed like I was in a dark suit, white shirt, and tie. He flagged a bellhop as I signed in, and we crossed the lobby and rode up in a glassed-in outside elevator. It felt like falling upward.

The room was on the tenth floor, drab and angular, furnished in several shades of brown with brown cinderblock walls and a floor you could feel through the thin carpet. A unit in a vertical motel. I tipped the bellhop and he left.

I was looking out the window at the low buildings, the

palm trees, brown, dry-looking hills, a baseball stadium, and, surprisingly, a snow-capped mountain—Disneyland —when I heard a woman's voice behind me.

"Hi, I'm Lou."

She was leaning against the doorjamb, a tall woman with orange hair held in place with a red band; she had on green pants, a white blouse, and sandals; her toenails were painted. For a moment, I thought she must have the wrong room; but she looked me in the eye like a man.

"Joe Burke," I said.

"Hey, have you got a view." She walked over to the window and bent her face close to the glass. "You can see everything from here."

"You sure can," I said, looking at the green pants that fit her like the skin on a cooking apple.

She turned her face back. "I know what you're thinking," she scolded. "It's okay. I'm cool. Why don't you close the door?"

On legs I couldn't feel, I crossed the room and shut the door, came back, and stood behind her. For all I knew, she might be crazy, or somebody's wife. My heart was pounding so much my whole body shook with it. I reached my arms around her, afraid she would scream.

"Aaahhh, that's better."

We stood looking out at the Magic Kingdom, the turrets and pennants of a castle, bucketlike cars moving on overhead wires, the elevated track of a monorail. I reached a hand up under her blouse, which was all she was wearing, and felt a breast as heavy as margarine in a plastic bag. We watched a red-and-silver monorail car glide into the park.

"How about the other little fella?" she said. And I complied.

We left her blouse on a chair by the window, her green pants on the brown, box-shaped couch, and my pants, shirt, tie, shoes, and underwear in a heap on the floor, forsaking the fantasy land outside for our own within, until we broke through into another reality that left us hushed, dazed, and touching. Then we both slept.

When I awoke, the sun was coming in through the window at a low angle and Cool Lou was sleeping as though poleaxed. My watch said four-thirty and my stomach was growling. I got out of bed quietly, gathered my clothes, went into the bathroom, and stood under the shower. She was, beyond doubt, a hooker, sent and paid for by the National. A lifetime of looking at girls who don't look back has left me with few illusions about my own magnetism. At every convention, while the Cannons held their own caucuses, they assigned people to keep certain delegates distracted. Not only women. Young field-representative types were sent to the rooms of certain delegates with bottles of good whisky; or were obliged to drag delegates' wives all over the convention city sight-seeing. It had never been done to me before, but I'd heard about it. You were expected to lie back, let it all wash over you, attend a couple of general sessions and vote "aye," go home to your local and file such a modest expense voucher that they knew you'd done a hell of a job representing them. I found the attention flattering; and I certainly could have done worse than Cool Lou for a distraction. But what was I going to do with her when we weren't in bed? As I dried off and got dressed, my first concern was getting something to eat.

Sitting on the couch, I watched her sleep, the toughness gone out of her face, lying on a pillow smudged with make-up. I could have some food sent in, but that was like being prisoners; and if we ate downstairs we were bound to run into delegates who didn't know me well enough to know she wasn't my wife, and there would be those awkward introductions. Looking out the window I decided I'd take her to the park. With all those rides and all those people, there must be dozens of places to eat, enough to hide in.

Cool Lou rolled over onto the empty side of the bed and woke up, rubbing a lashless eye and wanting to know what time it was. I told her, and asked her how she'd like to have dinner in Disneyland. She looked at me sideways, then broke into a laugh that collapsed into a rattling cough that left her red-faced and whispery.

"Sure," she wheezed, "that'd be a gas."

She got up, wearing nothing but a cigarette, gathered her clothes, and went into the bathroom, leaving the door open so we could talk.

She was from Vegas, a show girl, or, rather, a woman who wanted to be a show girl, sang a little, danced a little, had worked at a night club once, at sales meetings more often, and at conventions a lot. She'd been booked for this one through an agency that supplied girls for any occasion that you could squeeze into the category of "modeling." They had an office and stationery and a file of pictures, from which she and several other "models" had been chosen, paid top rates, flown to Disneyland, and moved into private rooms. She'd been lying around the pool this morning, she said, when a young guy from the union had come by, given her my room number, and said, "Go to it."

"Who are you, anyway, the Teamsters?" She leaned on me while putting on her sandals.

"Construction workers," I said.

"You pay good bread, whoever you are. Let's eat. I'm hungry."

The outside elevator got us to the ground without going through the lobby so smoothly that I wondered if that wasn't its true purpose. Stepping out, we walked to some stairs and climbed up to a ramp where a single cement rail swept by the building in a wide arc. A group of people, none of whom I recognized, stood waiting, taking pictures of each other.

Toylike, a red-and-silver car glided to a stop before us, a door slid open, and we got on. The car had a low roof and curved windows that let in too much sun, and Cool Lou had to hold her hand up over her eyes. When the car moved it flowed with engineless quiet that had the passengers smiling approvingly at one another, except for those aiming movie cameras out the windows. The attendant who took our fare said that if we signed the register afterward, we'd get life-membership cards.

The ride was not so much memorable as brief. In practically no time we had stopped and everyone was getting off, moving toward the main gate, where more people were photographing each other against a backdrop of a gray castle. In front of the castle a swan floated serenely on the clear blue water of a moat. Everything seemed incredibly clean and orderly.

Suddenly, from the entrance where everyone was converging, there came a dreadful howl that awakened everybody as if from a dream, and even those people taking pictures turned to look. Some sort of argument was going on, involving a security guard standing behind a turnstile at the main gate.

"Presentable! Who's not presentable!" cried an angry, disbelieving voice that I recognized even at a distance as Baxter Bragg's.

Leading Cool Lou by the hand, I made my way to the outer edge of the crowd waiting to go inside, close enough to hear, but not near enough to be recognized.

"Those are the rules," the guard was saying with forced calm. "You go get cleaned up, get a haircut and some decent clothes, and I'll let you in."

It never stopped. Even here they were fencing him out,

191

making rules, using his wants to make him meet theirs. And he was still talking back, refusing to go along with what everybody else did.

"God damn it, I *am* cleaned up!"

"You just watch your language," the guard said, growing angry. "There are women and children present."

The people were trying to push through the gate, to get around the disturbance without noticing it, not wanting to have their day spoiled by someone causing trouble.

Cool Lou was impatient, wanting to join them, but I led her to the other side of the crowd, just in time to hear Bragg slide into his cold negotiating voice.

"You're open to the public. You can't turn people away just because you don't like the way they look."

"It's a private park and we can do whatever we like."

"No beards?"

"No beards."

"No long hair?"

"No long hair."

"Okay," said Bragg. "Suppose that monorail stopped over there and Jesus Christ got off with the twelve apostles. Beards. Long hair. Robes. Sandals. The works. What would you tell them?"

"The clergy are exempted from customary park regulations."

I heard Sally laugh, raw and derisive. But the cop wasn't joking. He was, at bottom, as serious and earnest as the fantasies he guarded. Even Bragg realized it.

"All right," Bragg said, his arms outstretched in resignation. "I'll go. There couldn't be anything in there more fantastic than this."

The guard sulked. The crowd parted and people moved away, looking displeased. Bragg was walking through them, complaining noisily, while Sally giggled.

"Banned!" he cried. "Banned from Disneyland!"

They passed nearby without seeing us, and I didn't call out or even wave.

"What a creep," said Cool Lou. "Making such a fuss."

"I know him," I said. "He's an official of our union."

"Well, I can see why you didn't want to introduce him," she said.

And passed, with a wiggle, by the very gate guard who had sized up Baxter Bragg and found him wanting.

19

Potter is upset. Since I brought him back inside the office, he's spoken to me only when he's had to; most of the time he stands at the dispatch window, mechanically collecting dues and stamping books, and assigning men new jobs. Sometimes when I walk through the outer office I feel him staring at me. I suppose he thinks I've written him off. Actually, his business-agent term was only temporary. I knew I was putting him in over his head and so did everybody else. If he'd only admitted his inexperience the foremen and stewards would have covered for him; but, resolved to make it permanent, he tried to bluff his way, pretending to know about conditions when he didn't, belittling people who opposed him, antagonizing everyone. If I hadn't pulled him back inside, I'd have had to fire him. It was a disappointment, but not a failure, and he'll get another chance if he's patient. Meanwhile there's this feeling between us that neither can talk to the other about: almost anything bad that happens to me is an opportunity for him.

This morning he walks into my office stiffly and slides a

card across my desk without a word, waiting, big-eyed, for my reaction. It's an application for a transfer from another local, a routine matter normally, except that the local this time is Bragg's and the name is Paul Eisan. Potter watches me. The moment is crucial to him. Grimes and Buxton are already here; now Eisan wants in. If Bragg's men start clearing into our local in numbers, next thing they'll be taking over and Potter will be sidetracked without a chance for advancement. I ask Potter if Eisan is here; still watching, he nods, and I tell him to bring him in.

I make up my mind to look at Eisan's face without staring at it, but this time it's his clothes that startle me. He's wearing tar-spattered blue overalls and thick, tar-caked work shoes, and carrying a set of crusty, blackened canvas gloves. I can almost see the hot tar clinging to his face as he stands with Potter across the desk.

I'm still holding his card. "You want to transfer into this local? What for?"

"The Safety Committee's been abolished," he says, tense with anger. "And the paper's discontinued."

It doesn't seem possible. So soon?

"Why? Who's doing it?"

"Silk. He's taking over."

Lenny Silk. An amateur, without convictions, wanting only to be liked. Then I remember: Bragg had suspected him. One of us, he said, had been informing. I didn't believe him, but some hidden ambition must have ached in Silk even then. Give him credit, he's no fool. This is his chance. Toad honors few things as he does his debts. If Silk helped Toad then, Toad would help Silk now.

It would cost Eisan a lot to come here: a semiofficial position, seniority. And he knows it. "I don't want to belong to any union if I can't do something about changing it."

195

I explain to him, for Potter's benefit, that we don't have a Safety Committee in this local. "In fact, we can't even afford a full-time business agent."

"I'll do it on my own time. I'll work as a roofer here."

What would it be like for him, standing beside a smoky, stinking tar trailer, feeling the heat and roar of the fire, looking down at the ooze in the cauldron, remembering?

"We still can't afford you. I couldn't pay your expenses or even give you time off to go check on the jobs."

"I'll make the calls on my lunch hour. I don't care about the money."

"You don't live in our jurisdiction."

"I'll move."

He stands rigid, arms stiff at his sides, the knuckles of one hand white against the blackness of his work gloves. For a moment the two of us seem to be alone, and I suddenly feel close to him.

"I'm not going to get away from you, am I?"

He looks me straight in the eye. "No. Or him."

I get the idea that Potter feels excluded, so I ask what do you think, do we have another spot for a roofer? He shrugs and scuffs a shoe and says he guesses so. I tell Eisan that Potter will fix him up with a job, and that for the other work we may be able to arrange a remission of dues. Potter turns back toward the outer office. Showing no gratitude, Eisan follows him.

I turn and look out the window. Lenny Silk. Already, they are crawling out of their holes, convinced that, with Bragg dead, all the strength has gone out of the revolt. Business as usual, time to go back on the make. Surely, of all the things in the world that people are willing to do, change must be the last.

Potter comes back in and plants himself across the desk, feet apart, hands on hips, staring at me.

"I want to know where I stand," he says, eyes glowing with suppressed anger. "I've been here four years, I've done my job, and now a bunch of outsiders is coming in and taking over. What gives?"

I tell him to close the door and sit down, giving me a moment to think. He does, impatient; and I tell him flatly what I've been meaning to say to him for months. That there are two things holding him back: inexperience and cocksureness. "One or the other is always tripping you up. I made you business agent before you were ready for it, so I brought you back inside. But that doesn't mean you won't get another chance."

He waves it away. "That's not the reason. I'm not one of Bragg's crowd—that's it."

"That's not true."

"It is!" he shouts, tears of rage in his eyes. "You want to be Bragg; everybody knows it. A big-time fucking labor leader. Well, I hope you make it, all the way. I hope you get what he got, so the rest of us can go back to a normal life."

Stunned and angry, I turn away from him again and look out the window. Let it come, I'm thinking; let the blast come smashing through the glass and knock me bleeding into his lap; let him have what he's asking for, and then try to live with it. I couldn't wish him worse.

"I didn't mean that," he says in a subdued voice. "It's just that, I don't know, I'm tired of being at war with everybody. Why does it have to be this way? Why do we have to fight his battles? Why can't we just do our work and be left alone?"

For a moment, I feel trapped. Life is a mess, death waits like a bandit; what men won't do to each other, fate will.

The sun comes bursting through the window, warming me and lighting the whole room.

"It doesn't have to be like this. You've got a choice. I've chosen."

197

20

The convention opened with a formal banquet breakfast.

At half an acre of white-linened tables, ten delegates to a table, we sat in assigned pink chairs, the officers of all the locals and the area representatives, the loudmouths, the ethnic leaders, the ideologues, the strong-arms, the middlemen, the errand boys, all wearing blue badges, talking in a steady murmur and eating noisily.

At the speakers' table, where the National officers sat, a small group of puffy-looking men took turns eulogizing one another. Monsignor Dunn, a fat, self-assured-looking priest, read the invocation and saluted Old Tom Cannon for forty years of unswerving anti-Communism. Young Tom Cannon, overseeing everything, put his arm around the monsignor, whom he described as the church's highest-ranking holder of a paid-up hod carrier's card, and ushered him back to his chair. Then Cannon read a telegram of welcome to the delegates from the President of the United States. After that, he waved Martin Morrison to the microphone. Morrison gave a long speech in which he called Old Tom "the most important single force within the life of our union, a man of vibrant personality, human sympathy, historical perception, profound philosophy, and unlimited energy, dedicated as a madman yet absolutely sane."

Young Tom was standing, turned toward the old man, applauding until the rest of the men at the speakers' table and finally the rest of the audience were shamed into doing the same, pushing back chairs and rising, napkins tucked in coats, brushing cigar ash out of laps, until Old Tom at last got to his feet, a huge, wounded bird, bald, his right arm and leg stiffened by a stroke, and gave a feeble, backhanded wave.

While all this was going on at the head table, Bragg, in the audience, was moving around from one small table to another, walking up and introducing himself to each group of men, sitting in an empty chair if there was one, or crouching beside the table and speaking, gesturing emphatically, so that at each table the proceedings were ignored as the delegates listened, staring at his hair, mustache, and unusual clothes with bewildered interest, until Bragg finished what he had to say and moved on, leaving his listeners looking confused and disturbed.

The consistent congratulatory dullness of the speeches aided Bragg by making almost any distraction welcome; even if you believed that the Construction Workers were led by the most courageous, hard-working, and devoted band of men in the history of organized labor, it grew tiresome to hear it repeated over and over. Around the room, the delegates yawned and puffed cigars and waved discreetly to one another, pretending to listen attentively and applauding dutifully.

My mind kept wandering to Cool Lou, in bed upstairs. Of the eighteen hours since we'd met, she'd slept fifteen, allowing interruptions only for food, making love, and brief readings of an astrology magazine. In Disneyland, all she'd done was eat; the rides would only mess her hair, the children were cute but noisy, and being in crowds made her perspire. We'd returned to the hotel early, made love with abandoned suddenness, and she'd gone to sleep again, motionless except for heavy breathing, waiting for that something which, if she were rested up for it, might come. I'd left her like that this morning, hugging a pillow, and had hung a do-not-disturb sign on the door that I was sure would still be there when I returned.

One of Cannon's young field-management trainees came over to the table, called me by my name, and asked me how everything was going. He appeared to be in his late twenties, a wise-looking kid with a long pointy nose and teeth that showed crooked as he grinned at me knowingly. For a moment I thought he was going to announce to the table that I was shacking up with a National whore, and I was prepared to call him a pimp in return, but he seemed satisfied to let me know that he knew what was happening, and spoil things a little, and left, advising me that he'd be seeing me.

Feeling a pang of guilt, I began paying more attention to the meeting.

Young Tom Cannon was speaking now, telling a long story about how the Secretary of Labor had been duck hunting on the Cannons' farm, and the Secretary, a wonderful fellow once you got to know him, had said, Look, Tom, all most people know about labor is the Auto Workers and the Teamsters and the Steelworkers, the big unions that grab all the headlines and are in hot water all the time. But the professionals in labor, we know who's really looking out for the interests of the workingman— it's the unions like yours, the men who are out on the jobs, settling disputes, quietly improving conditions day by day, instead of agitating in blocs for more and tying up the whole economy—it's those unions who represent to me the real backbone of labor in this country.

In the weary applause that followed, I wondered how much Cannon actually knew of the day-to-day work of the men he represented; he had inherited the union presidency from his father, and had never done a day of construction work himself. There had been a brief period when he had served as a National field representative, but even then he was being groomed for the top spot, and what local official was going to start an argument with Old Tom's son? What he had learned—the brokerage of favors, the string-pulling, the dispassionate playing of man against man, the reprisals—was management. He only called it labor.

From the table behind me, I heard a familiar voice.

"Hi, I'm Baxter Bragg, from the San Francisco local. We just signed a new contract that pays an average of six fifty-one an hour. How are you fellows doing?"

There was a silence I could feel even with my back turned, as the group of men waited, dumb with surprise. Sure, this was a convention, and everybody was supposed to be friendly. You even wore name tags to help you get acquainted, but you didn't just go around introducing yourself to everybody, not unless you were drunk or crazy or something. Bragg, I knew, looked like he could be almost anything.

Either sitting or squatting by the table now, he continued.

"Personally, I don't feel that's an unreasonable amount of money, an eighty-cent-an-hour increase spread over three years, what with the rising cost of living. And the contractors found they could absorb it—though they screamed at first. We've actually got more men working now than we had at the old wage rate. The only trouble I've had with our pay raise is that the union thinks it's too much."

"The *union* does?" a voice at the table asked.

"That's right," said Bragg. "Right after our contract was signed, Tom Cannon, Junior, came out and held hearings on behalf of the National. When I got into the hearing, the first thing he said to me was that five fifty-one an hour for this union is too high. I told him it was six fifty-one, and he damn near fainted."

There was sympathetic laughter at this; almost every delegate there had been yelled at or had a friend who had been bullied by Young Tom. They felt none of the affection for him that they had for his father, and anytime anyone threw a jab at Young Tom that hit the mark, they could all appreciate it.

"He had these hearings," Bragg continued, "and they were recessed after one day, with no decision. We all thought the charges had been dismissed, because nothing had been proved. Two weeks later, I get a letter from the GEB telling me I've been found guilty of intimidation and unbecoming conduct. Now I've been reading over the constitution, and everything I find in there seems to say that whenever a man has been charged, he has the right to defend himself. Don't you agree?"

The men, though still sounding skeptical, agreed.

"So what I intend to do is raise the matter from the floor, and make an issue out of it at this convention. I'd like your attention when I do it, and if you agree with me, I'd welcome your support. Thanks."

He went away then, and out of the corner of my eye I saw him approach another table, while I listened for the reactions of the men behind me.

"A maverick," one voice said disapprovingly.

"Like to have him negotiating *our* contract," said another. *"Six fifty-one an hour!"*

"Hell, I'd settle for five fifty-one," said a third voice.

"He's building an empire," the first voice said authoritatively. "Trying to weaken the National."

"What did the National ever do for you?" said the second voice.

"What did the National ever do for anybody?" said the third.

At the speakers' table, Martin Morrison was talking again, his speech smoothly paced and easier to listen to than most of the others. He kept looking from the audience back to Old Tom Cannon, sitting two chairs down the table.

"Tom, there's no way we can ever repay you for the years of leadership you've given us, for the burdens you've carried and the battles you've fought, for your democratic spirit, your friendliness, your openness, and your interest in people; but as a small token of the love we all feel for you, on behalf of all the officers of your union, I'd like to present you with a gift."

Reaching into his coat pocket, he took out a set of car keys and dangled them aloft.

"Outside in the parking lot is the brand-new Fleetwood Cadillac that goes with these, a gift to you from all your brothers who've chipped in and bought it for you."

He handed the keys to the old man, who was wiping his eyes with a table napkin.

"God bless you, Tom. We love you."

In the audience, there was a surprised silence as the delegates looked at one another. Recorded music, piped in through the ceiling, played "Auld Lang Syne." Old Tom got up, assisted by his son, hoarsely sniffled "Thank you" into the microphone, and was led by a pair of field representatives out the side door to claim his prize.

At the speakers' lectern, Morrison was leaning over now, listening to Bragg, who was standing toward the front of the audience with his hand raised, talking in an animated, angry fashion. Morrison was paying attention, but he kept his hand over the microphone, so that few

203

delegates could hear what was being said. Morrison said something back to Bragg and nodded, but he waited before the side door had closed behind Old Tom before he removed his hand from the microphone.

"Brother Baxter Bragg, of the San Francisco local, has informed me that what we have just done is illegal."

From the speakers' table, there was a chorus of moans, boos, and laughter, as if they expected the delegates in the audience to join in, and Morrison shook his head in exasperated agreement, as if they had.

"Apparently there is a regulation that a National officer can't accept gifts from the officials of his union. Is that right, Brother Bragg? Well, I know what Tom Cannon would say to that—if the rule and the men are at odds, the rule's got to give. What do you say, Brothers, are you in favor of giving a new car to Tom Cannon, who's worked so long and hard for us?"

"Yes!" shouted all the men at the speakers' table, and most of the delegates in the audience. But a number of the delegates were silent, and at the table behind ours, where Bragg had stopped, the men were calling toward the speaker.

"Question! You've got a question here!"

Morrison recognized them. "Question from the floor! Yes, go ahead."

A big, puzzled-looking man with thick, tangled-looking eyebrows got up from his chair and spoke.

"Look, I'm all for the old fellow, and I'm sure he deserves the car, but this is the first I heard about this. I mean, are these contributions voluntary or what?"

The man's question was relayed by Bragg to Morrison, who replied.

"The man wants to know if the contributions are voluntary. Of course they're voluntary; nobody is being forced to contribute anything."

Bragg had a question. "What's that?" said Morrison.

"How much?" said Bragg. Morrison had forgotten to cover the microphone.

"How much is each man's contribution? How much is each man's contribution, Jack?" Morrison turned to the young, bald-headed man who assisted him, sitting at the end of the speakers' table. The young man got up and walked over to the lectern, and the two men conferred for a moment. This time, Morrison kept his hand over the microphone.

Just down the table, Young Tom sat staring at Bragg and breathing with great, angry heaves of his shoulders.

"Yes," said Morrison, turning back to the delegates. "We wanted to be sure we got the best automobile possible, and, believe me, we got a terrific deal on this one through a friend of Jack Kalb's." The bald-headed man smiled and took a little bow. "Of course, since the old man is incapacitated now, he needs help, so there's a chauffeur who goes with it. The whole thing comes to a hundred and fifty dollars a man."

There were apprehensive whistles, and some of the delegates looked around, counting heads and figuring up the total. That brought Young Tom flying to the microphone in a burst of enraged energy, his eyes wild, and his cheeks red.

"You want to make a federal case out of this, is that what?" he said, trembling with fury. The delegates were suddenly dead quiet. "We bought my dad a car. Big deal. A man who built this union, by himself, from nothing. You wouldn't even be here if it wasn't for him. Now we want to show him a little appreciation. You'd think you'd jump at the chance, and here you are acting like a bunch of cheapskates. What's the matter with you, anyway?"

Morrison touched his arm gently, and Young Tom shook off his hand violently, and glared at the audience.

"Of all the puh-puh-petty . . ." he started to say, and then, in frustration, turned and left the speakers' table, stormed out the side door and slammed it with a booming echo.

Morrison, pale now, looked around at the other officials at the speakers' table, but none of them was volunteering help. When he spoke into the microphone his tone was soft and almost pleading.

"I think what we ought to do is refer this matter to committee, where we can discuss it calmly and without emotion. Does everyone agree to that?"

There was general relieved consent, quiet, with some nodding of heads. But Bragg wasn't going to let it go. His hand was up again.

"Yes, Brother Bragg," said Morrison, with a pained grimace.

Bragg walked right up to the table, and everyone could hear him when he spoke. "Don't you think we should delay taking possession of the car?"

Morrison didn't seem to understand.

"Shouldn't we send someone after the old man and tell him to wait?" Bragg said.

"Hey, now, just a minute—" One of the officers at the table began to rise.

"We can tell him the insurance has been held up," Morrison said to quiet the man. And he sent two field representatives outside to bring Old Tom back in.

The room was full of confusion now; with both Cannons gone, no one seemed to know what to do or how to act. The delegates were standing, talking to each other in little groups and looking around nervously for instructions.

"This meeting is adjourned," Morrison announced hastily. "This afternoon there will be work sessions in committee, and seminars tonight on union law and bargaining.

We will reconvene in a body here at ten o'clock tomorrow, no breakfast."

Music started coming out of the ceiling again, and the men at the speakers' table got up and began filing out. The side door opened, and three field representatives came back in, one holding the door and two helping Old Tom Cannon, who was looking from one face to the other, questioning. They sat him in a chair near the door, where he watched the standing, milling delegates, moving his mouth and looking neglected, until Morrison came over and began consoling him.

Waitresses and bus boys began clearing the tables, hurrying among the delegates, who were slowly moving out. By a pillar to one side of the room Bragg was standing, addressing nobody in particular, his dark eyes burning with intensity, his brows shrunk.

"Of all the nerve—buying him a Cadillac and making us pay for it."

One of the delegates, on his way out, reminded Bragg that the contributions were voluntary.

"Sure. What do you think would happen if you refused? It's a sad state of affairs when your job or mine depends on a kickback."

Several of the delegates stopped to listen.

"Look. Imagine—just imagine—a contractor asking his employees to chip in and buy him a Cadillac. They wouldn't think of it. Yet here we are, in our own union, expected to fork over the money without a word. It makes you wonder what else has happened that we don't even know about. Let me tell you what happened to me up in San Francisco. . . ."

More delegates stopped. He was making sense to them; it showed in their faces.

I turned away. I'd heard it already. But there was something more. I had noticed something in Bragg that I had never seen before, and the recognition of it struck me like a physical blow. Bragg had disrupted the session, spoiled the presentation of the automobile, embarrassed Morrison, humiliated Old Tom Cannon, and enraged Young Tom. He had revenged himself on all of them for finding him guilty in a rigged hearing. Yet still he hounded them, tormenting them even as he was winning with a savagery that made me shrink from him inside myself. Never, in any of his battles, had Bragg won a man over. He defeated enemies, but he never forgave or forgot. They remained enemies, as though he knew and feared that in the end, in becoming reconciled with the beaten, he would lose the power that challenged and drove him: their hatred.

I groped my way through the lobby and went outside; the light and heat of the sun bore in on me, and the air seemed unbreathably warm. Off to one side people were laughing and splashing in the hotel swimming pool, and the playful noises drew me, as escape from all the bitterness inside. I walked over to the fence and through the gate to the pool. Children were paddling in the water and jumping off the diving board, and a few women sunned themselves on patio furniture around the sides. Sally Bragg was one of them, wearing her large sunglasses and holding a book that was bigger than her bathing suit. I walked over to where she was sitting.

"Nice day," I said, feeling hot and awkward in my business suit.

"Well, hello." She laughed, surprised. "Here, let me move this stuff." She leaned over and picked up a towel, a hairbrush, and a plastic bottle of sun-tan lotion that had been on the chair next to her, and my eyes were drawn to the whiteness of her skin where it wasn't tanned. She asked me how things had been going inside, and I told her untruthfully that everything had been routine. She was so young and pretty it was hard to talk to her. My throat went tight and I had to remind myself not to stare. She adjusted the back of her chair, flattening it; I noticed with surprise the muscles in her stomach; then she lay down on them and closed her eyes.

"Mmmmmm," she said, getting comfortable.

Where had I been keeping myself, she wanted to know. Just around, I said, meeting people, getting acquainted. Thinking of Cool Lou, who suddenly seemed pale and pulpy. Lucky Bragg. I sat back in the sun-warmed chair, and in the heat I began to doze.

Across from where we were, facing the pool, was a row of large, ground-floor suites, set back behind a thick, low growth of flowers and ferns. The plants and the shadow of the overhanging balcony above gave the suites a gloomy, secretive look, like the mouths of caves. As I looked at them, heavy-lidded, one of the sliding glass doors opened, and Tom Cannon came out, frowning at the glare from the pool. Turning, he moved down the row behind the ferns, lumbering darkly, like a prehistoric beast, to a suite at the end of the row, where he opened a glass door and went inside. The minute he closed this door another door up the row opened and Old Tom came out, clinging to the arm of the bald-headed young man, Jack Kalb. They shuffled slowly down the row and entered the same suite Young Tom had. I sat up in my chair. A few minutes passed. Then Toad came out of a third room and entered the suite. Soon after, the torpedo who'd been at the hearing came out of a fourth room and hurriedly joined the others.

I sat squinting in the sunlight, thinking about the trouble they'd taken to avoid being seen. They were caucusing, in secret, and there could be little doubt what they were caucusing about. It made my resentment toward Bragg vanish. For all his shrillness and savagery, at least he acted openly; he fought you face to face. Now his openness had driven them all into one hotel room, too ashamed of what they were doing to be seen walking down a hotel hallway.

Excusing myself, I told Sally I was going to find her husband.

21

The Black Thing stands across the street, beside the walnut tree in the Olmsteads' yard, outside but not moving: waiting. I noticed it just after dark, as I took an old maid's look out the front window, standing back, moving the curtain away with a long arm, scanning up and down the street, careful not to be seen noticing the parked cars, a forgotten lawn sprinkler left to run all night, an old man out walking a spotted dog, Iris Baker bellowing after her son LAA-REE, the Olmsteads' white cat, stalking, and there —there, darker than the dark, taller than a kid, broader than a woman, out there all alone, standing still, facing our house, is Somebody.

"Hoxie, somebody is standing across the street, watching the house."

He looks up from the paper, gets reluctantly out of his chair, sweeps the curtain aside, and looks out. Then he returns to the chair and resumes reading.

"Aren't you going to go see who it is?"

"No."

Lazy, no-good cop, caring only about his own precious skin.

211

"What if he starts shooting, are you going to do anything about it then?"

Hoxie puts the paper down in a heap. It's your neighborhood, he says. Suppose I go over there and roust him, show my badge, make him identify himself, put his hands up against that tree and search him, maybe—and he turns out to be a real-estate man, or some poor guy with a heat on who I'll have to arrest. How do you think your neighbors are going to feel about that?"

His excuse surprises me, it makes so much sense. I take another look through the window. Still there.

"Suppose it's the real thing. What happens if we let him stay there?"

Hoxie thinks a moment. "Well, he sees you're not alone, maybe, and he goes away. That's if he's smart. If he's dumb, he tries it. He's out there, you're in here. He's got to come to you, and you've got an armed police officer, a telephone, and a houseful of lights. That don't give him much chance of making it."

He smiles at me, proud of the easy way he turns aside my questions. But it doesn't stop the fear or change the cockeyed unfairness of it all. Or the fact that I'm a prisoner here.

"What if the two us go out there, and I take just one quick look at him? What if I could identify him?"

Hoxie considers it. A risk. But a chance to make The Pinch, a big arrest that might win him back the advances in money and grade he's lost. Or, if I get shot, maybe cost him even the job he has.

"No. We're gonna stay here."

It's final. He's stubborn beyond desperation.

I go into the kitchen, bossed around in my own house. The refrigerator is full of Pepsi, and I have to take out three or four bottles to reach the milk. Pouring a glass, I sit down with it at the counter.

Somehow, I have to get away from this: escape the trap in which I am the bait. I feel pained and dull, numb and sensitive at the same time. The sounds outside are enormous. A car door crashes shut. Someone is driving up the street with a raw angry noise. Voices are like cries for help: LAA-REEE! My head is heavy, my eyes ache. Sentenced to death, without trial. Who is it that waits outside, calm as a hangman? Trapped, like I am. If he tries again, the odds against him go up. If he kills me, he may be killing himself. If I went out there alone, and got a quick look at his face—"he saw me, how could I go through with it?" —that might release us both.

In the cabinet beneath the sink, back of the scouring pads and the liquid dish soap, is a hunting lantern, box-shaped, with a big battery and a beam so powerful it seems it could go through steel. I keep it next to the spare fuses, because our switchbox is outside. Up close, flashing at you suddenly, it would be blinding. It feels cold and heavy in my hand.

In the living room, Hoxie stares at television.

"At the end of four full innings, it's the Dodgers nothing and the Giants nothing."

I ease the back door shut without a sound. It's moonless out, and thick with crickets: good cover. Aiming the beam down, I flick the lantern on once to test it, and the glare lights a patch of our garden like the sun. I turn it off and start around the house, keeping my thumb on the button.

From our front yard, I can see him waiting, wide, dark, unmoving. Who else would stand that long, that calm, outside in the dark? He knows what he's after, and he's certain that he's going to get it. There's no escape from someone so patient; you have to break the pattern and catch him by surprise.

Lights. A car is coming up the street. I duck behind my car in the driveway. When I look up, he hasn't moved.

213

Across the street now, moving quickly, head down, then crouching behind another parked car. I can see the details of his body, big head, broad shoulders, fairly tall: not someone to tangle with. Just shine the beam in his eyes and haul ass out of here before he can see enough to shoot. I'll *know* then, and that part of it will be over.

Around the car, still crouching, holding the lantern up so that the beam will hit his face, across the Olmsteads' lawn, a step at a time, keeping the tree between us. The closer the better: the bigger the surprise. Until I'm right next to the tree and can hear his heavy, troubled breathing and his body moving slightly in his clothes. I swing the light around, stepping out from behind the tree. Aim it. Press the button.

"AAAAAAAA AAAA!"

Mary Olmstead, John's daughter, stands blinded, screaming hysterically, hair messed, her face puffy. The dark-haired boy whose arms she's been in is squinting, grimacing with fear and anger, one hand up against the glare. Caught Making Out. Standing out here, silent and soulful. All alone in each other's arms. And then this.

"I'm sorry," I say softly. "It's me, Joe Burke."

But the light still has her shrieking.

"He's got a gun! He's got a gun!"

In every house on the block, a light goes on.

"Mister Burke from across the street. Doug's father. I made a mistake. . . ."

The boy has found his courage. "God damn it, get out of here! Get the hell out of here!"

"Mary?" comes Olmstead's voice from inside the house. "Is anything wrong out there?"

I keep trying to explain, but it only makes it worse. I thought you were somebody else out here watching my house. Sounding more and more like the crazy, bearded neighbor. Mary has her face in her hands, crying. Doug

214

used to take her out. Peg McCabe is standing on her front walk in a bathrobe, her hair in curlers, listening. Suddenly, Hoxie is there; he's bounded out of the house and across the street. He takes the lantern out of my hand and turns it off.

"All right, let's go home now," he says in his policeman's move-along voice.

"Look, this guy jumped out of the dark at us—"

"I know, I know. I'll take care of it. You just go inside now."

The girl has stopped crying, and the two of them take a few steps back toward the house, then turn and watch, making sure I leave. Hoxie and I start across the street. Some of the neighbors go back inside. Peg is standing in an indignant pose that says it all: LABOR-UNION GANGSTERS.

"You can't tell me anything I haven't already said to myself," I say to Hoxie, anticipating. "I took a chance, I upset the neighbors, I risked getting shot, I made a fool of myself."

"You're off your ass."

That I hadn't said to myself. At the time, there had been a logic to what I'd done; it had made a kind of sense. Now, it seemed that perhaps it was the crazy logic of a strung-out man going mad. Maybe Hoxie is right. Maybe they won't have to shoot me after all.

22

I never meant to go inside that room. If I'd thought he'd want to—if I had thought at all—I'd never have told him. If I could take that moment back today, I would give everything I own. There's only one thing about me that is really dangerous: I am without guile. A secret is, to me, a burden, which I haven't courage enough to bear alone. I pass it on, so I can know what others think. Anything, to avoid deciding myself. I'm one of life's loose planks, for others to trip on.

I found Bragg standing in the hotel lobby, still talking excitedly to a pair of loyal listeners, dissidents from eastern locals who were staring at him, fascinated by the outspoken subtlety of his speech and the odd way he combined force with self-control. He looked pleased by the success and attention the morning had brought him, and when I touched his arm, he greeted me noisily, throwing the arm around me and asking me where the hell I'd been keeping myself.

My mind was in a tunnel: one thing was all I saw. "The Cannons and Morrison are caucusing with Toad."

He studied my face for a moment, up close. I could feel his thoughts racing. Turning away from the others, he took me over to a corner of the lobby and asked me anxiously exactly what I'd seen. I told him that they'd gone one by one into a room by the pool. On the end.

"Morrison's," he said, recognizing it. "Sneaking bastards. They knew I had Grimes and Buxton covering the hall. Well, let's go."

He started walking.

"Where?" I said, standing still.

"Inside," he said. He looked at me challengingly. "Are you with me?"

To have followed him this far meant nothing unless I would go on. I would be just another faint heart who failed him in a crisis, no longer worth his friendship. I guess I knew then that if it came to them and him, I was with him. I began walking with him, and he grinned.

"It appears they've lost the desire to do battle with us in the open. So we'll outflank them. It's time to bring them out of the hotel rooms and onto the battlefield."

As we walked, I could feel my face sweat. Guests and hotel employees stopped and glared at him; at the desk, a tiny white dog in the arms of a fat woman went into a frenzied yapping as we passed. All this, Bragg was too preoccupied to notice.

Grimes joined us at the entrance to the hallway, walking alongside Bragg, explaining eagerly that he'd seen them all, that each of them had gone into his room about a half hour before and hadn't come out. Bragg listened, smiling to himself and me, and continued walking until he came to the last door. He thumped his fist on it, and Grimes's pinched face widened and fell.

There were surprised voices inside, and muffled discussion. After a pause, the door opened, just a crack; the torpedo was standing behind it like a second door.

217

"What do *you* want?" he asked contemptuously.

Bragg challenged him, loud enough to be heard inside. "Cannon and Fuller, and I know they're both in there."

"You got the wrong room."

"Everybody knows it. We saw you from the pool."

The thug looked surprised.

"We took your pictures." Bragg grinned at him.

Confused, the thug turned away, and there was more discussion inside the room. Then the door opened wide. Morrison was holding it, his big face forced into a tolerant smile, a drink in his other hand.

"Wellll, come in, come in. We're always glad to welcome any of the brothers." He ushered Bragg and me into a roomful of stiff, staring men: the Cannons, Old Tom and Young Tom, sitting side by side on the couch, faces set, not even their eyes moving; Toad, stuffed into a small chair next to them, his face so pale he looked sick; Jack Kalb, standing, fidgeting with a glass. There was a table with a cloth thrown over it with more glasses, a bucket of ice, and quart bottles of bourbon and Scotch. The room had an air of suspicion and fear so strong I could feel it myself; I had an urge to go along with Morrison and pretend we'd stumbled on a simple social gathering, have one drink, make an excuse, and leave.

"What have we got here?" Bragg asked brashly. "Another trial?"

In silence, the men glanced at one another to see who, if anyone, was going to deal with the intrusion.

"Just a friendly get-together," said Morrison quickly. The sound of his own voice seemed to reassure him, and he relaxed a little. He asked us what we were drinking, and I said I'd like bourbon. Bragg didn't want anything. Morrison handed me a glass and, lifting his own drink, gave a little salute. I raised my glass, too.

On the faces in the room, surprise had turned to hatred.

Again he had burst upon them and thrown them back, startled and inflamed at his appearance. Outraged, helpless, they seemed unable to oppose or stop him. They squirmed with resentment, knowing that he was enjoying their uneasiness.

"We've had our differences," said Morrison, trying to cover, "but that doesn't mean we can't be friends now that the smoke of battle has cleared. After all, when you come right down to it, we're all on the same side."

He drank and I drank. The silence was painful. I concentrated my attention on my glass until half my drink was gone. When I looked up, Bragg was grinning in a way that made me shiver.

"I came in here to give you hell," he said softly.

Everybody tensed. The room went quiet. Morrison was caught still smiling. Only Young Tom seemed to respond. He jerked forward, jowls working, about to stand; but his father suddenly came to life, stopping him with a small touch of his usable claw of a hand.

The old man spoke to Bragg with the naïve voice of a boy.

"Why do you always want to make trouble?"

Bragg walked over to where he was sitting and got down on one knee, his face close to the old man's.

"This union's sick to death of the way it's being led. They've got us headed into a dead end . . . letting jobs be destroyed . . . undermining working conditions . . . it's got to change, because if it doesn't, it'll die!"

Young Tom leaped to his feet. "What do you mean?" he interrupted hotly. "We got a headquarters going up in Washington, it'd knock your eye out. Who's dying?"

Standing, Bragg took a deep breath to steady himself. "You can't do it the old way any more . . . black-listing . . . drumhead trials . . . beatings . . . conspiring with contractors. You've got to get off our backs. We can't carry you any more."

Young Tom leaned forward, ready to spring at him in fury. "We haven't been firm enough with *you* people," he cried. "That's the trouble! Bunch of hotheads, rocking the boat! You're hypocrites! Sure, you want to tear down the Establishment—so you can put up one of your own!"

He stopped and seemed to think that over. His voice became calm, shrewd, mocking.

"How much you making now?"

"Me?" said Bragg.

"Yeah. How much?"

"Thirteen thousand, salary and expenses."

Young Tom shook his head and laughed in a joyless, belittling way. "Thir-teen thousand . . ."

"It's enough," said Bragg, with an edge to his voice.

"It's chicken feed. You want more. Okay, how about a raise of ten grand? Twenty-three thousand—that's two less than I'm getting. We'll make you a general representative of the National."

Bragg shook his head.

"Either you're dumb or stubborn," said Young Tom, growing impatient again. *"I'm inviting you in."*

He stopped, letting the offer sink in. We were all watching Bragg, who looked up with a hairy half-smile.

"It isn't worth the extra dough to be your flunky."

For a moment, Young Tom looked at him, his face frozen in a pout. Then he turned to his father, still seated on the couch.

"Let's go, Daddy," he said gently. "It's beginning to stink in here."

He helped the old man up, and they started slowly across the room toward the door, the father clutching his son's short, fat arm.

Bragg should have let them go. But he wouldn't. Or

couldn't. No matter how angry he made people, no matter what the consequences, he simply didn't know when to stop.

"Why don't you open the window you used coming in?" he taunted.

Young Tom halted. He was breathing hard; his jaw was shaking.

"You're dirt!" he shouted, his face inflamed. "Your clothes are dirty . . . your mouth's duh-dirty . . . your mind's dirty!"

Bragg didn't move. "Dirt's no disgrace to a working-man," he said calmly.

I don't know who gave the goon the signal. Perhaps, like a dog, he was just responding to the excited pitch of the voices. He seemed barely to move, the distance he traveled was so short. Two steps and a little punch that looked like a shove, and Bragg flew backward, dragging a lamp by its cord, his head thumping against the wall, his body sliding limply to a sitting position, his mouth agape. The thug wheeled and turned on me then, eyes wild, his fist cocked. I froze. Still flushed, Young Tom hustled his father out the door.

Morrison put a placating hand on the thug's massive shoulder.

"That's enough, Norman," he said soothingly. Norman waited; the voice could have been coming to him from far away. "I said *that's enough,*" Morrison repeated with some stress. The goon shrugged angrily, but turned away and numbly followed the Cannons into the hall. I took a look at Bragg. His eyes were open and distant-looking, as though the wind had been knocked out of him, although he was breathing normally. I wrapped some ice from the bucket in my handkerchief and held it against his fore-head.

Morrison put his palms out apologetically.

221

"I'm sorry, but he shouldn't have come in here and started shooting off his mouth like that."

"He should have wised up," Toad said in a shaken voice. "Doesn't he know he got off easy last time?"

The coldness of the ice seemed to revive him, and he tried to brush it away with his hand. He blinked his eyes and shook his head. While Jack Kalb carefully replaced the lamp, I helped Bragg, wobbling, to his feet. He was surprisingly thin and light. Then I assisted him out into the hall, as one Cannon had helped the other. Grimes and Buxton were waiting there, full of too-late threats and safe indignation. Bragg wasn't saying anything. Shaking off my hand, he led us into the nearest hotel lounge, where he sat down heavily in a corner booth and ordered us all drinks.

An hour later, the four of us were still there, sitting at the same table, listening to Bragg over rows of empty glasses.

"We've got to take it to the locals now, that's all. Travel around . . . start brush fires . . . I thought I could talk to them, but it's no use . . . they're entrenched . . . completely out of touch."

He pounded his fist on the table.

"They'll have to *go*."

Anybody could have been listening, but Bragg didn't care. He must have sensed that he had passed a certain point beyond which what he did threatened himself as well as his enemies. And still he didn't care. An uproar was growing, and I knew the only way I could escape it was to leave. I told him I was going. He looked disappointed, but he thanked me for coming along with him, and I could tell he meant it. He was a lot more upset by what had happened than he was willing to admit.

I rode up in the outside elevator alone, feeling myself

222

falling even as I was rising, longing to clutch and hang on to the tidy, secure lights growing smaller and moving away below. The earth was like the sky, with the lights the stars.

When I got to my room, the door was open. The bed was empty, and Cool Lou was gone. There was no note. The word was out already.

23

The short, earnest insurance salesman is hunched over my desk most of the morning, showing me tables of figures, watching me with small, greedy eyes, speaking in a soft, insistent voice.

"You know you're lucky you decided to take out some additional insurance now. If you'd waited much longer, you might not have been able to get any at all. Certainly not in an amount like this. You're still a young man, of course, but not twenty-five any more. And a hundred thousand dollars is a big risk, even for a company like ours."

With double indemnity, that's a hundred thousand for Doug and a hundred thousand for Rose.

"The premium, of course, will be higher than if you were taking out a policy at age twenty-five or thirty-five. But it's not too much for a man in your position. You have to look on it as buying you not a lump sum, but income, *income* for two people that continues coming in every month even though you're not here to earn it."

He begins sliding his tables and brochures back into a

limp blue plastic case. "I'm assuming now that you are a good risk, that you don't go home and hook yourself up to a kidney machine at night. You don't do that, do you? Good. Health is priceless. And your work is here in the office, mostly. You're very fortunate. You *will* have to take a detailed physical examination, though, perhaps even two examinations, because this is a large amount of money. If we threw our money around carelessly, we'd have none for your son and your—your other beneficiary. You understand? Good. Good."

Anxious to close the sale, he gives me a preliminary agreement to sign. The physical will be in a matter of days, and coverage can begin in one week. We shake hands on the policy and he leaves, breathing deeply, satisfied. At last, I am learning how to lie.

Alone, I reach for the telephone and sit with my finger in the dial, listening with one ear to the tone, waiting with the other for footsteps until I hear someone approaching from the outer office and put the receiver down, almost with relief.

"Oh, I'm sorry," Beverlee protests. "I didn't know you were on the phone."

"That's all right; it can wait." I push the telephone away and turn to her with exaggerated interest, feeling secretive and guilty.

"There's a delegation of the men here to see you."

"*Our* men?"

She nods, looking concerned, and I tell her to bring them in. There is a heavy, shuffling noise and, looking self-conscious, they file into the room and stand along the far wall: Grimes and Buxton, Paul Eisan, Mike Sullivan, Clarence Equals, and Billy Hildebrand, grim-faced, a jury looking at me across my desk. Beyond the doorway, Potter stands on tiptoe, trying to see inside.

Eisan looks at the others and takes a step forward, declaring himself spokesman. "We have a statement to read."

I knew having him in the local would mean trouble, but I felt a job was owed to him. Now it looks like I'll have to pay even more.

"Go ahead."

He reaches inside his tar-spattered windbreaker and takes out a piece of white typing paper, folded lengthwise, and drops his head to read.

"It has now been three weeks since Brother Baxter Bragg, President of Construction Workers Local Seven, was cruelly and cold-bloodedly murdered in the streets of San Francisco. Never before has anything like this happened to a leader of labor in this city. With burning indignation and deep disgust, the rank and file of this local have noticed that the top officials of the National Brotherhood have made no attempt to bring the perpetrator of this foul act of gangsterism to justice. And that the National has now launched an attack of its own on our local and its surviving leaders. We have therefore decided to take action of our own."

Eisan glances up. "This part is a proposed resolution." He looks down again. "Whereas Baxter Bragg, President of Construction Workers Local Seven, of San Francisco, has been assassinated, and

"Whereas Joseph Burke, President of Construction Workers Local Two Fifty-two, Madrone County, has been physically attacked in the local office by men claiming to represent the National, and

"Whereas the leadership of the National Brotherhood has opened no investigation, posted no reward, nor even expressed a word of concern or regret for either act, be it therefore

"Resolved that we of Local Two Fifty-two hereby declare ourselves and this local disaffiliated from the Na-

226

tional Brotherhood of Construction Workers, its constitution and bylaws, its officers, elected and appointed, its assessments, dues, and penalties, effective immediately.

"Be it also resolved that we pledge our full support and aid to our own democratically elected union officers. That we promise to uphold the principles of honest, participatory trade-unionism, to combat dictatorship and corruption of the principles of organized labor. We call upon all unions, organizations, and individuals of the United States to support and aid this cause of justice."

Carefully, he lays the paper flat in front of me, on my desk.

"We want to introduce this at the meeting Tuesday."

I look around at the men, who are staring back, not surprised by what they've heard, and my eyes stop on big, dumb Billy Hildebrand, hands stuffed into the pockets of his white carpenter's overalls. Can he possibly realize what it means? I pick up the paper and pretend to read, trying to think what I should say.

Folding the paper, I hand it back to Eisan.

"Use your heads," I tell them, trying to minimize it. "They won't stand for this." I reach for my suit coat. They look at one another, disappointed. "I've got some calls to make. We all better think this over."

I move, starting to leave, but nobody moves with me. Eisan stares, examining me. "*They* won't stand for it! What about *us*?"

Us. Impossible to move—and he moved them. Impossible to stop—and he's gone.

"I mean," says Eisan, almost pleading, "did he die for something, or not?"

The thought stops me. Eisan is still talking. How can we go along with them, after all this? It's like we were all in on murdering him. But as I stand, pretending to listen, his voice evaporates. A new feeling—did he die for something?—fuses with an echoing thought. It's only people like you who can change things. People who have the option to join the squeezers, and don't. His obligation. Mine.

"Either we do it now—" I hear Eisan say—"or not at all."

The words nearly choke me as they come bursting through.

"All right."

For a moment, they don't seem to understand; they have been waiting, nervous, expecting opposition. I put on my coat. Eisan begins babbling, a man suddenly freed from a dangerous burden.

"You're not alone in this now . . . remember, we're with you—all the way. We'll back you up. We'll do whatever you say."

We crowd through the door in a bunch and tramp noisily through the outer office. Grimes is grinning. Billy looks confused. Equals, who wouldn't take a union officer's job, smiles in satisfaction: he has another reason not to.

"We'll get them out on Tuesday," Eisan says in the hallway, almost whimpering with relief. "You can count on it."

"Just like it used to be," Buxton says.

Outside, I climb into the back seat of my car, while Grimes slides behind the wheel and Buxton sits next to him, elbow out the window, looking tough.

Eisan sticks his dead, expressionless face through the window on the driver's side.

"You take care of him now," he warns Grimes and Buxton. "We've got us a *leader* again."

At six o'clock, when I return, alone, the office is dark, the door is locked, and the shades are drawn. It's quiet in my office. There are no interruptions, no listeners, no more excuses for not doing what I've already done in my mind a dozen times. I reach for the telephone again.

Part of me keeps saying that I'm betraying Rose, that I'm doing something wrong—not morally wrong, because I don't think of myself in those terms, but inconsistent, something too ruthless for me to have done just a few days ago. While another part of me says go ahead, that what has happened has only released a desire and power that were always there, and that to deny them is to be a coward and a hypocrite, and betray myself.

The voice that comes out of my throat is husky with anxiety and dread, and not my own.

"Hello, Sally?"

"Yes."

"It's me, Joe. Joe Burke," I add, before she can ask Joe who.

"Joe! Where the hell have you been?" she says with emotion, sounding really relieved at the sound of my voice. Her response is all I'd hoped it would be. "I've been hearing terrible things about you. I was worried sick."

"Everything's changed," I tell her. "*I've* changed. You remember the things we talked about before?"

"Yes, I remember."

"I wasn't ready to go through with them then, but I am now. There's no stopping point any more."

"Really? That's wonderful, Joe. What a surprise. Oh, I shouldn't be surprised at all, really. Baxter always said you could be counted on. I'm so glad you're going to help. When I saw you I wasn't sure. Then I heard what they did to you and I wanted to talk to you, but it's so hard for a woman to pick up the phone and call."

"When can I see you?" I say, fighting to hold back a flood of emotion.

"When? Any time."

"How about if I come over tonight?"

"Tonight?" She sounds surprised. "What time?"

"I'm at the local now. I could eat somewhere and come over around seven."

229

"Eight," she insists, quickly hard-voiced.

"Okay, eight."

"See you then," she says, speaking softly again. "Terrific news, Joe."

I hang up the phone, palms sweating, short of breath. It's done. If she'd said no or discouraged me in any way, I'd have backed out and forgotten the whole thing. But she wants it, just as I do. Bragg's wife, Rose's friend—and we're going to collide.

I walk down the hall to the bathroom and wash up, staring at the mirrored beard as I dry my face. What will she think of it? Suppose everything goes as I hope, and as I drive into her in full passion and reach the ultimate place where he has been—will she call me by his name? The whole business is so ghostly, I'm nearly overwhelmed by the thought, until everything is clouded over by a panic of desire: I'm middle-aged, short, paunchy, certain never to be rich; it's my last chance at a girl like this.

Young. A flower.

I turn off the office lights, lock the door, and walk out to my car. Driving through the town of Madrone, looking for a restaurant, I begin to worry that someone will see me. Hoxie's partner, maybe, catching me out at night without my police dog; or one of Doug's friends. Or Rose. I pass the last familiar drive-in, turn onto the highway, and head toward the bridge and the city, devising strategy.

She'll want to talk union politics, and try to get me to make promises. Make them. Tell her anything. It's a game. Besides, she *wants* to. I wouldn't be doing this if I didn't know that, would I?

At a glass-walled cafeteria on Polk Street, I have a roast-beef sandwich and sit alone at a table like the other loners there, staring, not talking, forced by the coldness of the surroundings to finish in a hurry. Maybe we can begin where we left off; maybe she'll simply open her arms as I walk in; or we can have a drink first. Maybe it's all differ-

230

ent now, the way the magazines say it is, with the pill and the new morality; maybe you just say the word, and that's it.

A bus boy starts cleaning up after me, so I get up and walk outside. It's seven-fifteen. I buy a paper, walk up the street, unlock my car, and sit behind the wheel, reading. I'm halfway through the lead story on the sports page when a car pulls alongside and stops. The man inside points to himself and my parking place. So I start the car and pull out. Seven-twenty.

At a gas station, I read the front section while the attendant fills the tank, checks the oil and battery, and cleans the windshield; when I drive out, it's only seven-thirty. I feel ridiculous, killing time like a high-school kid. What's the difference if I show up early? So she's in a slip or a housecoat. So much the better.

Feeling hard, decisive, I press the gas, jump a signal, and head across Market Street into the Mission. I'm moving so fast now I get hung up turning off on the wrong cross street, have to pull into a driveway, turn around, and head back.

At twenty minutes to eight, sweating with anxiety, I turn into the alley between the gas station and the machine shop and drive slowly up before Bragg's house, past the first worn Victorian house and the second, past the cars parked or abandoned on the sidewalks, looking for a space and breathing with difficulty.

Double-parking at the third house, the one with Bragg's number, I open the car door and start out, resolved now to drop the game and come out with the truth and confess to her what I've been afraid to admit even to myself—that I want her to the point of doing anything she asks.

As Leonard Silk closes the front door and comes down the steps, handsome, freshly groomed, a shaving kit tucked under one arm.

I fall back into the seat, closing the car door. I see him

for maybe half a minute before he sees me. And stops. Even with the beard, he recognizes me. His even-featured face falls and he seems rooted to the spot, as startled as I am. We look at each other without a word, both foolish, betrayed, used. We are each other, and the realization of it fixes us for a moment, unable to speak or move. Dazed, embarrassed, desiring only escape, I put the car in reverse and back waveringly out of the alley, looking back and glancing forward, while Silk stands watching, a lonely figure, growing smaller, still motionless in front of Bragg's house, until I back out into the cross-street traffic and join it, losing sight of him completely.

As to a life of misunderstood intentions, bad guesses, and missed opportunities, I ruefully mark down another of each.

24

Joe—the fire is lit!!!

All I did was strike a match . . . to throw a little light in a few dark corners here—and whoom!—years of rubbish went up! It's incredible—you think you know what every other local is like on the inside . . . that you understand just how bad corruption and chiseling can get . . . and then you find out you didn't know a tenth of what's really going on!

I sneaked into town two days ago to meet with Morgan Rogers and Mario Lombardi . . . a couple of young guys who have been trying to start an insurgent faction here. . . . They know all about what we're doing through the *Free Press*. We're their model . . . "You cleared the path," Mario told me, "we'd almost given up hope . . . and there it was . . . somebody actually reforming the union from within."

We spent all day yesterday roaming around the city . . . walking . . . Independence Square . . . Downtown . . . (Did you know Philadelphia is a seaport??? I saw ocean-going ships here.)

Joe, the union here isn't a union at all—it's a racket, run with the Cannons' blessing . . . everybody's in on it . . .

233

and it's been going on this way for years!!! Mario and Morgan told me how it works.

Every year, the contractors get together and divide up the city construction contracts . . . they decide in advance who submits low bid for each project! Any outsider who comes in and doesn't want to play along is harassed by the union . . . the business agent calls a walkout . . . the stewards start overpolicing the union contract and assessing fines . . . the contractor's labor costs are driven up so high he can't bid!!

Meanwhile, while the union's fining and harassing the outsiders, they let the contractors who are in on the stealing get away with murder!!!! hiring scabs . . . working men overtime and paying them straight time . . . using material below specifications.

The city inspectors go along with this . . . they're in on it! Morgan told me every contractor allows a certain percentage of his gross receipts for bribes. The take runs into the millions!! The local officers here are rich . . . and as always, the people get screwed!!

I took it all down . . . names, dates, places . . . I told Mario and Morgan they've got to fight—they've got to start shouting and compel the grand jury to start an investigation . . . I told them that they could do it . . . that crooked officials and contractors are the most frightened people in the world. They base everything on the conviction that the rank and file won't act . . . can't act—because anyone can be bought off or intimidated. When you start screaming—it's the last thing they expect! There's nothing they hate and fear more than exposure . . . respectability means everything to them!! When you yell, it leaves them naked, and exposes them as the cowards they are!!!!

Mario and Morgan got all excited . . . they said they'd do it! I told them I'd run the whole story in the *Free Press*, demand a grand jury investigation . . . and send them enough copies to cover every rank-and-file man in their local . . . plus every public official.

They said, "Send us the papers, and we'll do the rest."

Things are beginning to burn, Joe . . . we're going to scorch this union clean—like burning off dead paint . . .

234

and the Cannons are going to feel the heat all the way in Washington!!!

Keep up the fight!!!

Fraternally (ha!) yours,

Bax

I met a man you'd really like—his name is Gordon Christiansen.

He's a quiet, easygoing guy . . . reminds me a lot of you . . . and he runs what he calls "a government in exile" . . . a sort of acting-conscience for the construction local here . . . which is corrupt. About twenty years ago, just after the war, they elected a Communist party member president . . . it really happened. There was a cell . . . they ran things off at night on a mimeograph machine . . . it was all like a J. Edgar Hoover nightmare . . . Christiansen was recording secretary then, and he decided this man had to be unseated . . . but he couldn't do it alone. So he helped a big, dumb Irish setter by the name of Mike Farraday run for the office . . . and he won.

Well, as it turned out, this Farraday was worse for the union than the Communist ever was . . . he had no political convictions at all—which meant he was dedicated only to getting rich!! Chris estimates he's taken three-quarters of a million dollars in bribes—and nobody can get him out. Chris can't run against him—can't even get nominated—because everything is rigged!!

Finally, a couple of years ago, using all his own money, some of his friends', and some from a few honest contractors, Chris opened a union office of his own . . . started investigating conditions within the construction industry here . . . and published a nonprofit newsletter. He's been beaten up and his life's been threatened, but he won't scare. He's quiet, but I think he is the toughest man I've ever met—and he's with us!!!

235

Just imagine, Joe—us pushing from the Coast—and Chris working back here—we can pinch Fat Tom Cannon till he squeals!!

One more thing—Christiansen still has this thing about Communists. He wanted to know what my feelings were about them . . . I think he was worried that I might be a party member. I told him I had no use for them . . . or any other conservatives!!

Brother Bax

Chicago, Illinois
March 18

I'm still learning.

Today I found out what happens when an International officer gets caught. Nothing!! A man here named Swanson . . . union officer . . . was tried, convicted and sentenced for extortion . . . he threatened contractors with goons unless they paid him . . . he did it so openly that finally the contractors all got together and brought criminal action against him . . . He was sent to prison, and the local finally got up the guts to kick him out of his job . . . they even rewrote the bylaws to prohibit convicted felons from holding union office.

That was two years ago. Now he's out . . . and Cannon is reinstating him as a union officer!!! He's cleared it with the GEB. They ruled that the ban on ex-convicts doesn't apply to this man . . . since it was written after his conviction.

At last . . . a stand on principle!!!

With clear eye and sick stomach,

Bax

Indianapolis, Ind.
March 21

More of the same.

Here, it's a member of the housing authority—who's also a

union officer . . . Webb's his name, appointed by a mayor who wanted to put a labor man in a responsible office . . . as an example. Oh, what an example!! Webb—in charge of construction contracts—leaked confidential cost data to contractors who were willing to pay for it. Those who weren't willing got such stiff inspections on the work they had done that they were discouraged from bidding at all.

I begin to wonder . . . if things don't change, will there be any useful purpose left to unions at all? Soon, we will be nothing more than another special-interest group . . . with no responsibility to the society in which we operate. I don't know . . . maybe it's me who's out of step . . . I enjoy my job . . . I have no perspective of living anywhere else, or doing anything else . . . the greatest pleasure I enjoy in living is bringing to fruition an idea . . . successfully . . . by the process of struggle . . . fighting for lofty ideals is an obsession with me . . . might be my own individual religion. Maybe I move too fast.

I don't know . . . I find myself thinking, more and more . . . Am I out of my time?? Is Labor???

Deeper and deeper,

Bax

25

As soon as the phone rings, I know who it will be. Don't ask me how: I sense it. I've known that he would try, and that it would probably be at night, and soon. I've been waiting for it to ring since dinner.

"Joe? It's me, Toad."

I take the phone into the bathroom and close the door.

"I want to talk to you, alone. Is the cop there with you?"

"Yes."

"Can you get rid of him?"

"Not without leaving the house."

He's quiet for a moment, thinking. "Okay, I'll meet you. You come alone, and I'll come alone. Name a place."

Unable to trust him, and unable to refuse, I tell him to name a place instead, hoping that will make him give away his intentions.

"You know the freeway exit you take to get to my place? There's a Texaco station on the corner just as you come off the ramp. I'll be standing there, on the corner, in the light. You come by and pick me up, and we'll go wherever you like."

In my mind, I see the exit. I can come off the freeway at forty and circle the block without stopping. Even if Toad's setting me up, the odds are against a shot at that speed; and once he's in the car, they won't dare try.

"Okay."

"Twenty-five minutes?"

"Twenty-five minutes."

I open the bathroom door, and there's Hoxie, staring at the telephone in my hands. He looks at me suspiciously. Now he's seen everything. I'm certain it's all up—but that isn't what's on his mind. Instead, he walks past me, lifts the lid on the toilet, and unbuckles his belt. Quietly, I close the door behind me and set the telephone back in its niche in the hallway. As I'm backing the car out of the driveway, I hear the toilet flush.

I drive across the bridge into the city, thinking of all the times I've crossed it and wondering how many I have left; the traffic is light, and nobody seems to be tailing me. I climb up onto the freeway and into the fast flow out toward Toad's, and I start preparing arguments, anticipating his.

The turnoff comes up fast, before I'm ready, and I take the turn at more than forty, tires screaming. Down the hill, heavy on the brakes. Across the intersection is the Texaco station, and standing in a pool of light beside a tire-sale sign, wearing a gray sweater like a tarpaulin thrown over a large, wide machine, is Toad. I barrel on through the intersection as Toad stares, surprised, recognizing the car, and continue around the block. There were two cars in the station at the pumps, but Toad was alone. And no lights behind me. Slowing, I make a turn, drive a block, and make another. Then, very slowly, I approach the corner where Toad stands waiting, reach over and open the door.

239

He gets in without a word, doing a double-take at the beard and the blue denim work shirt. They seem to sadden him, and he looks out the window and sighs. I start driving up a dark, empty street lined with trees that all look like they have been planted by the same gardener. Toad clears his throat and hocks an oyster out the window. Then he turns toward me, laying one of his big arms on the back of the seat.

"You want to tell me why you're trying to commit suicide?"

I'm not, I tell him.

"You sure act like it . . . letting those creeps from his local in yours . . . taking on the National. . . . Now I hear you're going to turn renegade. Even he never did that."

I take a left turn into a long, wide street lined with discount furniture stores, taco and hamburger joints, and car lots.

"You were never a hard-core 'aginner,' like him," Toad continues. "Hell, you were just as likely to support me as oppose me. Nobody's got an ax to grind with you. What happened?"

"A man was killed. And I was told I was next."

"A warning, is all. And you didn't take it."

"I began to wonder why—and I started thinking about the things Bragg had said."

"Let's stop and get some coffee," Toad says.

I pull into a drive-in, brightly lit, where a bunch of kids Doug's age are hanging around each other's cars and glaring at everybody. The carhop, a young, hard, pretty girl, fastens a tray to my window and takes our order. She reminds me of Sally Bragg.

"I hate to say this," Toad begins again, "because he was my friend once, but a man who made people feel the way he did, he deserves to be killed. Now I know you don't feel that way—it sounds horrible to you—but try to under-

240

stand—a lot of people do. People he threatened and humiliated. Anyone who comes along and tries to stir up some more of what he stirred up is going to be thought of in the same way. Good riddance . . . that's what they'll say. I'd hate like hell to see anything like that happen to you."

The girl comes with the coffee, and when I give Toad his I have to use both hands, I'm shaking so.

"Thanks. Sugar, too. That's it. What he started—a little tin-pot revolt—has happened in every union that there's ever been. It's always the same thing—one guy taking on the Establishment, so he can set up a dictatorship of his own. And it always ends up the same. The rank and file go back to work—they don't care. The guys in power stay in power. And the punks disappear. Face it—what he started is over."

Staring out the window, I can feel him watching me.

"That's why you got to stop them from disaffiliating."

"I can't."

"You can. You can table the proposal. You can call it out of order. You can refuse to recognize the man who makes it. You can stick it in committee and keep it there forever. You can do a hundred things. Of course you can."

"Knowing what I know, I couldn't do that and walk into that local office the next day. I couldn't, that's all."

Toad sighs and looks out the window again.

"Okay. All right. I know what your private feelings are, and I respect them. I want you to keep them. All I am asking you to do—asking, now—is to pretend. Go along. You think I don't go along with things I'm opposed to? That's my job! Believe me, this is nothing in comparison. Nothing. In a month, everybody will forget about it . . . even you."

Finishing his coffee, he puts the cup down and folds his arms. He seems convinced that he is winning me over.

"I know what that will come to," I tell him. "You do one

thing like this, and they hold it over you. Pretty soon you have to do another. And another. After awhile, you have to go along with anything, no matter what it is."

I can feel Toad squirm. I have described his situation, and both of us know it.

"I think," I say to him, more coldly than I have ever said anything before, "that if you had a gun now, and you took it out and shot me, you'd be doing me less harm."

Toad stares at me, wounded. I think I can see the beginnings of tears in his eyes. He turns away, rolls down the car window, and looks out. I flash the headlights until the girl hurries over impatiently and takes our tray away. Then I put the car in reverse and back out.

On the way back, neither of us says anything for a long time. Toad is breathing hard now, and he is in a sweat; some kind of fierce pulling-and-hauling must be going on inside him. I'm scared. My legs feel cold. At Toad's house, I pull up and stop with a jolt. The sweat is running down the side of his face, and his jaw is shaking. He grasps the door handle and wets his lips with his tongue.

"Look—if you've made up your mind to let them go through with this, then do it—but you stay home. Stay out of it. I'm *begging* you."

I shake my head.

"Then you are an asshole," he says.

"So maybe an asshole can count for something."

Toad gets out and slams the door. He storms across his lawn. About halfway to his house he turns and shouts something at me that I can't hear over the noise of the engine. And don't want to. I let the car and myself go, and roll forward.

26

The night after he came back, he made a report on his trip to the local's Executive Board in the auditorium of the Trades Union Building. Those who were there said he talked proudly of the brush fires he had started, and that he had just begun to realize how big a thing it was that they had undertaken, and that it was more important than ever now that they continue. Some of them thought he looked tired, and he left before the meeting ended. He went into his office, where two friends, allies from the Laurel City local who had come to him for advice, were waiting.

From across the street, you can see into that room, and whoever did it could have watched him as he talked to the two men, pacing restlessly and waving his arms, while they sat in a car with a shotgun and a pocketful of shells, watching him living, thinking of him dead.

At about eleven o'clock he left with the two men, and they went out of the building and down the street to a bar, where Bragg continued the discussion in his familiar manner, raising his voice, pounding on the table with his

243

fist, sipping a drink, getting up occasionally and announcing he was going to the bathroom to blow tanks, other customers staring at him, offended. At one o'clock, the three of them left together and headed down the wide, working-class-district street to the parking lot, where the two men from Laurel City got into their car. As they pulled out of the lot, Bragg started across the street to his own car. Less than a minute later, a block away, the two men heard a pair of echoing explosions. There is heavy truck traffic on that street. They thought the noises were backfires.

Hoxie says he was shot twice, first with a rifled slug, an ugly chunk of metal hunters use for wild pig. It hit him in the back, point-blank, as he was unlocking the door of his car; it tore all the way through his chest, spun him around, and flattened him against the side of the car. The second blast was buckshot. It hit him in the chest and the right eye, tore into a telephone pole, and blew out the window of a barbershop behind him.

Between the first blast and the second, flung around, face into the attack, hit and hemorrhaging, he knew. He realized that he was being murdered.

27

How I dread this meeting. This morning, Eisan bursts into my office almost hysterical with joy. He says they've got the votes. They've canvassed every rank-and-file man in the local, and there's going to be a record turnout tonight. He is dressed flashy again—no tar-caked roofer's clothes any more—but a gold sports coat, red shirt, and tight, tight pants. The regime has been restored. The old new regime. He says everybody's with me. I don't think I've ever felt so lonely.

For the first time at a meeting of our local, serious security precautions have been taken. Eisan has arranged for twenty extra sergeants at arms on the doors. Special passes have been given out to all the members. Nobody gets in who hasn't got one—even if he's a cop. As a final security measure, Eisan holds open his coat, and he's wearing a pearl-handled gun in a shoulder holster. I tell him it looks great on him, and he accepts it as a compliment.

There are all sorts of rumors: Potter says one of the men in to pay his dues told him that he heard Toad was going to be fired, and a secretary from the San Francisco local called Dorothy to tell her that Tom Cannon was supposed to be coming out to make peace. But nobody confirmed anything, and tonight is still tonight.

Still no word from Toad. Or from Sally—but what is there to say? It all seems to have been settled centuries ago. Men survive their way, women survive theirs. For a time I felt I had to tell Rose about Sally, that I would die poisoned of the knowledge of it if I didn't. But then I realized that to blurt out something like that to her, something that would make her angry at me, while making me feel noble and truthful, would simply be passing the burden along. And I have done all of that I care to do. Instead, I've tried to think of her as much as I think of myself, because that, as near as I can figure, is what love is.

Pulling into my driveway, I notice Doug's car for the first time in a long while. It's even uglier now than the day he bought it: a dull gray over all, with scorched blotches of bodywork. Half a front fender is missing, the colors of the wheels don't match, and there are no handles to open the doors or the trunk. It occurs to me that if I somehow survive this day and live twenty more years, I'll never see that car completed. It just can't weather Doug's constant attention. It erodes.

Rose comes to our house for dinner, and I broil some steaks for her and Doug, and for Hoxie, who is sulking, sore at me for cutting out on him twice now. He doesn't trust me at all any longer, and I suppose he never will. I'm convinced he told me the details of Bragg's death only to scare me into doing as he says. I've grown to like the man, but we are tired of being around each other. And he is eating and drinking me out of house and home.

After dinner, Doug and Hoxie volunteer to wash the dishes, and Rose and I walk out into the back yard. It's getting lighter in the evenings now, and soon I can begin cooking outside. There seem to be more birds around, and some of the fruit trees are beginning to bud and bloom. The bushes look overgrown, and the grass needs mowing —I'll have to get on Doug about it. Rose slips off her shoes, so she's shorter than me for a change, and we walk across the grass to our dilapidated glider. I slap some of the dust off the faded canvas seat so she can sit down, and we start rocking gently back and forth.

"Nice as it is right now," says Rose, "I wish tonight were over."

"I do, too."

We sit like old people listening to the croaking of the rusty glider springs. Here I am, threatened with murder, relaxing in a garden. I think maybe I should be running down the street screaming "Help me! Help me! I don't want to die!" but I don't feel like it, I don't know why. I wish that things were different, that Bragg were still alive, but I don't know any way I could have changed it. I keep getting the idea that it was always going to happen.

"Will you call me when you get home?" Rose asks.

"Sure."

"Even if it's late. I want to know."

"Okay."

It's sure to be a noisy crowd. That alone was once enough to nearly scare the life out of me. The men will be in fever, like the night we voted to strike. But worse—with those avid, hungry, unforgiving faces: Grimes and Buxton, Eisan, Potter, Equals—to all of them, I have become something apart from myself. And to whoever else sits with a shotgun, waiting.

Hoxie said that if they were willing to die in the attempt, he couldn't stop it; and if one man couldn't, I don't suppose twenty could. They'd just get in each other's way. The killer could wait in a car beneath the tree in our parking lot until the meeting ends, then cross the lot and shoot

247

me through my office window. He could shoot me on the way to the hall, or coming back. He could kill me in my bed if I stay home. If it happens, it happens.

Doug calls to me from the kitchen window. Grimes and Buxton are here, come to escort me to the meeting. They're waiting out in front. I get up from the glider, help Rose up, and kiss her, feeling her mouth press with urgent need against mine. Her eyes are shut so tight they're squinting, and her breath is as labored and difficult as my own. Holding her so hard it hurts, sweating, scared, I turn and walk with her up the lawn toward our house.

If this past entry seems hard to read, it's because it was written in a moving car. We're here. Around me, the local's parking lot is jammed. From inside, I can hear the murmur of the men. Grimes and Buxton are looking in all directions, nervously.

A month of fear and anguish, and I have no answers. Only deeper questions. Time to go.

From where?

To where?

It shouldn't be a long meeting. I should be home early, unless I get shot.